Amityville House of Pancakes
Omnibus, Volume 1

Edited by Pete S Allen

Amityville House of Pancakes Omnibus, Volume 1

Edited by Pete S Allen

ISBN 1-894953-26-6

CGP-4001

This book is a work of fiction and all characters and events herein are products of the authors' imaginations.

All stories are copyright ©2004 their respective authors, and published in this anthology with their permission.

Published in Canada by Creative Guy Publishing.
www.creativeguypublishing.com

Cover art by Kris Dikemann

The Amityville House of Pancakes

"You don't have to be dead to eat here, but it helps."

Please Wait to be Seated

All right, all right, don't stand there gawking. Here's your menu, now follow me.

Hey! You ain't dead. What gives?

Well, no harm no foul I guess. I'll give you a table, but don't get any funny ideas. Listen up, kid, here's the scoop. I don't know what tour bus you got off of, but if you're slumming, you've come to the wrong place. This ain't no Callahan's or Cowboy Feng's or Restaurant at the End of the Universe — you aren't going to find interdimensional yahoos in here swapping stories.

What you're going to get is the biggest, greasiest breakfast this side of Hell, or Sheol, or Gehenna, or whatever watering hole you're used to hanging out in. Don't bother anybody, mind your own business, and you might get out of here without anybody noticing you ain't dead.

Nah, they're not necessarily a rough crowd, but what? You haven't been to a greasy spoon after the bars close before? Not exactly Granny's Sunday dinner.

All right, sit down and I'll grab you some coffee.

Non-smoking? What are you, a wise ass?

The Girl in B33

by J.D. Welles

The Carmine's wasn't sitting.

The leftovers were sitting – right under his ass and those of his son Jack, his daughter Julie and his lovely wife Shirl. But inside Arnie Moines' prodigious girth, the Carmine's was declaring a full scale war.

Arnie ran through a litany of possible culprits for his upset – the anchovies on the Caesar salad, the cream or the vodka with the penne, the veal, the cheese, the two bottles of wine he split with his wife minus the sips for the kids. Well, half a glass for Jules. She was only seventeen.

Or it could be the crap on stage. The kids picked this one – *Revolution!* – because history was too hard for them if they actually had to read it. They wanted history shouted at them in soft rock ballads and pounding show tunes.

And when there were perfectly good revivals of *Fiddler on the Roof*.

At least the only seats they could get were up in the balcony. He could close his eyes without offending anyone. Yeah, he'd catch some Zs if the stab in his gut would leave him alone.

Arnie expelled a bomb burst of gas as a bevy of chorus boys in ragged blue chased a couple of others in red coats off the stage. Shirl gave him a sharp look he didn't bother to apologize to. Jules never heard; she was in the kind of ecstasy that made a man muse on how many years of drama school he'd have to put her through before she started slinging joe at Starbucks.

Jack, on the other hand, was asleep, his mouth open and head back. History was history whether it was delivered by Mrs. Herrnacker, Franklin Pierce High's number one bore or Graham Hardy, Broadway's number one musical comedian.

Arnie couldn't blame him. The Hardy guy was overrated.

"Jeeesus."

The stab rolled into a tear. Is that possible? Could turning fish or too much booze rip a hole in his belly like mad cow ripped holes in the head?

But that didn't hurt. The brain didn't have nerves.

The belly had nerves.

"Are you all right, Arnie?" Shirl whispered through the applause. The boys had scurried off and that Hardy guy replaced them.

"Yeah, hon," he grimaced. "No."

His eyes widened. Yeah, ripping was the word for it, like his guts were coming apart inside him.

What the hell had he eaten?

"Arnie, you're making me worry."

Arnie groaned and bent double. "Just...gas."

He raised his head again and it seemed as if there were a hundred little hands pressing against his fleshy cheeks, his fat chin, his weak forehead. They were clawing and pushing through the skin

Shirl saw fingernails.

Arnie, his brain uncomprehending, his mouth still working against the pressure, turned to his wife and exploded like a giant pulpy firework.

Shirl screamed, but not for the shell of her husband, clinging to her clothes, to their children, to the walls. In her husband's bloody place sat a prim little girl carelessly dressed in a short, tattered party dress, her legs sweetly crossed at the dirty anklets of her lacy socks.

"This is my seat," she said inside Shirl's head.

Shirl screamed again. Again and again and again.

"A ghost."

"That's what she said." The officer scratched a note to himself on his pad before slipping it away. "Brooklyn told us to talk to you, said you helped out there with a serial killer or something."

"A werewolf."

"Yeah, whatever," The cop looked over the young man across from him. Good-looking in a craggy sort of way, thin as the thin man, dark hair, light eyes. Lazy. A killer – with the ladies. "Brooklyn said you could help."

Nicholas Brown, the object of his scrutiny, smiled wanly and against his better judgment. He never involved the police last time, his roommate Kylie did, and he never gave them any information, but that the Coney Island killings would stop.

When they did, like he said they would, he acquired a reputation. And consulting was supposed to pay some money, unlike his website, Urbanlegends.com.

His dream job, his website. Ha. Should have gotten in before the new millennium.

Nick hated economic downturn.

"So tell me what happened."

"This is what I know." The cop popped open his notebook, paged through it. "Right. So it's 'bout quarter to nine, the first act of the show is finishing up, this guy, Graham Hardy, gets up to do this big solo – he's Benjamin Franklin, get that! – and our man, Arnold Moines, literally explodes on the balcony. The actor and Arnie's family are the only witnesses we secured and they're saying the same thing. This little girl – a ghost – was sitting there, pleased as can be, in B33 the second of Arnie's demise. We're looking for more of the audience, the crew. Apparently the house staff wasn't actually in the house until after Arnie became graffiti."

Nick glanced up and over the off-white balcony walls. Graffiti was a fitting word for the spray the cops were scraping off the walls.

Nick hated carnage.

"They all saw a ghost."

"Except the boy kid. He was sleeping until a great chunk of his Dad landed in his throat, blocking off his windpipe. His sister heimliched him, but he's not doing much talking."

"I don't blame him."

"Me either."

"Where's the actor? He had the best view."

"In his dressing room. You want to go up?"

"Sure. I'll talk to him where he's comfortable."

"First floor." The officer pointed towards a curtained door marked "Authorized Personnel Only."

Nick sighed with relief. Nick hated stairs.

There wasn't a star on the dressing room door like in the movies, but he knew it was Graham Hardy's. He could hear the actor squealing behind the paneling.

Nick knocked.

"Who is it?"

"Nicholas Brown. Nick. I'm with Urbanlegends.com. And the police."

"The press?" The voice went higher, setting off the dogs the crew kept for the "Ethan Allen and the Green Mountain Boys" number.

"The cops!" Nick shouted and the door cracked open. A blood-shot eye and large mouth appeared, looking him over.

The kid was boring to look at with blemishless skin like a baby, too much weight around the middle, light hair, dark eyes. Energetic. Sexually ambiguous, probably gay.

So Hardy let him in. "All right," the star said and the dressing room opened all the way.

Clearly, Hardy had been indulging in some kind of meditative relaxation technique. Aromatherapy candles littered every available surface not already occupied by yoga texts and empty booze bottles. The room smelled of expensive perfume and sweaty derelict.

Nick hated candles. And bums.

"You want a drink?" Hardy offered, dropping himself into his makeup chair.

"Sure. What have you got?"

"What you see." Hardy gestured vaguely around the room, then buried his head in his arms.

Nick found a bottle of scotch with a snort in it lying across a palette of flesh-toned powders. There was no glass into which he could pour it.

He shrugged. Down the hatch.

"That's twelve year-old, you know."

Hardy hadn't lifted his head from his dressing table.

"It's...okay." Nick put the bottle down empty and took out his palm pilot. "Shoot."

"Shoot what?"

Nick hated actors.

"The shit, Hardy."

"The shit, as you so eloquently put it, is that some bastard spontaneously combusted on my big first act solo – 'Electricity, Bifocals and The Stove.' That is 'the shit.'"

"Not really. Spontaneous combustion is clean. A little pile of ashes here, a black stain there. I don't know if you've been in the balcony, but that was not clean."

"All right, all right. Imploded. Exploded. Whatever. Died in the middle of my big first act – 'Electricity, Bifocals and The Stove.'"

"And you saw a girl."

"I saw a ghost. Right where that poor bastard was sitting. Grinning." Hardy turned in on himself. "How could I know she was grinning? I can hardly see a thing up there. Not a facial expression, anyway."

"A ghost."

"Yeah, a ghost. Aren't you the spook hunter? Aren't you the only one required to believe me?"

"Supposed to. But I don't often have to deal with theatrical personalities."

Hardy had been accused of carrying half a dozen diseases – Legionnaire's, Cat Scratch, Lyme – not to mention the average go-around of personal and professional defects.

But theatrical personality – said like that.

"Listen, buddy." Hardy raised himself to his full five foot four, 185 pound glory. "I know this house like the back of a chorus boy's ass. There was never never never a spook in this house. Never. But when we got in here for tech, they were doing a wham, bam, thank you ma'am rush job through the renovations and I'll tell you, that chiquita up there ain't happy—"

"Renovations?" Nick finally got his word in.

"Yeah. Renovations. They added a couple dozen seats. In the mezz and up in the balcony. Supposed to restore the theatre to its former capacity when it was a vaudeville palace. A shame with this piece of shit show. They can't fill the seats they had already."

Then, like catastrophe or something else mostly disconcerting, in came a burly bearded troubadour, decked out like an aging hippie in a cowboy hat, a t-shirt and old jeans. A band of duct-taped leather held a battered guitar to his back.

"Oh my God! Guys!"

Hardy had a roll in his eyes, even if he didn't put forth the effort to actually roll them. "This is Sammy Winstrom. Our composer."

"And lyricist. And producer. Part producer."

"Nice to meet you." Nick held out his hand, but Winstrom was already moving past him to Hardy.

"Graham, this would make a great musical."

"Better than *Revolution!?*" Hardy asked innocently. Nick knew what he meant.

Nick liked actors.

"Better than *Revolution!*. The best! And I can see you as the fat guy, Arnie Whats-his-name. Perfect."

Hardy pretended to be interested and not insulted. "What kind of percentage are we talking? For me?"

"Two. After profit."

"Before."

"Okay." Winstrom smiled, deal done. There was only the little thing of writing the musical. No problem. It'd be in workshop in two weeks. "What's your name again?"

"I never gave it. Nicholas Brown."

"Nick, you're coming to the show tonight."

"Thank you, Mr. Winstrom, but I don't really do Broadway. I'll come after—"

"Don't do...? I can understand if you don't like the old stuff, the pop music of its day, but not the pop music of today. Now me, on the other hand, I'm the people's composer, making the music of today for the audiences of tomorrow. You'll love the show – and you'll learn something. It's all history. Our history in song."

Nick hated composers. And history.

"All right."

"Two comps'll be waiting for you." The same smile. Another deal done.

"In the balcony."

"In B31 and 35."

Nick nodded. "Perfect."

It was not perfect.

"The werewolves called. They're having trouble with the therapist. Again. Why don't they just eat her and get it over with? I know, I know. That's why they're in therapy." Kylie looked over her roommate.

Nick was a thin, pale specimen, a study in bourgeoisie concepts and contrasts, a socio-political study in light and dark.

It was kind of sexy. They'd slept together once in college, but never did again.

That wasn't her fault. She was a sweet petite woman, by the grace of God, a little pug-nosed, maybe but blond, by the grace of Clairol. In graduate school, Kylie authored a revolutionary physics breakthrough, the "Just Sorta Happens" theory of time-travel, as yet unpublished, but sometimes practiced. She supported the communist causes of the 1930's ("a heady time," she reported, after returning from the grocery with twelve cans of SPAM expiration date Nov. 30 '39) and she supported them despite the most catastrophic failure of a political system in modern history.

Modern, schmodern. She believed in the past. When it didn't offend her.

"Nick, what's wrong?"

"It's too terrible."

"Who died?"

"I don't know. Some little chick. Some guy." Nick plopped down at the kitchen table and pushed Kylie's calculations away from him, creating a tidal wave of thought that tumbled to the cracked pre-war tiles.

She ignored the mess. For the moment. "Did you see it? Them die, I mean?"

"No. Kylie, who cares about the dead? I have to go to a Broadway show."

"A play?"

"A musical."

"Oh, man. Alone, I hope?"

11

"No," Nick moaned. "I have two free tickets. You're going."

"I'm not!" Kylie began piling the papers back on the table, deliberately in front of Nick to demonstrate her displeasure. "Musical theatre is an offense to the working classes. Bourgeoisie entertainment—"

"Please." He lifted tortured eyes to her, pleading.

Kylie stopped. There was only one thing she held closer to her heart than her communist principles. That was her "Just Sorta Happens" theory of time travel. But after that, Nick.

"Okay. I'll go."

"Thanks."

"You owe me."

Nick brightened a little. Maybe she'd ask for sex. That would be...okay. "You got it."

Kylie considered asking for sex. She settled on "Chocolate cake. And that new bio, *Misunderstood: The Joseph Stalin Story*."

"Done."

Better luck next time.

"Is this seat taken?"

Nick froze, a helpless woodchuck in a pit bull's sights.

Sammy Winstrom laughed. "B33. You couldn't pay me to sit there. Mind if I take 37?"

"Be my guest," Nick said politely.

Nick hated politeness. And enthusiasm.

"Great! I really hope you like the show. And that the ghost shows up. I really want to see what kind of song to give her, you know?"

Nick was grateful the composer hadn't brought his guitar.

"And who is this beautiful woman? Your date?"

"My roommate."

Kylie pursed her lips, squeezing them into a half-assed smile. "His roommate. Kylie Strong."

"A pleasure to meet you. Can I put you in my show?"

"Uh."

"Sammy's writing a musical based on the recent theatrical events."

"On the ghost? Just what she needs – an ego trip. They come back for attention, Sammy, 'cause Mommy didn't love them enough' or whatever pissant problem they had in life. The last thing you need to give her is validation!"

"Thanks, Kylie. Can I do my job, please?"

"I'm just saying, Nick."

Sammy grinned at both of them, moving his head back and forth with their words. This was better than opera. "Do you two want to be in my show?"

"Do we have a choice?"

"No, I mean, be in my show."

A majestic trumpet call cut off their reply – which was, not surprisingly, not an actual trumpet call, but a synthesized one – as did the entrance of Graham Hardy in his Franklin get-up – stringy wig and bald cap, wire-rimmed glasses perched on his nose and an underage chorus girl clasped to his arm.

This was the War of Independence. Broadway style!

At least it was short. The show, not the war, which apparently dragged on for eight years. Short and sort of sweet, if the audience definition of euphoniousness included a Founding Father in a hoedown with his slaves.

Nick hated Founding Fathers. And euphoniousness. And slavery.

"So..." Kylie said as the applause around them died down and the house lights came up. "Did I miss her?"

"Did you enjoy the show?" Winstrom immediately wanted to know.

"No."

"No?" Winstrom's voice broke and tears began quivering at the corners of his eyes.

"I can only answer one question at a time," Nick said.

Nick hated multiple questioners.

"No, I didn't miss her?" Kylie tried again.

"Yes. No. She didn't show."

"So, what'd you think then?" Winstrom asked, forcing himself to be brave, like Mommy always told him to be. He could take it. He could –

Nick blanched. "Of the show?"

"Of the ghost."

"Oh. She's a brat. We're going to need stronger methods."

Kylie nodded knowingly, knowing nothing really. "So there's only one thing left to do."

"Yes. Hold a séance."

"Great! So what did you think of the show?"

The David Belasco apartment was secreted high up in the theatre bearing the great producer's name, far removed from the prying eyes of spying wives, but not the sweet charms of discreet chorines.

The apartment served more as an office than a living space, although there was that rollaway bed, no doubt for those long nights spent over plots to screw the cast and crew. Figuratively, literally – whichever.

Everything was kept exactly the same as it was when Mr. Belasco left the Broad Way on May 14, 1931 at the ripe old age of 71.

The house manager let in the ragtag mediums, Nick, Kylie, Graham Hardy and Sammy Winstrom, with a weary sigh. "Mr. Belasco will see you now."

He closed the door behind him.

Nick waited.

Nick hated waiting.

"Mr. Belasco?" Kylie offered into the uncomfortable silence.

She felt a brush and a breeze as if a heavy fabric had passed over her shoulders and then settled down around her.

"Cropped hair is back in style?"

Belasco had seated himself beside her on the rollaway, his cape, a fiction in her universe, but quite real in his, floated gently an inch above her skin.

"Jesus Christ!"

"May He have mercy on all of our souls," Belasco moved closer to her, draping an arm suavely behind her on the couch. "Now what mercy may I have on you, my dear?"

"Nick, is the ghost...hitting on me?"

"Yes. Mr. Belasco, we have business with you, not pleasure. Alas. Alack."

"Alas, alack, yourself, boy. What kind of business could you living possibly have with the Bishop of Broadway?" Belasco turned back to Kylie, who smiled weakly and scooted to her right.

"Your Eminence, does she look like an altar boy?"

"Actually, she kind of does," Hardy said.

"Shut up, Hardy."

Belasco stood, his gentlemanly white hair standing on end like a mildly put out house cat. Sweeping his cape aside revealed his dress – that of a priest's, down to the dog collar. A servant of the Savior on his way to the Met.

"This guy is so in my musical!" Winstrom swung his guitar from around his back and began tuning.

Belasco ignored him. "What is your business, living? I don't have all day."

"What do you have to do – when you're dead?"

"All day, all night with breakfast, lunch and dinner in between." Belasco sat himself – if something immaterial could be said to sit – behind his ancient desk, resting his chin on his steepled fingers. "Shoot."

"Shoot what?"

Nick frowned at Hardy, then proceeded. "We need your help, sir. A ghost problem. A girl who won't leave her seat."

"And kills any poor bastard who tries to take it," Hardy added.

Winstrom began to make little "ma-mee-may-moe-moo" noises in the corner. They ignored him.

"A girl?" Belasco raised a ghostly eyebrow.

"She's eight, sir. Was eight, sir. Is eight, sir," Nick said.

"Oh. I see. Not one of mine then. What does she want?"

"We don't know. She wouldn't show for us."

"Wouldn't show, eh? Stubborn. Only eight, but already a woman."

"Excuse me?" Kylie interrupted.

"A touch of the vapors, my dear?"

Nick laid a warning hand on Kylie's thigh. "He died in 1931."

"Is that a problem?" Belasco asked. "Are things so different?"

"Actually, no," Kylie shrugged as if to say go on, then. She loved the past – so long as it didn't hit on her – or offend her.

"All right, then. This may require more strength than I have on my own. I must call in the reinforcements. I may be the elder statesman on the Way, but I don't control, nor even grasp, every creature's connection."

"There are others of you?" Kylie asked.

"Of course! Every theatre has its spirit. Where do you think the tradition of the ghost light came from? A producer's philanthropic desire to contribute to the electric company's coffers?"

"And they'll come here?" Kylie wasn't sure if she wanted any more spirits in the intimate apartment. Especially if any of them were feeling amorous.

"If I put out the call, they'll come. Let me have a moment, please."

Belasco made a show of picking up the cobwebbed phone on his desk and dialing it. A rotary telephone! The producer said nothing into the receiver, only entering number after number, the dial pulling forward, then slipping back.

After several minutes, he put the phone back onto its cradle. "They'll come."

"When?" Nick glanced at his watch.

Nick hated waiting.

Belasco frowned. "Now."

The apartment, already chilly, grew bone cold, pulling tiny puffs of breath from the lips of the four living souls. Winstrom rubbed his hands together and grinned. "I should have brought my gloves. Well, here's what I've got."

He struck a 5/7 cord and sang "Mister Belasco/takes his toast with Tabasco/the dirty old rascal/the Bishop of Broadway!"

"Goddamn it, David, you ain't payin' the breather for that crap, are you?"

"Goodness, no, Two Beers – excuse me. Mr. Beck," Belasco addressed a new manifestation, a well-dressed, but earthy-looking man in a bowler hat. "Did you bring the children?"

"Here and present."

The second speakers, a man and a woman, stood huddled together as if moving away from the other might cause the dissipation of both. The fellow was dressed in denim overalls, a baseball cap and leather gloves. Around his neck, he wore a slip of rope decoratively, yet powerfully as a businessman wears his tie. His boots – he should have been wearing boots – were gone and his bare feet stuck out, the toes dirty and the nails broken and bruised. She, on the other hand, was a delicate slice of spectral beauty, diaphanous in body and in dress, her skirts and low-cut top emphasizing the suggestion of phantasmic flesh beneath.

She was majestic.

"And Junior?" Belasco asked, as Beck and his male and female companion parted like an ectoplasmic Red Sea. "Is Jamie with us?"

"I hate the theatre," came the reply to Belasco's inquiry. "This is hell."

The fourth spirit resembled his father, the early 20th Century thespian, James O'Neill Sr. – not that anyone in the room born after 1915 could identify the pater from the filis. Both bore a strong, long nose, funny Irish ears and dark hair that framed a thin, almost handsome face, given to fattening up with age and booze.

Junior squandered the opportunity to grow fat and aged. He died at 45 years old, two years insane of alcohol abuse.

Death gave him back his coherence and a thick feeling like the slow, heavy smoke from a hot fire wasted on wet wood.

"James O'Neill, Jr.," Belasco said by way of introduction.

"No doubt you've heard of his brother, Genie," Beck said. "If you haven't, you're missing a long night's journey into coma. The Siamese twins are Joe Harper, stagehand, died in the flies for the love of this gorgeous dame, the high wire act of the moment, Emilie Poupee. She fell 'mysteriously' to her death, a couple weeks after Harper broke his neck. On purpose."

"Pleasure to meet you." Harper gave Kylie a little nod, incising the circus performer to ruffle her tutu like a package of distressed cellophane.

"Now you are looking at her! Always the living! Always!"

"Well, no one warned me before I took the dive that all the dead ones were bitches."

"You–" Emilie burst into a semi-coherent string of multi-lingual obscenity that Beck listened to with impatience.

"Yeah, yeah. We know. Every time it's the same. That is love in eternity, kids. Learn your lesson. Die separate."

"Thanks for the advice," Nick said. "Tell me, Beck, why do they call you 'Two Beers'?"

"It's a long story. And it's got nothing to do with business. Which is?" Beck rendered the floor to Belasco who slipped it under the table to Nick.

"A ghost. A little girl in a party dress in the balcony of our theatre. She killed a man for sitting in her seat. A living man."

"No kidding. Living?" Beck shook his head. "That's the only time you folks can be bothered with us."

"And when we drop scenery," Harper said.

"When we open doors," Junior giggled.

"When you turn on faucets." Beck looked meaningfully at Belasco.

"That is not me," the Bishop sniffed.

"Sure," Nick said agreeably, wishing the ghosts would just shut up. "But you don't kill people."

"Right. So we're okay. Thanks a lot, kid."

"Listen, Beck." Hardy, stage veteran and the instigator of more than a few producerly squabbles, had reached the end of his tolerance for bullshit, otherworldly and otherwise.

"We need your help. Our show needs your help. Our theatre needs your help. I need your help."

Hardy's mouth was set, but a laugh, an uncomfortably familiar laugh – echoed through the apartment.

Nick knew it immediately. So did Hardy, turning white as, well, a ghost. In this case, his own.

"Graham Hardy?"

"Am I late?" a disembodied voice replied.

"But I'm–" Hardy stammered.

"Alive? I know!" the voice answered.

"But you're–"

"Dead! I know!" The voice took on a self-satisfied tone. "Time travel. It just sorta happens."

Nick glanced at Kylie. Yeah, there was the "I told you so" smirk. He'd be hearing about this all week. All month, probably.

Junior roused himself out of his supernatural stupor. "How did you pass on, fellow thespian?"

"Sitting through one of your brother's plays." That laugh. "Liquor, pills, autoerotic asphyxiation. What does it matter? I'm here because this affects me. In life."

"It does?" Hardy – as in the breathing embodiment of Hardy – managed.

17

"Oh, yeah, and it ain't pretty, honey." The voice was in Nick's ear. "There'll be pictures all over the place – the Post'll do a centerfold. I'd rather there'd not be pictures."

"From *Revolution!?* Who are you diddling – John Adams?"

"Alexander Hamilton, but that's not what gets me. I can't say more because it won't even be – if you can nail that little bitch."

"Why don't you tell me what you're whispering to the spook hunter?" Hardy demanded. He was jealous, he had to admit. Jealous of himself. Dead.

"Not for all the sheeps in Wales, Tony, which, if I were me again, I would avoid the second time around. They've got diseases."

"Thanks for the warning," Hardy said to Hardy.

"Don't mention it," Hardy said to Hardy.

"This is so a song –" And Winstrom sang in a folk-blues. "And Hardy said to Hardy/Better keep it in your pants."

Nick ignored him. "Who's Tony?"

"Me. My real name. Graham's from Fred Graham. You know, *Kiss Me, Kate*."

"Oh."

Nick hated stage names.

"So, gents, what do we do with the girl?" Beck shouted and Belasco, dozing at his desk, forced his eyes open.

"It's simple." The stagehand broke his embrace – or stranglehold – on the circus girl. "Get the usher."

Beck scoffed. "She won't leave her house."

"Tell her there's a seating problem. Someone doesn't have a ticket." Harper stopped fighting off Emilie and let her push him back down and halfway through the far wall.

"Anyone got a link to the old girl?"

"I fucked her."

"Yeah? You fucked me, Junior. Helluva lot a good it did you."

Junior giggled. "And all it took was two beers."

Beck glanced hellward. "Jesus Christ."

"You know something we don't?" Kylie asked.

"Only where heaven is and it ain't where you breathers think." Beck sighed. "Field trip, kids."

Strolling up Sixth Avenue accompanied by half a dozen spirits was a new, annoying experience for Nicholas Brown. It was enough that he knew they were there; it was more that Hardy's head shot from side to side and up and down like a man off his meds carrying on with the voices in the head. But the clincher was the looks from the sensitives – mostly homeless, although the occasional fat tourist in fanny pack and painted on short-shorts, favored them with a stare.

Nick hated sensitives.

The usher had never left her house – the Cort, a small-sized theatre on the wrong side of Broadway (Belasco would disagree, of course, as his domicile also fell on the wrong side of the street of dreams). Already blessed with a ghost, the theatre seemed to be also laboring under a curse. In ten years two plays had shuttered in their first preview performances – and the Cort stood empty between flops for months at a time.

The usher liked it that way. She preferred, like Garbo, to be left alone.

When the motley crew of living and dead arrived on 46th Street, the theatre was in its natural state. Closed.

"How do we get inside?"

Beck shook his head and Junior giggled.

The front door sprung open.

"After you, sweetie." Junior bowed to Kylie, who wisely chose to defer to the ghosts.

"Age before beauty, Junior." Beck pushed O'Neill through. "He may say he's a door-opener, but he's a bum-pincher too. Over-sexed in life, they never learn in death."

"Weren't you–?"

"Oversexed? Jesus! Judged by the company you're forced to keep. I loved my wife, kid. She was a pip."

"Is she with you?"

"Nah. She got the gravy train. I got my theatre. And I was happy, ready to let go, you know? Then the living gotta get in there and change the name on the place I built – with my own two hands – sort of – and all I get is a miserable brass plaque. Cost 'em $300 bucks. That's all I'm worth to them," Beck looked miserable, but like a good trooper, tried to dig up some righteous anger. "So, now I'm mad. I ain't budging."

"Where would we find her?" Nick did a quick inventory of the theatre. It was cold, musty and devoid of life and light. And the usher.

"Bobbi, you gonna seat us?" Beck called into the still air.

"Mr. Beck, she isn't a dog to come when you call. Miss O'Hara?"

Beck winked at Kylie. "Belasco's the charmer. I get the job done."

"Whaddya want?"

"Ah, the dulcet tones of my lady fair." Junior bowed again, this time towards the stairs. Then he fell back as if he'd been struck.

Nick and Kylie turned away in time to avoid a shaft of concentrated luminescence, bright and hot and hard as a laser, but white like the sun.

"Whaddya want?" the voice demanded again.

"The usher. We're looking for the usher," Nick shouted through a crack between his arms.

"Well, you found her."

The beam, emanating from a large ghostly flashlight of the damned, faded, replaced by a tiny, ancient hag draped entirely in black but for the lacy doily buttoned up tight around her neck.

"My dear." Belasco took her hand and kissed it. She absorbed his propriety as half-bullshit, half her due.

"How you doin', babe?"

"Good, Marty. It's quiet. No living 'cept for these four assholes. Whadda they want?"

Nick knew better than to address this spirit. He waited for Belasco to explain.

"That's a problem," she said when she heard it and she removed a cigarette from a silver case in her breast pocket. "Got a light?"

Belasco offered her a flame and she inhaled, leaning in to him, like they always did in the movies. Nick wondered what the ghost of a cigarette tasted like. He couldn't smell it anymore than the ghosts themselves, who had no discernable body odor.

No deodorant, mouthwash or shower gel in the afterlife. No perfume.

Nick had to admit, he liked the afterlife.

"Whaddya want me to do about it?"

"Do what you do," Nick said. "Throw her out. She hasn't got a ticket."

"Not my house. Don't know if she'll listen to me."

Nick noticed then that when the usher exhaled, the smoked billowed out from a metal disk inlaid in her throat like a broken piece of tile, and not from her mouth or nose.

"Cancer, Charlie. These things'll kill you." The usher hacked through a laugh, waving her cigarette.

"Nick. Not Charlie."

"Whatevah. Look, I'll give it a try 'cause I like you, Marty, and you came all this way for me. That's respect." She snuffed out the cigarette in the palm of her hand. "But I ain't promisin' nothin'."

"Thanks, babe."

The usher gave Junior a sudden hard look as if she'd just seen his slinking shade. "I know you."

"You remember me?" he asked, hopeful.

"Yeah. I fucked you. You were crap."

Junior's drunken smile drooped.

"But you served great booze. Jesus. I can still taste it."

The smiled popped back up and he offered her his arm. "Thank you, sweet lady."

The usher took it. "Don't let it go to your head, Junior. You were still a lousy lay."

The usher balked at Times Square. "I don't go through there."

"It's okay," Junior tried to tug her forward, but she stood immobile as the rush hour traffic.

"Not up here. I don't cross here. I'll cross down there." She pointed to 42nd Street.

"But we're going uptown," Nick whined.

Nick hated doubling back.

"I won't go there." The usher flung her grizzled head towards the statue at the far end of the square.

"Father Duffy?"

The gray statue glared a bit, as if annoyed that his eternal vista was of a gigantic, steaming cup of soup. Although the man wore the khaki and puttees of a World War I doughboy, the splattering of pigeon poop and the fat bird perched on his head erased any dignity Duffy might have possessed in life.

"Never fear, Miss O'Hara. He cannot harm you in death."

"But his voice."

"We're here for you. Take a step forward. One step. We'll be there," Beck whispered.

The usher shook her head no, but she did as he told her. She took a step. Then another. Then another.

When they arrived at the midway partition dividing Seventh and Broadway, Nick heard it. Like a dark rumble of thunder emanating from underground, a runaway subway in the street beneath their feet.

"Catherine O'Hara?"

"I hear him. I hear him," the usher whimpered, but her tiny orthopedic shoes kept moving.

"The Lord took your filthy brother in France. The Lord took your worthless son in the streets. But the Lord will not take you. Sinner! Sinner!"

The streetlight changed from the little white man to the orange right hand and the ghosts stopped out of deference to the living. The usher shook like a junkie coming off the stuff.

And the voice started up again.

"The Lord took your mother, coughing up her blood into the sheets. The Lord took your sister, bleeding her blood into the sheets. The Lord will not take you."

The light changed again and Beck gently pushed the usher into the crosswalk before turning back to the dour effigy.

"Why didn't your Lord take you?"

The pigeon on Duffy's head fluttered its wings, but the voice stayed silent under Beck's stare.

"I thought as much." Beck allowed himself a stiff smile. "Remember, kid, there are no atheists in the fox holes – and no lonely men either."

"How dare you, Beck! You've defamed a beloved and charitable man of the cloth." Belasco was offended.

"Who said that was Duffy?"

Their path continued unmolested unless one counted the bag lady who took her title literally, as she was nothing more than a grinning mouth swathed entirely in Hefty Gladlock.

Nick hated counting.

"Who are you?"

As obnoxious as traveling with an ectoplasmic entourage had been, suddenly feeling their absence was worse. Especially now, as they were staring into the expressionless face of the theatre's house manager.

"Nicholas Brown. Who are you?"

"No matter who I am. What are you doing in my theatre?"

"I'm with the police. Concerning the investigation into the death of Arnold Moines."

"Oh." The house manager barely opened his heavy-lidded eyes. "Officially, we don't believe in ghosts."

"You don't have to–" Kylie began to protest.

"I said officially. I didn't say that I don't believe in ghosts." He smiled wanly. "What are you planning for us today?"

"I'm going to bring a ghost–"

"Oh, no! The last thing this house needs is another ghost. I forbid it."

Nick felt another pulling away as if the house manager had the power to revoke the rights of entry. Like a priest.

The manager must have felt it too. He said, "During our certification process, we learn a few tricks of the holy trade. Unofficially."

"Why don't you banish her?"

"Officially, I can't. Unofficially, we have no revocation rights against those who emanate from inside our own house. Only the strangers."

"If you won't let my ghost enter, then there's only one option." Nick observed the manager's Armani suit and Knights Templar ring. He hit the house where it hurt. "Don't sell the seat."

"Don't sell the seat?" That got his eyes open. Wide. "Do you know how much that would cost us? Sixty-five dollars a night, eight performances a week, fifty-two weeks a year?"

Nick hated math.

"A lot."

"$27,040 to be exact. And the producers – and my bosses – are going to be very exact."

"Then let the usher in."

"The usher? I don't think I have her on our payroll..."

"This one's a freebie."

The house manager leaned back away from them and gave himself a moment's solitary thought. "All right. But officially, I never did this."

Then he flung his arms to the ceiling, as if to embrace the soft cupids painted above him. "Spirits near this earth, I welcome thee into my house. Be thee well until I send thee back to hell."

Nick was again cold, almost frozen. It was a relief.

"If that will be all, I have paperwork to attend to." The house manager pursed his lips and took his leave.

"Back to hell? Jesus," Beck said under his breath.

"They believe it carries more power if it rhymes. Damned doggerel," Belasco said.

But the usher put it most succinctly. "Fucking management."

The airless, arid balcony would have been appropriate to a tomb, but with seats. The ghost light shone as a straining blur below them, too weak to brighten the sullen coldness of the theatre's uppermost level.

At least it wasn't pitch black. That would have been creepy.

Nick hated creepy.

B33 hunkered below them like a squat toad among the princes.

"That the one?" The usher pointed to it out. There was an aura to it, palpable like cooked and rotted steak.

At her words, the little girl manifested herself, all smiles and welcoming arms. The usher frowned and made her way down the steep stairs in a sort of halting crab walk, one hand in front for balance – no railings – and the other flung back to grab a step if she tumbled backwards.

"Balcony. Balcony! I'm an orchestra usher. This is bullshit," she mumbled to herself as she jerked from stair to stair.

She lit the flashlight of the damned and for a strange moment, the ghost of the girl seemed to be too solid flesh and none too willing to melt. But then she shot out of the seat and grabbed the usher's arms and the two did just that.

Melted into nothingness.

"What happened?"

Nick rushed forward, tripping down the steps, barely holding to his feet, until an ice wall knocked him back onto his back on the stairs.

He blinked, fighting for consciousness, and everything was different. He was not in the balcony, for one; he was backstage, but he was still in the same theatre. He could see the balcony from where he was standing – sitting? – no, standing.

The little girl was there, truly solid, and beautiful in that soft, sexless way little girls could be.

The usher was only a few steps away from him and, like him, transparent.

A ghost of a ghost. Nick sniggered.

"What's so funny, hotshot?"

"Nothing."

Nick hated ghosts. Even if he was one. Technically. Even if he was one and he'd never yet been born.

Because this was clearly the past. His guess was the end of the teens or maybe the 1920's. Pre-Prohibition, but post-World War I, he could tell by the clothes, the hair and the drunks. The Lost Generation.

Well, he was lost anyway.

"Hell, the little girl's sure givin' us the business. This is her time. So hold the chuckles, hotshot, and watch and learn – hey, Marty!"

The usher waved, but, of course, she as a ghost of a ghost and completely invisible to the human eye. Even the human eye living in the past and now a ghost and...Nick was getting a headache.

"Didn't see me," she said to Nick like this was every day to her. "And there's Mr. Belasco and shit, did ya see the program? Vaudeville – I knew it. The half hour *Monte Cristo* – there's Junior. Jesus Christ."

Nick rolled his eyes. "I suppose Harper's up in the flies and Poupee is doing her tight rope thing? Are you in the audience or working the crowd?"

"If this is boring you, we could go back."

"Could we?" Nick was hopeful.

"Nah. Like I said. This is her show. Watch and learn."

The high wire act was disappointing. Barnum and Bailey's was better. Junior, in the flesh, was as appealing as he was in the ghost – drunk, horny, depressed. Belasco had retreated to the seats; Beck needed a Bromo.

Then the girl, the fleshy, living little girl, took the stage, all alone and on her own. She opened her mouth, to sing, to recite; it didn't matter.

Because nothing came out.

The little girl was staring hard at the balcony, at B33, and nothing, nothing came out of her mouth.

The curtain collapsed like a consumptive lung around the girl. A stage manager bustled her off. Nobody held her or comforted her or even acknowledged her.

She was only a little girl. She did what little girls did – she sat in a corner and cried.

The show was over. By the mercy – or maybe just a quirk – of the Just Sort Happens theory of time travel, Nick and the usher had been spared the rest of the vaudeville program.

"Thank God. I saw that *Cristo*. Good thing Genie got out."

Junior, on the other hand, had not; he was puking liquidy stuff like uncooked crème brulee into a fire bucket. The little girl sat alone below it, crying to herself.

The ghost light blinked on.

The house was silent.

The ghost light blinked off.

Nick blinked and saw the usher laying beside him on the balcony stairs. They were home.

"Whatta trip, eh?" The usher was smiling, as she dusted stray motes of dusty ectoplasm from her black skirts.

"What happened to her? What happened to the little girl?"

"Who knows? Those were strange times. Bad times. I remember. And they kept getting worse. First they took away our booze, then they took away our money. If I coulda skipped about 20 years in there, I woulda done it."

Kylie moved forward to disagree – the Depression days of Mother Bloor and Communist beauty pageants were not bad times – but Nick, like Dorothy, was overwhelmed with the familiar faces, color only a few minutes before, now rendered in ghostly gray.

"And you were there. And you were there. And you were there."

"Was I there?" Hardy asked hopefully.

"No. Hello, Hardy. But all of you were, but alive. There's something to this. If she'll come back, I want you two to talk to her."

Belasco looked at Beck, who shrugged.

"I need you to be producers. Make her deal. Then we're going to put on a show."

"Oh, God, no," Junior groaned and fell back onto the stairs.

"Oh God, yes!" Winstrom cried and began strumming his guitar.

Nick and Kylie left the spirits to themselves, feigning hunger. Well, not entirely feigning. Nick picked up some McDonalds in the faux movie palace franchise on 42nd Street, taking quiet comfort in the gaudy lights.

Then he headed them towards downtown.

"Where are we going, Nick?"

"Back home. To the web. I know who the little girl is and we're going to solve her problem."

"What happened to her?"

"A lot. I'll explain later." Nick smiled wonderingly. "How come we never thought of it before? Dumb ghosts. What's the point of remaining in this world for fifty extra years if you can't even figure the simple shit out?"

Kylie didn't know. She ate her fries and reflected on the armed uprising of the underclasses against their cruel corporate taskmasters as the subway slid out of the Times Square station towards their apartment.

It would begin on the trains, she decided.

When the little girl reappeared, it was half-hour. Or would have been, had it not been a Monday, the theatre's one dark night.

Hardy slept peacefully below a row of seats, part of him reverting back to the starving actor who'd lived in a shitty black box Off-off-Broadway to save on the rent.

Winstrom was halfway finished with his new musical, tentatively called *The Untitled Sammy Winstrom Project*.

"Do you think I could add a few ghosts to the apartment scene? You know, like headless guys and stuff, in like chains?"

Harper ignored him, but Poupee inched closer, leaning in towards the composer.

"Sammy – it is Sammy, is it no?"

"Yes, Sammy." He looked up from his guitar and right into her ample phantom bosom.

"Sammy." She snuggled into him and Winstrom was surprised at how real a ghost could feel – and feel up. "Do you not think I deserve my own song,

Sammy? Do you not? I sing very pretty like a little birdie, I sing."

As she spoke, her immaterial material hand slid between his material material thigh as her immaterial material lips laid next to his ear.

That was all it took. Winstrom was in love.

And in pain, as Harper's immaterial material foot connected with his material material crotch.

"Oh my God! Guys!" he screeched.

Beck and Belasco ignored him. They had business to attend to.

The two producers took seats on either side of the girl in B33, flanking her and hoping, perhaps, to prevent her escape if negotiations got a little rough.

The girl turned away from Belasco, concentrating her hard black eyes on Beck. He shuddered despite himself.

"I know you," he whispered, but he couldn't quite place her. A vaudevillian – maybe a sister act – no, she was alone.

She was alone.

"I do know you!" Beck stood and backed away. "Oh, Jesus, I know you."

The little girl smiled, her teeth broken jags in her little mouth.

"This is my seat," she said simply.

Belasco realized he'd lost his partner, but going on the nothing that Nick had told him, he became the producer he was. He produced.

"We're prepared to offer you a role, my dear, in a brand-new extravaganza. What is your specialty? Song, dance, elocution?"

She told him.

"Excellent. I'd like to offer you a contract. One show only. Next Monday. I can't promise you much except, perhaps, the fulfillment of whatever you have been seeking."

"I want my seat," she said.

"That you'll have. Let me draw up a contract. Do you have an agent?"

And did he demand a ghostly ten percent?

The little girl's face blackened for a moment, then she said, "I want my seat."

"Yes, we've established that. Come on, Beck, let's get to work."

"I know her," Beck whispered, pointing at the fading child.

"Yes, we've established that as well." Belasco cast his eyes over Winstrom, still clutching his privates, curled in a fermata on the floor. "Wake up the other living, would you, and come along. Now the real business must be done."

Back at the Belasco apartment, Beck was drinking and Junior, who'd long ago retreated to the comfort of the bottle, was sobering.

"What kind of show?" Junior asked, looking over Belasco's shoulder at the contract. "Should I get Dad up over it?"

"No, no. Nothing as drastic as that." Belasco removed a pair of reading glasses and loosened his clerical collar. "Beck, put down the whiskey and tell us what you know."

"Jesus." Beck's hand held the glass like it was a rough-cut diamond slicing its way through his fingers. They trembled. "That kid."

He sat himself down on the rollaway couch, pushing Poupee and Harper back inside it. "I know her 'cause I hired her – about 80 years ago – in a throwaway slot in a night of throwaway slots."

Emilie's head popped out of the couch, a scowl on her lips and an obscene gesture on her fingers.

"Sorry, Emilie, but that's what you were. Her Ma really wanted her to be in the show and the kid had some talent, so why not? I mean, I hate stage moms like all good and decent people do, but this dame was nothing like. She was kinda sweet, pretty pale, real quiet. So I said yes to the kid. If only I'd known."

"Known what?" The disembodied voice piped in.

"You here, Hardy?"

"Yeah. I couldn't take myself anymore. God, I'm an asshole."

"Back to the story, please, Mr. Beck." Belasco blew ghostly breath across the ghostly paper to dry the ghostly ink.

If Nick were there, it would have driven him mad to contemplate it. But Nick was not there. He was at home, solving the mystery of the girl in B33.

Or so he thought.

"The kid was a bitch! Fuck Mamma Rose–"

"No, thank you."

"You know what I mean. The kid was the problem. The dressing room's too hot; the dressing room's too cold; there's no food; there's no coffee; Junior's touching me in inappropriate ways."

"Did I fuck her?" Junior asked.

"Jesus! I don't know. Did you?"

"I don't remember." Junior looked worse than when the usher insulted his prowess. Being a lousy lay was one thing, child molesting quite another.

"So on the opening night, she goes out to do her thing, only she doesn't do her thing, she just stares up...into...the balcony!" Beck jumped up and kicked up his heels in a sort of German Irish jig. "Jesus, that's what she's looking for – why she wants her seat. Her guest! I always gave them a guest, Belasco, for the opening."

"In the balcony? How generous, Mr. Beck."

"You should have seen some of their guests. Jesus, who could she have been waiting for?"

"Her mother!"

Nick burst in melodramatically with Kylie, out of breath, at his heels. He should have been waving a computer printout that revealed all, but he didn't bother to print out the information. It was simple.

Kylie shivered. "Can't you people turn up the heat?"

Nick ignored her. "That's right. Her mother!"

"Well, obviously." If the ghost of Graham Hardy had had a body with which to make a dismissive gesture, he would have done.

"What do you mean, obviously?"

"The mother. I've known that this whole time. I come from the future death of Graham Hardy, right? So, duh."

"Why didn't you tell us?" Nick was annoyed.

"Not my fault the past tense can't keep up with the future. When you're the 'will be,' it's hard to lower yourself to the 'was not.'"

Nick hated the living dead. Or was it the dead living?

"You never finished the story, Beck." Harper rose up out of the rollaway. There was no sign of Poupee. "What happened after she couldn't perform?"

"The first night, she stayed in the theatre. Slept there for all I know. The second night, she was still there. Nobody paid any mind. Then the third night, she was gone."

"And nobody looked for her?" A mothering instinct was so post-feminist and Kylie prided herself on being a post-post-Feminist, but then why had she put up with Nick so long if it weren't just to have a big, lazy baby around the house? A big, lazy, occasionally wage-earning baby.

"Jesus, doll, it was a theatre, not a babysitting service. There was business to be done. Always business."

Kylie decided she was definitely on the little girl's side. "No wonder she's pissed off."

"Yeah, well. She's still a little bitch."

While the story was touching, yeah, right, Nick saw no point in discussing the girl further. "It doesn't really matter what happened to the kid. We need to find her mother."

Belasco sighed and picked up the phone. "Whom do you want me to call?"

"You can't call where her mother is. Hart Island."

There was a pause, the kind a film composer would be unable to resist filling with a pounding series of minor cords.

Before Nick could be grateful Winstrom was back at the theatre, Hardy – the ghost of Hardy future – obliged. "Dum, dum, DUM!"

No one was amused.

"What? What's the big deal?"

Like their living counterparts, the spirits of the future were less educated than those of the past.

"The dead do not go there."

"The dead do go there, Belasco. That's the problem."

"The homeless dead, Mr. Beck." Belasco sniffed. "The hopeless."

"The lost." Beck poured himself another drink, phantom whiskey in a phantom glass. "If you're going there, kid, you're going on your own. Our kind can't go there."

"Can't go there or won't go there?" Kylie asked.

"Won't. Maybe can't. I don't know what'd happen if we did. Maybe we'd just disappear. Maybe we'd be devoured. It might just be too much, having seen what happens to a spirit that doesn't have a place. It could bring on the second death."

Poupee, still entombed in the couch, trembled and the rollaway bucked and shuddered.

"The second death?"

"Obviously you know of the first, even if you haven't known it like we do. In the Biblical sense. The second death, though – well, sometimes it's a good thing. Like what we're trying to give the little bitch. We'll release her from her earthly need and bring on the second death."

"But if the second death is unsought and yet it comes..." Belasco held his palms up.

"There's only hell left," Junior said.

"The only club that'll admit you, after that."

"Right," Nick said. "So you're too afraid to accompany us?"

"Not too scared. Too smart. We leave the really stupid stuff up to the living."

Beck gave Nick a toothy, shit-eating grin.

Nick hated Martin Beck.

"Hart Island is a depressing place and not just because it's a skinny slab of worthless land floating out the back end of the Bronx. Nor is it solely because of the dead people (although they help a great deal). No, Hart Island is a sad place because it's the final subway stop on the way to oblivion.

Not that the subways go there, of course. Only the *Michael Corosce* makes the trip.

If one seeks to ascertain the level of sadness – on a scale from a hangnail to supervillian world domination, say – ask the prisoners from Riker's who shovel corpses there for 25 to 35 cents a day.

No matter which incarcerate you speak to, you'll get the same answer. "Hart's is some fucked up shit."

And that's from the necrophiliacs.

Because New Yorkers die, just like everyone else. And in a city lacking in a few of the social graces, in a city that runs with scissors, in a city that does not play well with others, sometimes New Yorkers die alone.

Hart Island is where those New Yorkers go, almost 3,000 a year, about 750,000 in all. The dead arrive by the boatload and some of them never leave.

Nick put away his palm pilot and frowned at Kylie, who sat still as the dead between him and a hefty tattooed mexicano called Raphael Manuel Gabriel Garcia Santos de Lopez-Ortega (née Stinky Gomez). The Virgin of Guadalupe stared back at him, her eyes bleeding blue pen ink down one badly rashed cheek.

Perhaps it wasn't the best of ideas to hitch a ride with the prison detail, but Nick's connections in Brooklyn were only able to get him on the Saturday burial duty before the coming Monday when the girl in B33 would be performing at last. He had to get to Hart's Island. He had to find the girl's mother.

He had to go on the prison detail.

Still, he felt a little sorry for Kylie. She was filet mignon wrapped in bacon in a boardroom full of ravenous CEOs.

Or a boat full of convicts, anyway.

The *Mikey C*, the prisoner's pet name for their transport, drew further and further away from the quaintly Victorian City Island and Kylie drew closer and closer to Nick.

She hoped to distract herself with the vista. But Hart's did little more than depress her until she remembered a late night insomniac cable fit the month before.

"Shit! *Don't Say a Word* was shot here. Michael Douglas, right? I loved him in *Reds*."

"That was Warren Beatty." Nick reopened his palm pilot and set his pencil to it. He had stopped feeling sorry for her.

"So what? I'm expected to keep those bourgeoisie oppressors of the brown man straight?"

"They don't keep themselves straight, why should you?"

"*Island of the Dead*'s a better flick anyway. Man-eating flies."

"Mos Def, son."

"Man-eating flies!"

Nick carefully craned his neck back and found a tall, whippet-thin Irish-looking fellow face-to-face and fist-to-fist with a handsome, well-built black man.

"Mos Def, son," said Irish.

"Man-eating flies," said Handsome.

"Both suck," said Nick.

Irish and Handsome lowered their fists.

"You're right, of course," Handsome agreed.

Kylie sunk lower in her seat and closed her eyes, pretending to sleep. She was sick of this already. First the apartment, now the boat.

"What you in for, son?" Irish asked. He gave Kylie a long, lingering once over then, from her black toes – she wore sandals, on a prison detail, God knew why – up her ripped jeans and to her arms wrapped protectively around her small breasts. Her face – he was pretty sure she had one – wasn't important.

Irish licked his lips. "What the bitch in for?"

"A ride to Hart's Island. The bitch, too." Kylie shot him a frown, which gave Nick an ironic thrill. "What are you in for?"

"Murder One, niggah. But I done it in Delaware, so that that."

"And you?"

Handsome pursed his lips, contemplating an answer. "A white collar crime, which, to my dismay, turned very blue collar very fast."

"I'm sorry."

"So am I."

"Do you always do burial detail?" Nick asked.

"Every day." Handsome sighed.

Raphael Manuel Gabriel Garcia Santos de Lopez-Ortega (née Stinky Gomez) started to get up and Kylie and Nick went with him, afraid the bench might follow without his bulk to hold it down.

"Welcome to potter's navy, son." Irish flashed his teeth, 2/3 of which were a sort of gold color, most likely pyrite.

The convicts unloaded in a slow-motion shuffle like a line dance in *Night of the Living Dead*, heading towards the middle of the island and their work. Kylie and Nick waited beside the boat for some kind of assistance, but none came, unless one counted the ongoing presence of Handsome and Irish.

Nick hated counting.

"So, what, are you our guides?" he asked finally.

"True dat, true dat. Just waitin' for the instructions," Irish replied and started off in the opposite direction of the prisoners, towards a large, ivy-engulfed tower. It resembled a mill or –

"A missile silo?"

"The 1950's were a frightening time on this island. But that's where you'll find your answers. This path is your River Styx, we your Charon–"

Irish turned green, fit to puke. "Yo, what did I say 'bout muthafuckin' Charon?"

"Because you never bothered with an education, the rest of us are expected to suffer?"

"I graduate the muthafuckin' fif' grade, son, so don' you –"

"Shut up!" Kylie stopped them both cold, not with anger in her voice, but with fear. "What the hell is that?"

"I think you mean, who the hell is that?" Nick corrected softly.

Coming towards them out of the oppressive darkness of the silo was a young woman, probably dead in her early twenties. Not that one could tell from the damage life – and death – had done to her.

Her clothing, a poor thing to begin with, was no more than rags, dripping some sort of dark substance down the devastated hemline. Nick would have wondered what it was if the same stuff wasn't also leaking from her mouth and nose and from her eyes.

Nick missed Guadalupe's ink-wet tears. Because this woman's tears were blood. All of it was blood, slipping down her face and dripping between her thighs.

"Yellow fever," Handsome said.

"That shit be hardcore." Irish slapped Nick on the back, knocking the breath – and nearly the lunch – out of him. "And fuck my brutha here. That be muthafuckin' Charon!"

"You got Peg Leg Stuy down?"

"Of course! One mustn't hold an opening without at least one Stuyvescent in the house. It wouldn't be right."

Belasco and Beck had been busily scrawling out invitations to their ghost girl's first and hopefully final Broadway performance. They were nearly through their list of notable spirits – and with no help from the others. Jamie had passed out on the couch, the phantom whiskey bottle empty, its phantom shards shattered not far from his phantom hand. Poupee and Harper were off arguing or fucking or both and no one could tell if Hardy was in the room or not, so for the sake of their sanities, Belasco and Beck assumed no.

"You know, Belasco, I was thinking of putting up a broadsheet in Washington Square."

"If you'd like to attract that element, Mr. Beck."

"Hippies? Drug dealers? Shitty musicians?"

Well, they'd found Hardy.

"No." Belasco said. "Criminals, paupers, the strange fruits of the hanging tree."

Beck shrugged. "Somebody's got to fill the balcony. You think Peg Leg or Poe or Alex Hamilton'll sit up there?"

"No, no." Belasco carefully dotted his "i's" and crossed his "t's", adding a little flourish under his own name while leaving Beck's unadorned. "Go ahead. Put up a notice."

"Hot dog!"

Beck hardly made it to the apartment door before it blew open in his face. A warm breeze and a perfumed scent – Nick was wrong about the smell thing, actually – wafted through, filling the small office space.

"Ms. Thomas," Belasco said, in awe.

Indeed, it was Ms. Thomas. Olive Thomas, the New Amsterdam chorus girl who'd gone and poisoned herself over the kind of slight chorus girls went and poisoned themselves over – a sugar daddy knocking up their best friend on the line, having to sleep with an ugly producer, stolen stockings.

Olive's reasoning was lost to history, but she was not. In death, she preferred living construction workers to ectoplasmic money men, but obviously word about the show was out.

She pouted at them both and spread out her legs. "Marty. Davey. Don't you like me?"

"Of course we like you!" Beck gave her a chaste kiss on each cheek. "You're still gorgeous, baby."

"Naturally."

"Unnaturally," Beck said and they both laughed.

"Davey?"

Belasco rose to pay homage, placing his lips gently on each of her tiny hands. She clutched a blue bottle in the right one and Belasco carefully avoided it.

It contained the poison that killed her, or so the gossip went.

"Have a seat." Beck pulled out a chair, afraid of what might put her too close to the couch – and Jamie.

"Thank you, Marty." Olive smiled primly, but recrossed her legs on the seat, giving the boys a split second vision of paradise.

Belasco actually grinned. "What may we do you for, my dear?"

"I'm looking for a spot in your little show."

"We're not doing a line nor anything on par with the Follies. A few recitations, a song or two –"

"That's what I want. A solo song."

Olive Thomas was not the stereotypical chorus girl. She didn't speak in the squeaky tones of a Maltese on helium. In fact, her voice was husky, like ripe corn as it's ripped open on a warm August night.

Unfortunately, she couldn't sing for shit.

"Uh, doll–"

Fate intervened then and, as Fate is oft to do, it intervened for the worst.

"Guys! I wrote the song – for Poupee! Where is she?"

Winstrom was all teeth and glad hands until he laid eyes on her. On Olive Thomas.

That was all it took. Winstrom was in love.

He dropped down on one knee in front of her, holding out three pages of battered sheet music like a scepter. "My angel, I would like to present you with this song." Then, as an afterthought. "Do you sing?"

"Of course, I do!" Well, she thought, he's no beefcake, but at least he's breathing.

"Then please do me the honor of performing this on Monday."

"Okay, honey." She gave the producers a triumphant pout. "So, I'm in, right, boys?"

"Yes, Olive," Belasco said wearily. "You're in."

She squealed, a sound like an alligator's orgasm. "Let's celebrate, Mr.–"

"Winstrom. But you can call me Sammy."

"All right, Sammy. Have a drink."

She held out her blue bottle.

Beck took an involuntary step forward thinking "it's poison!" But then he thought "Is the world better with Winstrom in it?" But then he thought "What if he becomes a ghost – and chooses to haunt us?"

"Uh, Sammy, you might not want to–"

It was too late. Winstrom was already drinking.

"Louisa Van Slyke," the bloody spirit held out her hand, but Nick wasn't sure if he could – or should – take it. "What can I do for you fellows?"

"Excuse me?"

Louisa reared back in surprise at Kylie's female voice. "What they're doing to ladies in your living days! Not that we don't have a few of your kind down here, somewhere. Do you want to meet one?"

"No, thank you," Nick said. "We're looking for someone specific. From 1919, 1920, maybe."

"Oh, we have lots of retards from then."

"Retards?" Kylie was already offended and she was getting offendeder.

"What else would you call them? They've got no conversation. They're here, All right, but they don't know why. If you had something besides a retard, you'd have already solved your problem."

"We don't use that term any more," Kylie said.

Louisa's jaundiced eyes blazed. "You'd like me to call them what – spiritually challenged? You watch them and wash them and love them like I do. Catalogue them.

Try to understand them. Try to FREE them. And then you tell me what to call them, girlie."

"Sorry to offend. Jesus."

"If only. But we don't brook that path here. Patty, Reginald, take them away."

"Yes, ma'am." Irish took Kylie hard by the arm and Handsome took Nick's and, with a hearty yank, began to drag them away.

"Wait!" Nick pulled himself away from Handsome and went slipping and sliding back towards the missile silo and the fading guardian of the slow dead. "Louisa, there's a girl, a little girl, involved. If you give us her mother, that's one less for you to have to care for. We'll take her. If we have her, we can bring the second death – the good second death – to the both of them."

Louisa frowned at the living man, panting with the effort of his shouting, the waste of breathing wracking his sad form. He was handsome, she decided, in a sweaty, smelly, living sort of way.

"What is her name?"

Nick said it and Louisa immediately smiled. "I know her. Stupid, but sweet. A good girl. You can have her."

She called the name back into the blackness of the silo with the caressing tones of one hailing a beloved pet. There was a shimmer and a silence and then the woman came forth, rising from somewhere deep below.

She was easily as young as Louisa, but still beautiful. Her death had come so swiftly, it hardly marked her except for the pallor in her cheeks.

"Hart's Island was a tubercular hospital in its time." Louisa touched the woman who looked up to her like a dog or a daughter. "Go with these living and they will give you rest."

Mother shook her head no, but Louisa gave her a gentle push forward. "Go with the living, love, and they will give you rest."

Mother came towards them then and Irish let Kylie go. Mother was nervous, but Kylie was careful to smile broadly. "Come with us."

At the invitation, Mother followed, laughing at the grass on her feet and the two living souls who went along with her.

Nick was not laughing. Kylie was trying.

The *Michael Corosce* awaited them at the dock, the convicts already half-loaded. The prisoners who waited for their turn were wet and tired. Nick didn't envy them. He envied his prisoner guides.

"So how do you two get away with abandoning your shift?"

Handsome glanced at Irish as if to question the question. Then he headed straight towards Raphael Manuel Gabriel Garcia Santos de Lopez-Ortega (née Stinky Gomez), a fighter's glare fixed on his face, twisting it almost to ugliness.

"Watch out! That guy—"

Handsome passed right through the mexicano, who went green, then red, then white, then green again. Raphael stumbled away to throw up somewhere private.

"What was that?" Nick murmured.

"He saw what I did to be punished thus," Handsome said, turning back towards the boat. "Nice to meet you, folks. Safe home."

Nick watched wide-eyed as Handsome mounted the gangway and the prisoners parted before him like a white and brown Red Sea.

Irish found this all to be some mad funny shit. He laughed from behind his hand, but with his fingers splayed out so his pyrite-encrusted teeth twinkled between them.

"Peace out, sistahs," he said and disappeared.

Nick, Kylie and Mother went last after the prisoners were safely boarded. They saw Handsome and Irish sitting together in a corner and carefully avoided them, although Irish threw them a complicated gang sign which might have been an invitation to join them. Or a threat to their living lives.

As soon as they were far enough away from the two, Nick, having overcome his initial shock, leaned into Kylie and whispered. "They're ghosts."

Kylie rolled her eyes.

"What? So I'm not very sensitive."

"No shit, Sherlock."

Kylie was silent the rest of the trip, her arms folded over her chest in a gesture of defiance, not protection, although that was still a side benefit.

Unfortunately, Mother wasn't silent. She babbled, she moaned, she took off her boots and counted her toes.

She only got to eight.

She only had eight.

"What happened to your feet?" Nick asked.

Mother smiled and nodded and counted again. "One, two, three, four, five, six, seven, eight!"

Nick sighed. Still, in some ways it was more satisfying than conversing with Kylie.

Mother could count. That was better than Kylie.

Even if Nick hated counting.

"To drink that."

Winstrom guzzled and swallowed. "Why?"

"It's poison." Belasco felt ill.

Winstrom, perplexed, smacked his lips, retasting it. "No, it's not. It's gin."

At the word gin, Junior rolled off the couch and onto the floor. He picked himself back up as best he could, shards of glass stuck to his face so that his visage read "YEKRUT DLIW."

Olive took one look at Junior and slapped him hard across the cheek.

Jamie didn't react, only pulled the embedded glass out of his face with a sickening, slurping pop.

"Glad I'm not a bleeder," he said, dropping the pieces back on the floor.

"I wish you were, you...cad!" Olive stomped to the door, then rounded fiercely on the producers. "And my boyfriend better have a place in the show too! Or else!"

Then, remembering the impoliticness of her outburst, she turned to Winstrom and went down on her knees before him, a familiar position for her. Not that the composer had ever stood back up anyway, remaining penitent to his newfound queen. "That is, if he still is my boyfriend. There's only one aphrodisiac for me, after all. Talent."

She dragged out the final word, exaggerating the movements of her lips and tongue as she came closer and closer to Winstrom's mouth.

The dead could hear the inaudible groan from the living as she pulled away.

"My boyfriend's in – or else!" she repeated, then stood and swung open the door.

"Is that me? The boyfriend?" Winstrom asked.

Nick made the poor choice of taking this moment for his entrance. Olive passed right through him, pushing him back out of the door.

"What is it with you people? Why do you do that?" Nick shouted, shivering in his frost-coated skin. Icicles dropped out of his mouth as he spoke.

Then he shot forward and slapped Junior across the cheek, his hand passing harmlessly through the ghost.

"What was that for?" Junior rubbed his reforming jaw like it hurt.

"Momentary possession. Residual resentment." Belasco answered. "Welcome back, Mr. Brown."

"You mean that woman was...inside me?" Maybe playing ghost hunter wasn't so bad. There could be...perks.

"More or less. For a moment."

Belasco intensely disliked the living.

"Pretty! Pretty!" Mother bounced up and down as if she'd just noticed the disappeared chorus girl.

Belasco frowned. "Who is this sorry wrench?"

"This is Mother." Kylie walked the spirit forward, keeping her hands firmly anchored on Mother's upper arms to prevent the woman from bolting. The spiritually-challenged didn't realize they could pass through solid matter. Or else they couldn't.

Beck didn't quite believe his eyes at first, but yes, it was her in the flesh. It was the little girl's mother. "A pleasure to meet you – again."

Mother took in Beck, almost as if she knew him, then blew a loud raspberry, spraying the producer with ectoplasmic spit.

"Jesus!"

"She's stupid," Nick explained.

"Stupid?"

"The brain-dead dead. We learned all about it on Hart's. A charming slit of countryside, though I can see why you don't care for it."

"Stupid?" Beck repeated.

"Like you're being now, Beck." Nick took over for Kylie, leading Mother to the couch. She didn't sit when she got there; instead, she played with her lips, dragging the top one up over her nose, then pulling the lower one down over her chin.

Nick applied pressure to the spot right above her buttocks, and, like an obedience school C-student, she squatted.

"Sit, Mother." She dropped down on the cushions. "Good girl."

Now pushing Kylie in front of him, Nick quickly made his way back through the apartment door.

"Where're you going, Brown?" Beck had a sneaking suspicion of what was about to happen. Only because he'd done it himself, once or twice.

"Out. We're living. You're dead. You take care of her."

Nick closed the door behind him.

"Oh, no. Oh, no." Mother cried out, rocking herself back and forth.

"What?" Beck didn't want to know.

"Oh, no." Mother raised her puppy-dog eyes to the producer and pointed to the spreading gray stain beneath her.

"I'll never get that out," Belasco said.

"Jesus. Do we got any diapers?"

Olive Thomas' boyfriend turned out to be Dylan Thomas (it was easier for her to remember him since they shared a surname). A shame he never turned up for rehearsal. Or for the actual show.

"It was half-hour a half hour ago and where's your boyfriend?" Beck raised his voice in the way a storm rises to a squall. A few drops of rain, then streams of it, then the deluge.

Cats and dogs, indeed.

Olive was prettily put out. "I can't imagine where he might be."

"And has anyone seen Junior?"

"Has anyone seen Georgie's head?" Harper, serving as chief follow spot operator and prop master, interrupted. Holding onto his overalls' back strap was the headless body of a well-dressed gentleman.

Georgie was George Fredrick Cooke, a venerable old ghost from St. Paul's Chapel way who, in life, had donated his head to science (upon his death, naturally). When that time came, his skull proved little useful for its intended purpose and the men of learning passed it on to the only people who might find a use for it – actors. George's head went on to feature prominently in half a dozen productions of *Hamlet* and two *Macbeth*s and Georgie, headless for so many years, was jealous.

The skull certainly wasn't and, as the only fame it had ever experienced came after it was separated from its body, it had no desire to rejoin with its former master.

The skull had developed a habit of running away. No. Don't ask how.

Merely, this was the problem Harper was attempting to solve. Where to find the head. Or any head for that matter.

"We can't hold the show for him. Put Poupee on."

"It doesn't matter anyway. We can't get Mother to come in." Kylie pushed her way through the ghosts to Belasco, disrupting their spiritual forms and generally pissing them off.

"Hey, doll, you look good. If you weren't living."

"Thank you, Mr. Beck." She blushed and actually curtsied, although the movement more resembled a small child in her Sunday best letting out gas at a garden party than a grown woman showing proper respect.

"You're welcome. So what's the problem with the broad?"

"She's scared, I guess. Really, really scared."

"We can't hold the show. I'm sorry." Ghosts could sweat and Beck was dripping. "We gotta go. He's just gonna have to get her up there. Somehow."

Nick wasn't sure if it was the rabble filing its way up into the balcony or the balcony itself, but Mother wasn't moving. She had enjoyed watching the notables enter, doing their delicate social dance – how Peg Leg Stuyvesant hobbled in on his cane and finest frou frou, how the Burr wife and daughter carefully avoided Alexander Hamilton so as to prevent any mention of that messy dueling business, how a whole series of Tammany Hall mayors still argued over whose corruption charges were more impressive.

But now that it was time for her to enter the theatre, she was afraid. She stood before the balcony entrance, specially reopened for this performance only, shaking her head no.

"Why not? Why not!" Nick heard the sounds of a haunted overture kicking up inside the building and almost burst into tears.

He hated retards. And ghosts. And retarded ghosts.

Eh eh, Kylie corrected inside his head. *Spiritually challenged*.

"Can I help you, sir?"

"No. No one can help me," he moaned.

Then from behind his eyelids he saw a bright blazing light as penetrating as any beam emanating from the bellybutton of God himself.

The flashlight of the damned.

"Except maybe you."

The usher really grinned, exposing her last good teeth. The both of them. "Come on, honey, show me your ticket."

Mother immediately obeyed, producing the billet on command.

"We're going upstairs, in the balcony. Come on, honey. There, you hear that pretty music? That's the show starting."

Neither Nick nor the usher could keep up with her then. As they climbed the six flights of stairs, the usher kept groaning about always being in the orchestra and Nick wondered why there wasn't an elevator.

Nick hated stairs.

But when they finally arrived at the top, there was Mother waiting at the entrance to their section, near panting like a soon-to-be walked hound.

For safety's sake, Beck gave Nick B31, but as the only living person in the gallery, Nick was beginning to think his safety had nothing to do with it.

Even in the slight light reflecting up from the stage, Nick could tell that far too many of his fellow theatregoers had died from the involuntary snapping of the 2nd, 3rd and/or 4th cervical vertebra. If the knife wounds hadn't killed them first.

But he couldn't leave Mother to them. What if she went off with one and missed her little girl's number? The theatre's management would be dealing with exploding patrons for the next decade.

Or forever even.

The first act on the bill was to have featured Mr. Cooke reciting from Shakespeare, but as his skull was still AWOL, Poupee, re: Beck's instructions, replaced him with her high wire gymnastics.

Ghosts could twist themselves in the most interesting positions. The rousties in the balcony enjoyed it anyway, showering the circus girl with catcalls, wolf whistles and obscenities.

Nick worried about Mother's – oh, innocence, he supposed – but he shouldn't have been nervous. She was already asleep, gray drool dripping from her lips onto the shoulder of his second-best sweater.

Did ectoplasm stain?

"'We always hold in having it, if you fancy it/If you fancy it, that's understood!'"

"A little of what you fancy does you good. Yeah, I know." Beck had heard enough English music hall, especially the dirty ones. He didn't even have to look. "You're drunk."

Junior answered for himself and the now unconscious, bloated poet he propped up with all his strength. "Yes. We are."

"Certainly brings back the memories, doesn't it, Mr. Beck?" Belasco was floating two inches off the ground in his satisfaction with everything. Not even the collapse of Junior and Thomas on the boards could sink him.

"Yeah, the bad ones. Olive, go."

"But, Marty, I'm not warmed up!"

"You'll be great, kid." Beck almost choked on the encouragement.

Beck hated lying.

Winstrom, pathetically as living as Kylie and Hardy beside him, jumped at the chance to lapdog his lady. "I'll go out with you. I believe in you."

"Oh, Sammy, you're a death-saver." Her lips brushed past his cheek, fresh like a shot of Febreze.

The audience greeted Ms. Thomas' entrance with great enthusiasm, an applause so loud Mother briefly awakened from her slumber. She blinked twice, yawned and went back to sleep.

How she managed that, Nick couldn't fathom. The gorgeous ghost – who had been inside him, he reminded himself – opened her mouth and the most horrifying noises, syllables that might have been whole words, but put back together backwards and upside down, emerged from it – and not softly, but at an ear-splitting volume.

Ear-splitting to three of the four living persons in the building. Winstrom was in a trance.

Winstrom was in love.

To the well-bred patrones dell' arte, there was only the discomfort of an unrecognized tune, making them feel undereducated and, therefore, unappreciating. To the rabble, Olive was a babe, so who gave a fuck what she did, so long as they could see the milky tops – if the milk were skim gone gray and transparent – of her ample breasts.

Unfortunately, New York City's banshees population, long time residents of Hell's Kitchen who immigrated in the holds of Black '47 ships, couldn't help themselves. They screamed along.

Nick wasn't sure exactly when the number – if one could count it as a number and Nick, as it's been mentioned, hated counting – mercifully ended. When he carefully reopened his eyes and ears, a headless body, carrying three sticks in one hand and three plates in the other, was alone on stage.

The body, Mr. G.F. Cooke, according to the playbill, began spinning the plates, first on the left hand, then on the right, and finally, with a flip of ghostly levitation, on the stump of his neck.

Nick clapped, despite himself, rousing Mother who, for the first time, took an interest in the proceedings.

The plates still spinning, Mr. Cooke began to dance, each little jiggy jump bumping the plates up into the air. Each time, he caught them again, drawing gasps and laughs from the crowd.

This was too much for the skull, who had sequestered himself in the tank of the star's toilet. He bounced past the grinning producers and edgy living, his muscle-less jaw flapping out the immortal words of Shakespeare.

"'Alas, poor Yorick. I knew him, Horatio. A fellow of infinite jest, of most excellent fancy. He hath borne me on his back a thousand times. And now—'"

"Shut up!" came from the balcony.

"The hook! The hook!" came from the mezzanine.

The orchestra stayed silent – out of sophistication, not interest.

It didn't matter; the body couldn't hear anyway. Cooke merely continued to jig his way to the shoulder of the stage and with an energetic high kick, knocked the offending head into the left box.

Peg Leg Stuyvesant caught it and held it aloft like a trophy. "Ole Hesh Horseman could use one of these, eh?"

The crowd laughed at the joke, although no one was willing to make the journey up to Westchester to give the Headless Horseman his prize.

Cooke took his bow and the audience went wild for him, culminating in a wholly spontaneous standing ovation. George Fredrick Cooke had found his rest.

Backstage, the drunks were unconscious, Winstrom was seeking comfort in the arms of Miss Thomas and the little girl was ready for her entrance.

"Go kill 'em, kid."

With her most innocent eyes, she replied, "They're already dead."

"Good point. Now get out there."

The tiny costume, tattered in its most earthbound incarnation, transformed into its former glory as she skipped into the spotlight, the frills and flounces bouncing fully around her plump, pale legs.

"She's kind of cute," the disembodied Hardy said.

"When she's not killing people," the living Hardy said.

"When she's not killing living people," Beck said with some satisfaction. "Shut your traps, breathers, and watch this."

When the little girl reached the center of the spot, she stopped and looked up into the balcony. Nick felt her cold eyes on him, but only for a second before they settled on Mother.

The moment Mother was in her gaze, purpose and meaning erased what eighty years of aimless waiting had wrought. Mother stood and with a clear, bell-like voice called out, "I love you, sweetie!"

The little girl opened her mouth and recited "Mary, Mary, quite contrary, how does your garden grow? With silver bells and cockle-shells and pretty maids all in a row."

"Nursery rhymes? We went through this for nursery rhymes?" The living Hardy plopped down on the nearest Equity cot, a convenience required by the actors' union and often utilized for between show liaisons. This time, it settled for supporting Hardy's ass.

"It was a novelty thing. Big in those days." Beck smiled and the girl made her way through "I love little pussy" and "Ride a cock horse."

He shook his head. "What a dame."

"When did you start speaking like that?"

Beck knew the voice, a mother's caress and a lover's spanking. "Weezie. There was a revival of *Guys and Dolls* in the house. It took."

"*Guys and Dolls?*" Weezie, Mrs. Louise Beck to everyone else, took the producer's hand and smiled. "Never mind. I like it."

"The show's almost over." The light from the stage was becoming unbearably bright.

"Wonderful. Are you coming with me, Martin?"

Beck shrugged, smiled. "Why not?"

If Kylie and Hardy hadn't been so completely swept up in the romance of the Becks, they might have noticed the romance of Winstrom and Miss Thomas, now climbing the stairs up into the flies. They weren't arguing, but going solemnly as if to a wedding – or a funeral.

"Just a few more steps, Sammy, and we'll be together forever," she was saying.

But Hardy's head was on Kylie's shoulder and they were both sighing at their own solitary status.

"If only I could find a man like that," Kylie said.

"Me too," The living Hardy said.

"You do," The disembodied Hardy said and there was a breeze and a passing like the end of something.

Which it was.

With all the force and light of a nuclear bomb detonated in the dimension kitty-corner to their own, the theatre filled with a rushing, sucking wind and a blinding flash.

When the living reopened their eyes, the theatre was vacant except for those annoying black splotches dancing through their vision, the final side effect of the damned.

"Are we all clear?" Hardy shouted out into the seeming emptiness. When he didn't shout back at himself, he understood.

The ghosts were gone.

Just to be sure, Kylie dragged the ghost light from its hiding place backstage and onto stage left. She plugged it in and felt satisfied – no, safe – basking in its single sixty watt glow.

Hardy carted a few folding chairs into the center ring formed around the light. He sat them up, four of them, around and inside the light, then held his hands palm open to the naked bulb, as if warming himself before a campfire.

"You guys all right?"

"Fine, Nick," Kylie answered. "Come on down. The stage is fine. Quiet, even."

Nick hated stairs, but he'd never in his life done them with such enthusiasm. It was over; the ghosts were gone.

"Not quite, Mr. Brown."

"Belasco?" Nick froze on the final set of balcony stairs. He couldn't see anything in the pitch dark, but he shivered in the cold.

"We worked together so well and I'm not accorded the respect of a Mr. Belasco?"

"Mr. Belasco?"

Nick hated Mr. Belasco.

"I only wanted to say thank you. The ghosts of Broadway have had so little purpose of late, so little reason to be. Oh, there are still the superstitious in the theatre, the old guard actors, the classically trained, the stagehands and the ushers, still but one or two generations out of mother Ireland in their belief in lore and legends. But it's all fun and games to these new ones, the chorus children with their musical theatre degrees and the hot young Hollywood boys who come here when their films aren't being made. It's positively depressing. But you made us feel again that we could change things. That we have changed things. And that we matter to the living."

"Blame that kid who killed Arnie Moines too."

"I thank her as well." Although he couldn't see, Nick understood that Belasco was fading. "You have an open invitation to visit any time, Mr. Brown. You know where the apartment is. We'll be waiting."

Nick had a feeling they would be.

Nick hated waiting.

"You okay, Nick? You look like you've seen...a ghost?" Kylie burst into laughter despite herself. Stupid bourgeoisie turns of phrase, oddly appropriate in this case.

"Belasco. Invited me up for a drink sometime," Nick threw himself in one of the folding chairs with an exaggerated yawn.

"That was fun," Hardy said, yawning along.

"Lot of help you were," Nick said.

"Hey, my ghost showed up. Where was yours?"

Nick ignored that, forcing himself back to his feet. "Let's go home, Kylie. I'm fucking tired."

"Hey, wait!" Hardy sat up, suddenly remembering. "Whatever happened to Winstrom?"

Kylie looked to Nick and Nick shrugged.

Some things, it was better not to know.

The Late Night Menu

You still ain't decided? Looking around too much, is that it? Look kid, I ain't kidding. You might want to spend a bit more time browsing that menu and a little less gawking.

Yeah, I'm dead. What gave it away, the occasional grub coming out my sleeve, or my lovely perfume? You're a bright one, I'll give you that. I know what the brochures say, we get about one or two of your type in here every six months or so — not that time means much around here. But seriously, this ain't one of those places where the working stiff (pardon the expression) comes in looking for a friendly ear to tell a sad tale to. Everybody doesn't know your name here, and frankly, nobody gives a damn.

Here, let me lean a bit closer so you can see my friendly promotional pin.

No, underneath the one that says, "Sally."

Yeah, you read right, "Eat and get out."

Dirk Moonfire and the Nefarious Space Women

by Jack Mangan

"So you see, Dirk, why this mission is so important," the President said. He steepled his fingers together and looked gravely across his desk. Dirk rubbed his ruggedly square chin and nodded.

"Yeah, I understand what I have to do, all right, but there's one thing I don't get."

"What's that?"

"Why would aliens want to come to Earth to kidnap Miss Lucilla Bloodsky anyway?"

The President rose from his seat and leaned against the edge of his desk. "Well, as I explained earlier, Dirk, Dr. Bloodsky is Earth's top Atomic Scientist. It must have something to do with the work she'd been doing on the MatterBomb project. We can only guess that the aliens plan to force her to give them the MatterBomb's secrets, then return in their flying saucers and use our own top secret weapon technology against us."

Dirk's jaw remained firmly set, even in the face of the ghastly possibility.

"But we don't really know anything Dirk, other than the fact that at about 6:00 this morning, the Bloodsky Estate's maids witnessed Flying Saucers descending upon their property and taking Dr. Bloodsky away with them. As soon as our agency was notified, we tracked the Saucers' deep space movements on our Space-o-scopes. We watched them fly all the way to Planet X."

"Planet X!" Dirk stood up, but then quickly composed himself and returned to his seat.

"Yes, Dirk, the newest planet found on the other side of the galaxy. It is very far away, but Dr. Bloodsky is too valuable to us to simply allow her to fall into the hands of potentially hostile aliens. We need you to find out the reasons why these aliens would kidnap Dr. Bloodsky and take her all the way there, but more importantly, we need you to bring her safely back to Earth. Do you accept this mission, Dirk?"

Dirk stood again and gave a manly salute. "Of course, Mr. President. Now about my crew-"

"Your crew will ready for you at the Rocket Ship tomorrow at oh-five hundred hours. Good luck, Dirk. God be with you."

The next morning, Dirk found himself standing at the base of the scaffolding supporting the Rocket Ship in which he'd be flying off toward Planet X. It rose high into the air above him, a beautiful, silver cone shape, its sleek surface only broken by its black spacewings, its windows, and the door. As Dirk climbed the scaffolding toward that door, he could see the ship's spectacular Spaceray Gun, which projected needle-like from the Rocket's shining nose. With a manly grin, Dirk walked through the door into the ship.

Seated inside the cockpit he found Blink Buzzard, the hotshot young cadet who'd made such a name for himself at the academy. Blink looked up with awe and saluted Dirk immediately. His shiny, slicked blonde hair gleamed under the overhead lights, just like his silver space uniform.

"Dirk Moonfire!" he exclaimed. "It will be an honor serving you on this mission, sir! Blink Buzzard at your service."

Dirk returned his salute. "At ease, Mr. Buzzard. And since we're going to be in these tight quarters together for a short time, please call me Dirk."

"Sure, Mr. – Dirk. Golly, this mission is going to be neat-o. Wait 'til I tell Old Tug."

"Old Tug?" Dirk frowned.

"Yeah, he's the third man on our crew. Hey, here he is now!"

An old man with white hair and a full, matching beard entered into the cockpit room through a porthole to another section of the Rocket's interior. He looked up and saw Dirk standing in the room before him.

"Well, well, looks like we have a real expert for a captain. Our mission is sure to succeed." The old man touched a salute to his forehead, just above his scowl.

"Tug, it's good to see you again," Dirk said quietly, also giving a quick salute. Blink looked back and forth between the two men.

Suddenly, a voice rang out from loudspeakers all over the scaffolding and Rocket Ship. "All crew and ground personnel must assume launch-ready positions. One minute 'til Rocket Ship launch. Repeat: one minute until Rocket Ship launch."

The three men moved to the three seats against the far wall and strapped themselves in. Each flipped the appropriate switches and dials at their control panels. Old Tug watched all of the needles and dials in his panel, and tore away the status printout paper to read it.

"All systems go," he announced. "Ship is ready to launch. Sir."

Dirk ignored the bitterness in the last of Old Tug's words and spoke in a strong voice. "Blink, prepare the cockpit to rotate up, to face forward. Make sure there are no loose items in the room."

"Aye, aye captain," Blink said, and clicked two big switches on his board. The cockpit immediately began to shift, rotating slowly until it finally locked into place, with the seats they were strapped into now faced directly up toward the Rocket Ship's nose.

"Space helmets on," Dirk commanded, and the three of them attached their helmets to the buckles on their suits' shoulders.

"Ready for launch," Dirk said, squinting out through the forward windows into the high, sun-filled morning sky. "Begin the countdown, Blink."

As Blink spoke the word, "One", he eased the throttle forward and the entire ship began to rumble; the engines below began to spit an enormous fire against the launch platform.

The Rocket Ship lifted gracefully off of the platform and shot up and away from the earth at amazing speed.

"Woooooo-eeee!" Blink shouted, but Dirk and Old Tug sat still and silent in their seats. Soon the blue and white of the Earth sky faded into a black field, punctuated here, there, and everywhere with shining white stars and constellations. Dirk scanned this great map until he finally found the eerie purple dot that was the image of faraway Planet X.

"Here we come, aliens," Dirk murmured. "To rescue Dr. Bloodsky and save the day."

After they'd flown for about an hour, past the Moon and Mars, Old Tug rose from his seat and excused himself, claiming that there were routine checks he wanted to get to in the engine room.

A few seconds after he'd passed through the porthole, Blink cleared his throat and spoke, "Excuse me, Mr. Moonfire – Dirk,"

"Yes, Blink?"

"Well, it may be none of my business, but there seems to be some bad history between you and Mr. Old Tug there…"

"Yes, it's all right, Blink," Dirk rubbed his square jaw thoughtfully. "Old Tug used to be a captain, just like me. But his better days are past him, and one day we were both sent on an exploration mission together. I was placed in charge of the mission over him. It hurt him deeply, as you can imagine, to be replaced by a younger man. I guess that also made him resentful towards me. I can understand those feelings of his though; I'm not angry with him at all. Tug's a good man, and we're lucky to have him with us on this mission."

The manner in which Dirk nodded seemed to indicate that the matter was closed, but Blink still looked puzzled. He sat back in his seat without saying anything further, though, keeping his thoughtful expression.

Finally, he seemed about to speak again, when buzzers and alarm klaxons suddenly sounded all over the cockpit. "What's going on, captain?" The room began to shake. A myriad of colors; indigos, magentas, teals, blood-reds, yellows, all splashed across the ship's window screens. Dirk squinted beyond them into space to see what it was that assailed them, but nothing could be seen. "What the hell have you steered us into?" Old Tug grumbled as he stepped back into the cockpit room.

"Tug, we've unexpectedly flown into some sort of energy field," Dirk replied calmly. "Check your sensors and see if there's a ship out there somewhere, or if it's just some kind of subspace anomaly. Blink, you try to steer us out of this mess."

"Yes sir," Blink Buzzard said through clenched teeth. "But the controls are fightin' me on that. I'm having trouble controllin' her!" As if to confirm his words, the ship began to lurch sickeningly back and forth.

Tug flipped a number of switches on his panel. In mere moments, it printed out the results of his scan. He donned his bifocal spectacles and read the fax with his mouth slightly open. "Negative on the presence of any other ships nearby, Dirk," he said, not taking his eyes away from the page. "But this confirms that we're smack in the middle of a huge field of distortion energy. Won't do any harm to the Rocket, but it's gonna be damned hard for Blink to regain control of the helm."

Dirk looked grimly out at the flickering colors of the energy field again. The ship began to spin wildly on its central axis, tossing and turning its crew in their seats.

"What do I do, captain?" shouted Blink frantically.

"Just keep fighting. Just keep fighting," Dirk said. He grimaced against the nauseating g-forces, but then spotted something through the flashing colors outside. He pointed. "Blink! Aim us for that planet there! Maybe we can park on that rock for a bit and wait for the energy storm to pass."

Blink wasted no breath answering, but tugged the ship's steering console with all his might. The Rocket Ship continued to bounce and sway tumultuously.

"It's working," Old Tug whispered fiercely. "Keep going, Blink; you're getting us there." Dirk saw that Tug's words were true; the planet they sought to reach was indeed getting closer. But as they drew nearer, he also began to realize that it was no world at all.

"What is that, some kind of asteroid?" he murmured aloud.

Old Tug shook his head. "Not like any asteroid or moon I ever seen."

It was actually a long, misshapen cylindrical body, with no sharp edges or corners anywhere on its massive form. It equally matched Earth's Moon for mass, but its shape was entirely wrong, and it seemed to be moving in a straight line.

Suddenly, the flashing colors and the rocking of the ship stopped abruptly. They found themselves floating just as peacefully as before, but now with this giant mass looming directly before them.

"Hey, we're out of the field!" Blink announced cheerily, but then dropped his good humor down a few notches to worry. "Captain Dirk, do you still want me to land... on that?"

Dirk squinted thoughtfully at it for a long second. "No. No, that's not what we've been sent out for. Steer us around it and get us back on course."

"Aye, aye – hey, I still don't have any control! They're still out!"

Tug spun a dial on his panel, then read the paper it spit out. "Yep, the controls are still fried."

"Can you fix them?"

"I can try, but I can't guarantee anything."

"Well go, man. We have less than two minutes!"

Precious seconds ticked by as Old Tug stood defiantly, staring Dirk down. But the young captain would not avert his eyes, and finally Old Tug went off through the porthole again to try to repair the ship's controls.

Meanwhile, Dirk and Blink watched the massive, colorless form looming ever larger in their front windows.

A full minute and a half went by like this before Dirk resigned himself to the fact that they were going to crash on its surface; Old Tug wouldn't be able to fix the controls in time.

"Tug! Get back here and strap yourself in!" he hollered. "We're going to hit in less than twenty seconds!"

Old Tug moved with surprising quickness back into the room and got into his seat, just in time to see the massive object blot out all the stars in their front windows. Looks of horror overtook each of their faces as the ground rushed toward them. Dirk screamed, a high-pitched shriek, as the Spaceray Gun at the tip of the Rocket pierced the surface...

...and plunged itself in, as if cutting through styrofoam. The ship's movement jarred to a halt, stuck upside-down into the object's surface, like a giant dart in a huge foam pillow. It wavered to and fro for a few moments before finally easing to motionlessness.

"Well," Dirk said, and cleared his throat. "Let's seal our suits and go out and have a look around, shall we?"

The other two nodded in agreement and Blink rotated the cockpit floor to reach the Rocket's exit door. They opened it with a hiss, and looked out at the ground where the Rocket Ship's nose was planted, about twelve feet below. Old Tug tossed his watch out the door, and they watched it fall to the surface.

"Gravity seems fairly equivalent to that of Earth," he said, almost to himself.

Dirk looked at his two crewmen to make sure they wore their zap guns in their hip holsters. Satisfied that they were both armed, he said, "I'll go first. Blink, you jump down after me and Tug will take up the rear."

Dirk eased his way out of the opening until he hung along the ship's outer surface, with his gloved hands gripping the ledged of the doorway. He then dropped the remaining feet to land easily on the ground. He got up from his crouched landing position and watched his two crewmen follow. Again, Old Tug surprised him with his agility.

Once the three of them stood together on the soft, somewhat spongy surface he spoke again, his voice crackling in all of their headsets. "We won't stray too far from the ship. We'll just do a sweep around to make sure we don't have any company. Then we'll head back, let Old Tug fix the controls, and get us off of this strange world, back to our mission. Let's head over to those craters over there first."

Three of them walked across the odd ground, headed toward the field of craters Dirk had indicated.

"The density of the ground seems inconsistent," Tug said, his head tilted to look at his feet. "The terrain we're on right now is kind of rocky, but there are patches everywhere of thinner, supple soil. Those seem to absorb our steps much more. I'd advise that we stick to the rockier turf while we're walking." The other two nodded and they continued on.

Finally, they found themselves in the midst of the craters, but still there were no other landmarks to be seen. The three of them climbed the lip of the nearest crater and looked down into its bowl. Blink got himself up and sat on the crater's ledge, as if on a fence.

"Now that turf in there looks even spongier than the patches back behind us," Tug said. "Very peculiar..."

Before either of the other men could protest, Blink jumped down onto the crater's inner floor. As soon as his feet touched the colorless surface, they kicked high up into the air. Blink did a quick backflip and bounced again off of the ground.

"All right!" his voice crackled in Dirk's and Tug's headsets. "This is like a trampoline in here!"

"Buzzard! What the hell are you doing?" Old Tug growled.

"Blink, get out of there! We're on an alien world; we don't know what could be here."

"But you guys should come in here and try this," Blink said, bouncing higher and further toward the crater's center. "It's lots of fun!"

"Blink, that's an order. *Blink*!"

The two older men looked on in horror as Blink Buzzard came back down from his jump, but his feet failed to stop when they hit the ground. Right near the crater's center, his feet and legs passed through the ground and the rest of Blink's body followed after. In a split-second, the ground had swallowed him up and he'd disappeared.

Dirk leapt the wall and ran toward the center of the crater, trying to keep his footing on the springy floor.

"Dirk, move carefully," Old Tug called, following after him. "That pocket he fell into seemed to be somewhere near the center."

Before Dirk could respond though, he and Tug both stopped in their tracks, frozen with a kind of horror. Two dozen figures suddenly appeared beyond the far edge of the crater and began to traverse it, slipping down into the bowl. They were fierce-looking, multi-limbed creatures, each of them shaped like an octopus with mouths full of razor-sharp teeth. On the tips of their tentacles were black, scythe-like claws that whipped about wildly as they approached. Each Octopus-Man emitted a horrific roar as it moved across the crater's surface toward them.

"Dirk—"

"Fire Zap Guns!" Dirk shouted. "Get them all before they get us!"

Beams of red burst forth from both men's Zap Guns, cutting into Octopus-Man flesh, but the minor wounds only seemed to anger them further. They roared louder and kept coming; Dirk noticed that they seemed to be skirting the central area where Blink had disappeared. Six more Octopus-Men appeared on the crater's far ridge.

Then, suddenly, amazingly, three human figures jumped up out of the ground in three different places inside the crater. Each human was covered from head to toe in an unfamiliar, shiny golden uniform striped with red and black. They held huge rifles, which they immediately began to discharge, firing at will upon the Octopus-Men. The fiery bursts from the guns assailed their targets mercilessly.

Their weapons were much more effective than Tug and Dirk's beam weapons had been; the Octopus-Men roared with pain and fury with each hit. One who was hit directly crumpled to the ground in a mass of smoldering tentacles.

Dirk and Old Tug watched in amazement as the terrible creatures were quickly defeated by the weapons of the three mysterious humans. In mere seconds, all of the surviving creatures had fled the crater, retreating over the edge by which they'd originally entered.

Once they were gone, it was time for Dirk and Tug to look in wonderment at their three rescuers, who stood amidst the charred, smoking ruins of their defeated enemies.

Each of the three humans moved in identically the same motions, as if choreographed. They dropped their rifles down slightly, to be held with their right hands, and then used their left hands to unsnap and remove their helmets. Once the helmets were cradled in the crook between each left arm and body, they all shook out their long hair. Dirk stared in amazement at the three most beautiful women he'd ever laid eyes upon.

The first had long blonde hair and blue eyes like the Earth from space. Her sensual full lips were held in a tight line on her stern face. The second, a black woman, appeared less stern, but even more beautiful than the blonde. Her dark eyes seemed to hide the secrets of the universe in their depths. The third had red, wavy hair. She was unable to hold her smile, but her expression and beauty were just as cold as that of the other two women.

"Remove your helmets," the blonde spoke harshly. "If you are human, than this atmosphere will sustain you." She gestured once with her rifle to let them know that her suggestion was to be obeyed without debate. Slowly, hesitantly, Dirk and Old Tug removed their helmets to face the women.

"I'm—" Dirk began, but the redhead interrupted him.

"A man," she seemed to spit the words.

"Kill them," the black woman said calmly.

"No," the blonde said. "We will take them to the Lady. It is up to her to decide their fates, not us."

With that, the black woman and the redhead hurried forward and gripped each of them roughly by the arm. Dirk stared defiantly into the face of the black woman as she took his Zap Gun from him, but she was unfazed.

"Let's go, *sir*," she said, with even more disgust at the word than Tug had shown earlier. Dirk snarled at her, but allowed himself to be led by his arm. To his utter surprise, they did not walk them away from the place, but rather began to step downward, right through the very ground at their feet. The women's feet disappeared up to their knees as they descended beneath the surface, pulling their two captives down to penetrate the mantle along with them. Tug looked equally shocked as they stepped through the spongy crust and into the earth below. It was amazing how easily the layers on which they'd just been standing gave way to the push of their bodies, once force was applied.

A moment of panic gripped Dirk as his face reached the ground, but once his captor had pulled him below the surface, he found he was still able to breathe somehow, even with his face engulfed in the foamy soil. Dirk felt an odd sensation as his skin made contact with the supple earth, as if a second conscious mind had awoken within his; surrounding his; parallel to his.

After a few minutes more of pushing straight through the loam, they emerged into an underground cavern, adorned with a number of corridors leading away in all directions. He looked up, but could see no holes in the ceiling he'd just passed through.

"How–?" he began, but the black woman interrupted him with a sharp crack of the butt of her rifle across his jaw.

"Shut up, male. You are forbidden to speak until the Lady allows it."

He glared at her and rubbed the welt she'd raised on his square chin, but followed quietly as he and Old Tug were led down one of the adjoining corridors.

The hallway seemed to twist without end, going further and further into the earth. There were countless other branches at many crossroads in the tunnel, but the three women led them on without hesitation.

They finally emerged into a vast, high-ceilinged hall, more ornately decorated than any room Dirk had ever seen on Earth. A luminous, golden throne rested empty at the top of a high, bronze-plated stairwell. Dirk was overjoyed to see Blink Buzzard standing at the foot of the stairs, grinning nervously back at them.

"Blink!" Dirk called, but remembered just in time to block the end of the rifle before it could make contact with his face again. Dirk and the black woman stared hotly into each other's eyes for a long moment before the blonde woman jabbed him in the back, nudging him and Old Tug forward to stand with their friend before the throne.

Once they were in place, the redhead and the dark-skinned woman receded, but the blonde walked up and stood on the second step before them.

"You men will wait here for the Lady to take her throne and give you her judgment. Any of you who steps away or speaks before she comes out will be executed." With that, the blonde woman whipped her hair about her and strode off, exiting through some unseen door behind them.

The three Earth men stood still and silent a few moments at the foot of the stairs and waited, occasionally exchanging questioning glances. Then the three simultaneously noticed the clouds of smoky fumes that had filtered thickly into the chamber from, carefully concealed jets in the floor.

"Hey is that–?" Dirk began, but slumped unconscious to the tiles below before he could finish, landing next to Blink and Tug's inert forms.

He dreamt of parasites weaving and winding their way through his flesh and blood, weakening him, sickening him, saddening him...

He awoke to a hand shaking his shoulder roughly. He moved swiftly to catch the hand in his own grip, but cracked his eyes open to see that it was Blink who was attempting to rouse him.

"Captain Moonfire, you awake? The Lady's here, she wants to talk to us."

Dirk opened his eyes fully, then rose quickly to his feet. They were still in the throne room, but now it was full of beautiful women of all varieties, all dressed in elegantly sensual, gold, shining outfits. Each woman was more beautiful than the next, though none quite equaled their three captors, who stood at places at the top of the stairway. It was there that Dirk's roaming eyes came to a full stop, unable to move anywhere else.

Upon the throne sat a woman of jet black hair and eyes, of the most terrible, incisive beauty he'd ever seen. The black and gold gown she wore flattered and made ever-more mysterious her figure's many finer aspects. His gaze could not resist or deny her; he looked into her cold stare, spellbound.

It took some effort to tear his gaze away, but when he was finally able, he saw her lone superior in the universe, regarding physical comeliness. Another woman stood leaning slightly on the throne, her wavy blonde hair cascading gently upon the shoulder straps of her green dress, which decorated and flattered her curvaceous, sensual figure. All the natural thoughts and feelings of sexual attraction fled from his mind, though, when he looked upon her open, wide-eyed face; the face of innocence. Gazing into the limpid green waters of her eyes, he felt compelled to rush to her aid and protect her, even though she was currently in no danger at all.

This one descended the steps, staring from one to the next of them with growing amazement. She drew close enough to Dirk so that he could smell her sweet, soft perfume; he fought the impulse to take her in her arms and kiss her mouth passionately. He heard her quick breaths as she stood nearby and realized she was actually taking in his own masculine scent. She moved on to Blink and did the same, then came to Old Tug. Her mouth gaped in open astonishment at his face. She turned to look up at the woman seated on the throne.

"Look at this one here, Lady," she said with child-like wonder. "His hair even grows on his face." The woman on the throne nodded, her lips pressed together tightly. She moved her hand ever-so-slightly to beckon the blonde woman back to her place by the throne. Dirk couldn't help but to stare in amazement and admiration as the woman climbed the steps back up to her place.

"We fully agree, Mr. Moonfire," The Lady upon the throne spoke in cutting, deep tones. "The female of the species is the more beautiful. Not to mention the more intelligent, the more empathic, and the more deadly." She smiled wickedly. Dirk stood frozen, unsure how to respond, to counter. He was unable to handle the intimidation of so much physical beauty at once. She spoke again in her voluptuous whisper. "You men do nothing truly to advance the evolution of our species. The only thing you're good for is your part in the creation of future generations."

"Where are the other men here?" he said, fighting the waver in his voice.

The Lady gave a short, sharp laugh. "Ah, we apologize for being so rude. Welcome to the Slug. We are its ruler, the Lady Macbetha Quasar. And there are no men here, except for those occasions when we take one from Earth to breed more girls. And also on those unfortunate occasions when one of us births a boy. That infant is only here for mere days, however, before it is dropped in some Earth-side orphanage."

"There's no one to sit at the head of your table then!" Tug grumbled. "And for whom do you cook the meals? Who's there to fix things when they break?"

The hall was filled with gasps of horror. Dirk wished prudence would have allowed him to bury his face in his hands. Lady Macbetha merely smirked though, and the woman in the green gown who stood near her throne pursed her brows in puzzlement. Before Dirk could apologize and reprimand Old Tug before the court, Lady Macbetha spoke up again. "Ah how quaint. Mr. Tug, is it? We can see why you were made obsolete by your younger colleagues." Old Tug's face reddened with anger, but Dirk jumped in to speak before he could make any more social errors in this strange, somewhat hostile, alien court.

"We've come from the planet Earth on a mission toward Planet X to retrieve a scientist who was stolen from us. We would not have landed here on... Slug, but for an unexpected encounter with a deep space energy storm," Dirk spoke coolly, flashing his manful smile once as he spoke. He thought briefly that the Lady probably found him attractive too. "We don't expect or ask your help, but simply your leave so that we may move on to Planet X to rescue her and return her to Earth."

"That's a very touching story, Captain Moonfire, but we're afraid there is no Planet X."

The three men stared with shock up at the throne.

"Surely you're joking," Dirk sputtered. "We've seen... it's on all of our charts...We saw it from Earth from our Space-o-scopes..."

The Lady sighed. "What you saw was an image we were projecting for foolish Earth men to see. That energy field your ship ran into was actually the movie screen beaming the fake image of Planet X back to Earth. It was supposed to appear far enough away to dissuade you from getting into your little tin phalluses and come tromping across the galaxy to save her. We forgot though, that you men can't resist playing with your phalluses, especially when there's a damsel involved."

Dirk now felt his anger rising, could sense it also from the other two. "So you're behind all this! You kidnapped Dr. Bloodsky!"

The Lady nodded. "You've already seen that we have troubles with the other tenants on our Slug here, those repulsive Octopus-Men. Her MatterBomb will be just the thing to rid us permanently of them. We'll simply set it to seek out only the life forms with the Octopus-Men's DNA-coding; once we detonate it in the Slug, they'll all die while we'll be perfectly safe. Then we'll have the Slug all to ourselves. No one else to raid our settlements and disrupt our peaceful lives here."

"We were attacked by Octopus-Men almost right after we landed," Old Tug said. "Your Amazons rescued us bravely, only to turn around and take us prisoner."

The Lady seemed not to have noticed that he'd spoken, "Yes, those Octopus-Men are a menace, with all of their aggression and their tentacles. They're just like men. And they originally came from a different Slug anyway. They're always beaming signals back to it; why can't they just leave ours and go back there?"

"Your petty wars are of no concern to peaceful Earth-folk like Dr. Bloodsky," Dirk said sternly. "And she'll never give the secrets of the MatterBomb to a force of hostile, misled women like you, who know no other ways of diplomatic relations beside kidnapping and imprisonment. I demand that you turn Dr. Bloodsky over to us immediately and allow us to depart this place to head back home to Earth."

"Impudent man!" Lady Macbetha laughed, acting shocked. "She's actually just back behind these curtains here, we'll bring her out. You can ask her yourself what she wishes to do. If she says she wants to go back to Earth with you, then we'll allow it. Does that seem fair?"

Dirk kept his surprise hidden, but found himself unable to disagree.

"Fine. Oh Lucilla? Would come out here please, darling? For just a quick moment? Thank you dear."

The three men watched the Earth-woman who they'd only ever seen in pictures emerge from a fold in the curtains behind Lady Macbetha's throne. Everything about her seemed wrong. The way she stared straight ahead, her jerky, robotic movements; something felt odd to Dirk. She wasn't dressed in the typical clothes of an Earth-woman, but instead wore a shiny, gold, aluminum-like skirted suit, similar to the other women in Macbetha's court.

"Lucilla," the Lady spoke with amusement in her voice. "These gentlemen have come here all the way from Earth, and they want to know if you'd like to head back home with them. What do you say?"

When Lucilla Bloodsky answered the question, her monotone voice sent chills down each of the men's spines. "Negative. Must remain here on the Slug and complete work on the MatterBomb. Must build MatterBomb so that Lady Macbetha's people can be free of the Octopus-Men. The MatterBomb can subsequently be used to take revenge against all but a select few of the men on Earth–"

"That's enough, dear. Thank you," the Lady looked back at Dirk and spread her hands apart with a shrug. "Well, it seems you have your answer then. We're sorry, but she doesn't wish to leave. Therefore, you can't have her."

"Will you at least let us go, then?" Blink asked, unable to hide the tremor in his voice.

"Oh no," the Lady returned. "Your masculinity and poor attitude has offended us. We feel that you must be used and discarded. Guards."

Their original captors moved forward to take them into custody again, reinforced by a second woman taking each of their other arms. Tug and Blink began to shout protests, but Dirk merely stared at the Lady on her throne. She yawned. The blonde woman next to her watched them being shackled at their wrists with an expression somewhat resembling pity. Dirk thought he heard Blink whimpering.

The Lady finished up her elaborate yawn and spoke again. "Feed the old one to the Thing. Send the young virile one to the Chamber, and take that one, the captain, down to cellblock XY. Give him the Special Treatment." The room filled with a gasp at this last command. Even the black woman who gripped his arm softened her harsh gaze upon hearing Lady Macbetha's orders.

He looked at her lovely dark face and for the first time felt the seed of true fear within him. "What's the 'Special Treatment'?" he asked.

"You'll find out soon enough," the large woman clutching his other arm said with a malicious grin, "If you survive it." She punctuated the word, 'If', with the swift jab of a needle into the thick muscle of his upper arm. Intense drowsiness overtook him again, and he slumped unconscious against the black woman's body.

He dreamt vaguely of strange, sexual pleasure... and Lady Macbetha...

He woke looking into the muzzle of a Zap Gun which he quickly recognized as his own. He attempted to shake his head, but found that he was unable to; it was apparently locked into place in some kind of harness or frame. As his eyes came more into focus, he noticed that the hand holding the Zap Gun was hairy, far too masculine to belong to any of the women here. He attempted to move, but froze quickly as he saw the hand on the Zap Gun tremble slightly.

Dirk blinked wakeful clarity into his eyes, but then caught his breath, fearful that he might choke on the very comprehension and fear of what he was seeing. The ring finger on the hand holding the gun was scarred in exactly the same place that he'd cut his right ring finger as a child in the orphanage, when one of the older kids had slammed a glass-paned door on his hand. The patterns of hair growth, the shape of the fingernails, and the individual freckles to be found here and there on the hand all looked intimately familiar. Dirk feared that sheer horror would scoop up his mind in its arms and carry it far, far away, never to return to him again.

The hand pointing the Zap Gun at him was his own.

But the hand was not attached to any limb or body that he could see; it was amputated and cauterized cleanly at the wrist. Approximately fifteen thin metal poles of varying heights protruded up from the surface of a nearby table, their upper ends adhering to different points along the skin of his palm and fingers. The reflective chrome posts upheld the separated appendage in a position to aim the gun right at his face.

His lips quivering with sobs, Dirk glanced down and his horror quadrupled, then quadrupled again, when he saw that his own head – in spite of the fact that he still breathed and was capable of conscious, rational thought – was entirely disembodied, suspended in position on the same table as his hand, by another set of fifteen chrome support posts.

He then rolled his eyes up, and through the welling tears saw an unattached, unclothed torso that he recognized immediately as his own. It was hanging from the room's high ceiling, suspended by the same type of metal posts that held his head and right hand. Where the four limbs were missing, there were no holes, but seals of flesh, as if his body had always existed in its current form, with no extremities. Lower on the wall, to the right of his torso, a pair of bended, hairy, masculine legs hung in symmetrically opposed places. They also had sheets of skin where he'd expected to see grotesque, severed ends of blood vessels and tendons. Dirk twitched his right foot involuntarily at the sight, and watched toes jump in response, attached to one of the feet that hung far across the room.

It was then that Dirk Moonfire began to scream.

He did not let up for a long, long time.

When he finally stopped, he opened his eyes and an Octopus-Man stood directly before him, staring placidly at his face. It stood still for a moment, blinking its large reptilian eyes. It paused another second, then suddenly emitted a horrible, deafening roar, just as the ones on the surface had done as they'd entered into the crater.

Dirk answered with a terrified, throat-grating scream. They matched each other in volume for nearly a minute, until the alien's scream faded out.

"What a strange greeting you Earth people have for us," the Octopus-Man chuckled to itself and shuffled a few steps back. Dirk's high-pitched shriek cut abruptly short and he stared at the Octopus-Man. It seemed to be moving about freely within their room.

"Excuse me?"

"Well isn't that your manner of greeting? To holler your fool heads off? That seems to be historically what Earth people have done every time they saw us for the first time. So we've learned that that's how to greet you when we see you, to scream as loudly as we possibly can."

So those Octopus-Men weren't attacking us in the crater? Dirk thought. *They were just coming to greet us with all that roaring?* "You know how to speak English?" he said aloud, "And God in Heaven, what have they done to me? God, Jesus, look at my body all over the room! Can you help me?"

The Octopus-Man chuckled again, "You're actually pretty lucky. Statistically, only 36% of the men who receive the Special Treatment survive it. But no, I'm afraid that we're both prisoners of the Macbethans, and there's little I can do to help...unless maybe you have an itch somewhere that I can get for you?" Dirk suddenly felt itches at points all over his body, but kept his mouth shut and allowed the Octopus-Man to go on. "They taught me to speak English, to make it easier on them when trying to extract secrets from me by torture. But I still always revert back to my natural language when they apply the intense pain to my body. It seems that I always forget the words of your language in pressure situations."

Dirk felt his lip trembling miserably again; he looked morosely at the beam weapon aimed at his forehead, held less than a foot from his face by his own hand. He wished that he was able to move his head, even an inch.

"My name is XQJ47 Osmond," the Octopus-Man continued, seeming slightly uncomfortable, if an Octopus-Man could convey such an emotion to a human, "Oh, if they didn't tell you, you probably don't want to think about letting go of that gun you're holding. You probably don't feel your left arm because they've numbed it and taken over its motor control, but it's on posts directly behind you, aiming another Zap Gun directly at the back of your head. Drop the gun in your right and they'll just use your own left hand to shoot you. It's a kind of mental torture, you know? Your life and death in your own hands... Oh, and your ass is also hanging on the wall behind you, by the way."

Dirk closed his eyes in resignation. He wondered about the other body parts that had yet to be accounted for, but simply said, "You can call me Dirk, I guess. So what happens next? Is there any hope of getting out of here? Intact?"

"That's a complicated question," XJQ47 replied, "With a complicated answer. This cell is basically a big open room with one impenetrable steel door to get in and out; it's essentially escape-proof. Security ladies are constantly watching us from the central Computer Room; that's also where they have the machine that controls your left arm.

"But our situation is much more involved than just that. We're not currently on a planet, you see, like the one your species originates from; rather, we're inside the cavernous flesh of a massive, living SpaceSlug. It's one of a species of beings that travels along consistent courses throughout the galaxies. This Slug we're inside of now happens to travel a very desirable space-route past lots of good trading posts, which is one of the reasons for the struggle between Lady Macbetha's people and mine for dominion upon it. But there are countless Slugs out there, traversing the spaceways, crossing vast, cosmic distances. Whenever two Slugs meet in deep space, they always fight. It's a terrifically violent clash, always catastrophic for the civilizations living inside of the slug combatants."

"Disgusting and fascinating. What is the point of all this?"

"My Octopus-People have developed a deep space signal that can attract another Slug, and draw it off of its course. They've been transmitting just such a signal from the far end of this Slug we're currently riding, calling one of its brothers to come here and attack it. When I was last a free Octopus-Man back on the far side of the Slug, our astronomers had just confirmed that another SpaceSlug was indeed on its way to rendezvous with ours. It should be here very soon; I'll bet my people are making evacuation plans even now. Once the massive Slugs are done fighting, assuming this one survives, of course; my people will come back and destroy whatever is left of the human civilization here. Then we'll have the whole place to ourselves."

"Is Lady Macbetha aware of this?"

"Nope, they haven't managed to torture that information out of me yet."

"But didn't you say we're constantly being monitored by the security women in the Computer Room? What if they have this cell bugged to eavesdrop on our conversations?"

"Er–"

"Oh my, you survived. That's wonderful!" Dirk rolled his eyes in his stationary head and saw that a woman had entered their cell. XQJ47 gasped and exclaimed, "LP Zelda!" while performing what appeared to be his species' version of a bow. As she approached, Dirk was able to see that it was the blonde woman in the green gown from the throne room. He was surprised all over again at her radiant loveliness. The pitying look she gave him made his heart melt, wherever it was.

"You're a very lucky man, Captain Dirk Moonfire," she said. "Only 36% of–"

"Yeah I know; the other 64% percent die from the Special Treatment," Dirk interrupted testily. "Boy, I feel lucky." When the woman's face appeared hurt by his sarcasm, he sighed and attempted to spread his arms apologetically. He cut that motion short when he watched his right hand wave the Zap Gun in his face. "So you're royalty too? Are you related to Lady MacBitch out there?"

"She is my mother," the woman said. "I am the Lady-Princess Zelda Quasar of the Slug Women."

"Oh, ahem... Your mother? How is that possible? You both appear to be the same age."

"Yes, all Slug Women appear the same age."

"One of the many technological secrets that Lady Macbetha stole from my people," XQJ47 said. "The ability to halt the body's aging process. She tricked us into giving her that, along with interstellar flight, uncloggable plumbing–"

"Silence, Octo-Man," Zelda's eyes flashed hotly at the alien creature. "Once one of our girls reaches her physical prime, we administer the anti-aging procedure, and she remains perpetually young and beautiful. It is a gift from my mother to us all."

"So Zel, you wouldn't happen to be in that defiant stage where you're looking to shock and outrage your parents just to get attention, would you?"

Dirk felt his panic rise when she moved behind him where he couldn't see her. "Whoa, hey, take it easy, Your Graciousness. No offense intended," he said. She stepped back in front of him holding his left arm with the gun in its hand pointed directly at his face. "Watch where you point that thing," he felt his panic rising.

"Your friends are in need of your help, Captain Moonfire. For one of them, it may even be too late," she sighed. "Sometimes my mother just goes too far. I'm going to set you free so you can help them."

"And put me back together?"

She lowered his armed arm and walked across the room to a control panel set into the far wall. "As much as possible. Some of your parts are being held in other places within our Slug. One of them is in danger right now of being eaten by a giant, two-headed Tyrannosaurus Rex."

"What? By a what?" Dirk was aghast. "Wait – which part?"

She didn't answer, but flipped a lever on the wall that brought his torso down to where she could remove it from its posts. Her soft hands felt odd on his skin, far across the room. "Such a hairy, manly body," she said, smiling mischievously as she ran her fingers across his chest, carrying the torso across the room to him. She stopped along the way and took down his right leg too.

Once she had reached his head's table, she fitted the leg into the spot below the pelvic area on his headless torso. The flesh seemed to adhere together effortlessly at the seals of skin. She then stuck his left arm back in its place just as easily, taking the Zap Gun out of its hand. He tried to swipe the pistol back, but his arm refused to budge.

"I'm afraid my mother's people still possess all motor control of your left arm," the Lady-Princess said. "It will only obey the synthetic neural signals they send it."

He felt simultaneously sickened, soothed, and aroused as she removed his head from its posts and rested it against her bosom, stroking his hair gently. She carried it over and adhered it to the neck on his torso. He breathed a sigh of relief as he felt almost whole again, standing on his one leg, leaning against the table.

"Umm, not to seem ungrateful, your highness, but I seem to still be missing a few essentials here." He hopped across the cold metal floor and nudged his left leg down from its wall posts. He watched, fascinated and horrified, as the leg sealed itself seamlessly again to his sans genitalia pelvis.

"That dissection technology was ours too," XQJ47 piped up. Dirk barely heard him; he was watching the black woman who'd captured him as she entered the room. She strode briskly across the floor of their cell, the heavy steel door sealing shut behind her. Her icy gaze was fixed upon Zelda's face as she approached.

"Lady-Princess Zelda," she said with a slight bow of her head. "I carry a message for you from the Lady Macbetha herself. She has been made aware of what you're doing here, and she wishes...for me to remind you that if you continue to displease her with your actions contrary to her wishes, she will increase the intensity of the Mind Control device...until you see fit to obey her will again." The woman looked uncomfortable; her eyes flicked across Dirk for the briefest instant.

"Jane, you know that Macbetha's treatment of these men, male as they are, has been unfair and unjust." Jane, the black woman said nothing, but her eyes seemed to convey agreement. "Help me Jane, to give them a chance for freedom. It's the right thing to do."

"Yes, Your Highness."

Dirk sighed in relief. "But what's this about a Mind Control device?"

He felt an instant jolt of excitement in his loins, wherever they were, as Lady-Princess Zelda hiked her green skirt all the way up her leg. Though his eyes were fixated upon her lacy, purple, leopard-skin underwear, she pointed to a back garter bound high around her thigh. "Your Dr. Bloodsky has been fitted with a similar device," she said sadly. "Those of us who wear them have our minds bound to Lady Macbetha's through her Mental-o-Matic Machine. My Control Dial is turned way down on the Mental-o-Matic, but Dr. Bloodsky's is turned all the way up. She is a mere puppet of my mother's will."

"That's what you're going to be, milady, as soon as your mother finds out what you're up to," Jane said.

Dirk noticed that Zelda held the fabric of her skirt up with her right hand, but that his own detached right hand was still in her left. It still held the Zap Gun. Where the hell is my right arm? He wondered. Aloud, he said, "Well then why don't you just rip that garter off? Then she won't have any control over you."

"Oh, I couldn't do that," Zelda said. "If any flesh touches the garter other than that of my leg, even my own fingers or toes, then it will explode!"

"I see," Dirk said, wishing he hand a hand to use to stroke his manly chin thoughtfully. "Couldn't you just wear gloves?"

Zelda and Jane both shook their heads. "Someone tried that once. The garter recognized the grip of fingers and blew up anyway."

Dirk grimaced, then said, "Hmmm." He walked across the room to her, no right arm and his left arm hanging uselessly by his side, and dropped his knees painfully to the floor just in front of Zelda.

"What are you doing?" she asked.

"Just keep your skirt hiked up," he replied. "I'm gonna free your mind." He moved his face slowly toward her inner thigh, trembling slightly, and carefully clamped a lacy frond of the garter between his teeth.

"Don't let your lips touch it!" he heard XQJ47 say anxiously.

With increasing anxiety, he began to slide the elastic fabric down her leg, he could feel her eyes locked on him, watching his every move. Her scent was heavenly. He didn't dare exhale, expecting an explosion to scorch his face at any second. Sweat collected on his brow as he slid the band down around the swell of her knee and onto the widening section of calf.

"Almost there," she whispered. "Don't stop, Dirk."

"You're doing it," Jane said.

She raised her foot slightly as he passed her garter below the ankle, and hooked it around the bend of her heel onto her foot. When he'd moved it just past her toes, she yanked her foot out from it and breathed a deep sigh of joy and relief.

Dirk stood up and flung his head around like a dog to rid himself of the explosive garment; it brushed past his lips just at the last second as he released from his mouth, and the thing exploded harmlessly in midair, landing in a blackened ring on the table where his head had been just a short time earlier.

"OK," Lady-Princess Zelda beamed happily at him. "Let's go get your friends."

Dirk nodded, "And also my–"

"Wait," XQJ47 said. "Get your ass out of here."

"Well right, that's the plan, XQJ47."

"No, your ass. It's still on the wall over there. You're going to leave it behind."

"Oh," Dirk looked helplessly up at it.

"I'll get it for you, sweet man," Zelda said.

He had never felt more embarrassed in his life, than when he stood before the two beautiful Slug Women while one of them reattached his own rear end to his naked, sexless, one-armed body. Jane then opened a cabinet set into the wall and found a white length of material.

"Here," she said, carrying it to him and clasping it around his frame. "You can wear this as a toga."

Before he could say any words of thanks, though, his left arm suddenly sprang to life and flailed wildly about in its socket. He watched helplessly as it made a fist and punched him squarely across the jaw, knocking him to the ground. It continued the assault, pummeling his face and head. He rolled his body on top of it, but the arm easily worked itself free and hit him again, squarely in the nose.

He hollered in pain, just as XQJ47 slithered up to him and restrained the wild arm. Jane had gotten a hypodermic syringed from somewhere and injected a neon green fluid directly into a vein at the crook of his right elbow.

"That will keep it quiet for about an hour," she said. "To truly trust it to your own nervous system again, you'll need to destroy Macbetha's central control computer before your arm reawakens."

"In the meantime, I'll hold your hand," Zelda said. He saw his right hand in hers, still clutching the Zap Gun.

He resisted the urge to smash his head against the metal floor.

The two women then opened the door leading to the hallway just outside the cell. Dirk followed first, but he turned and nodded for XQJ47 to follow after them. "Unless you're planning to stay here?"

XQJ47 nodded his huge octopus head. "Right behind you."

As soon as Dirk had set his bare feet on the clammy, spongy surface of the corridor, he again felt the sense of another mind melding with his own, talking to him. Then a clear, unmistakable voice reverberated deeply throughout his mind. If not for the two women darting around bends in the network of tunnels ahead, he would have fallen and screamed in fear again.

"Dirk Moonfire, I have waited all your life for you to return here," the voice spoke. He looked all around to see if someone else was standing nearby, talking to him, but he knew that the deep voice was only speaking in his mind.

"Are you God?" he whispered aloud as he ran after Zelda and Jane, but quietly enough so that no one else would hear him.

"Speak to me without your mouth, Dirk Moonfire; I can hear the questions in your thoughts," the bass voices resounded in his skull. "I am not the omnipotent God of your species, though others have worshiped me as one. I am currently laden with two parasitic races, however, who neither respect nor worship me. They merely seek to use me and tax my resources until I am a mere hollow, lifeless shell, floating endlessly, without destination through the galaxies. After that, they will move on to exhaust one of my siblings to death."

"Are you... the Slug?"

"Yes."

"Oh my God." A thousand questions raced through his mind. He'd almost disbelieved XQJ47 when he'd claimed they were currently inside of a giant SpaceSlug, but now the thing was speaking into his own mind. He then remember something else XQJ47 had told him. "I have to warn you, Mr. Slug. The Octopus-Men on the other side of you have been calling another to Slug to come here and fight you! It's on its way here now."

"Yes, I'm aware that Hector is on its way. Should be here momentarily."

"Hector?"

"Yes, that is the name of the SpaceSlug who is being drawn here by the Octopus-Men's signal. Hector and I will fight to the death, as is our custom."

Zelda and Jane entered a large circular room and stopped suddenly, standing next to an extremely smooth patch of turf in the center of the corridor's floor. He'd been so engrossed in the Slug's speech, that he hadn't even noticed the muted sound of savage, cheering, female voices.

"The elder of your friends in locked in mortal combat just below us,"

Zelda said, gesturing toward the patch of smooth ground. "For us to continue to help you, Jane and I cannot go into the arena. You will have to go alone to aid your friend in his peril."

"Well–"

"Halt!" They all looked up to see the blonde and the redhead standing at one of the circular room's other entrances, surrounded by heavily armed women in sexy, shiny gold outfits. "Kill the man and the Octopus-Man! But seize the female traitors!"

Dirk dashed off to find cover behind a sticky column of slug-flesh in the room. Jane positioned herself between the guards and Lady-Princess Zelda, drawing her own small Beam Gun. The blonde and the redhead led the team of guards into the room, and they began firing at random, shooting energy beams and firing everywhere, searing the walls, floor, and ceiling.

"Zelda!" Dirk called. "Point my hand at them!"

Zelda aimed his hand toward the attackers over Jane's shoulder, and he began squeezing the trigger of his Zap Gun, firing a multitude of shots at the women, sending them scurrying for cover positions of their own.

"HELLOOOOOO!" XQJ47 roared fiercely, charging straight ahead into the group of guard-women, his deadly, razor-tipped tentacles slashing all about him. He took a handful of them out in grotesque fashion before the blonde woman blasted him with a fiery burst from her rifle.

"No!" Dirk called out, but XQJ47's blackened form fell over, dead at her feet. His finger began to squeeze off more Zap Gun shots, but it soon appeared that they'd be overrun. "Slug, please help us!"

At this call, the floor beneath his feet lurched suddenly up at a sharp angle. He and Zelda and Jane watched with sick fascination as the floor and ceiling where the women were suddenly rushed together. The bone-crushing noises made his gorge rise in his throat. He feared he would vomit right there and then.

"I'd close all of my passageways and kill every parasite inside of me, if I could," the Slug spoke again in his mind. "But in doing so, I'd only close off all of my ventilation and I'd suffocate myself."

"Dirk, snap out of it!" Jane spoke up hotly. "Your friend is down below right now, fighting a large, two-headed dinosaur, trying to keep it from eating him and your right arm. You probably don't want to waste any more time here daydreaming."

"But XQJ47..."

"The Octopus-Man is most certainly dead," Zelda said. "Go and help your friend, Jane and I will find you as soon as you come out. I'll hang on to this for now." She held up his hand with the Zap Gun.

Dirk sighed and ran towards the center of the suddenly much smaller room. The soft flesh in the center fully supported his weight, but gave easily as he pushed his foot down through it, in the same way he'd been led inside from the Slug's surface. The Slug's voice returned as his bare skin penetrated its way through the layers between levels.

"Precognition of fate is an ability that we Slugs share, but alas, we are unable to stray from pre-destiny's plans, even after we've glimpsed them. We can sometimes, however, choose between a few possible outcomes. In the case of my duel against Hector, I shall be the victor, but I will sustain terrible wounds. Ordinarily, such injuries to a Slug would repair themselves in time, but when the Women and the Octopus-Men return to inhabit my body, they will do even further damage to me. By the wounds they inflict through their wars and parasitic dwellings within me, my own demise shall come."

"What can I do to change this fate?" Dirk asked silently. "And incidentally, why have you tried telling all of this to Lady Macbetha? Or anyone else?"

"There are only two human beings who are able to hear me. You see, Dirk, you were born here on this Slug; that is why in all those lonely years growing up in the orphanage, your mother never came for you. She was one of Lady Macbetha's fiercest warriors, until she was slain in battle against the Octopus-Men two years ago." Tears formed in Dirk's eyes as the Slug continued.

"There was one other child born here the same day as you, to a different mother. To Lady Macbetha, to be precise. I was aligned perfectly with the sun of Alpha Centauri on that day, and therefore was able to grant those two children the special ability to link to my mind. But alas, you were shipped off to Earth before you could comprehend my speech, and the other has had her mind weakened and controlled by Lady Macbetha for her entire life."

"Zelda!" Dirk said aloud, into the foamy flesh that was pressed against his mouth.

"Precisely. She is still unaware of her empathy towards me, as even after you removed her mind-restraint device, her skin has still not touched mine. But this brings us to the answer to your first question. My only hope is if she becomes Queen among all peoples here, with a sympathetic link to my mind. It is the only way that we can all live in a harmonious, symbiotic relationship."

The voice grew suddenly quiet. Then finally, after many minutes of stepping downward through the Slug's solid, foamy flesh, Dirk's foot broke through a kind of ceiling, touching upon nothing but air. He moved another step down and fell through the final layers of membranous wall, only to fall twenty feet to the next floor. He looked up to his left to see Old Tug brandishing a primitive-looking spiked club, his bare chest looking strikingly fit for a man of his age. Just beyond Tug, Dirk's unhanded right arm lay on the floor like so much refuse. Some distance away to Dirk's right, towered a two-headed Tyrannosaurus. The crowd of Slug Women cheered his arrival with savagery and cat-calls.

"You're here just in time for the main course!" Old Tug quipped, obviously feeling it necessary to make a snappy comment. He then seemed to notice Dirk's empty right shoulder socket. "So that's your arm back there? I thought it looked familiar..."

And so Dirk and Old Tug devised a clever, daring, reckless, thousand-to-one plan to defeat the two-headed dinosaur...which worked perfectly. Their victory over the beast mostly silenced the crowd, but their strategy was so brave and crazy and ingenious that they even received a small amount of applause afterwards.

As Dirk stuck his right arm back in its place, Old Tug sat on the Tyrannosaurus' carcass, eying him appraisingly. "I appreciate your help in vanquishing that thing, Dirk. That was quite a plan you came up with."

Dirk shrugged, swinging his reattached handless right arm pleasantly. "You fought bravely, Tug."

"Well so did you, Captain. Maybe I misjudged you after all," Old Tug gave a small chuckle. "Thanks for coming here to save me. If you had a working hand, I'd shake it."

Just then, a voice suddenly emanated throughout the entire arena from hidden loudspeakers. They recognized it as that of Lady Macbetha, "My women, the insidious Octopus-Men have used vile tactics and summoned another Slug to come and attack ours. That opposing SpaceSlug can be seen even now on our long-distance telescopes. It will soon be here and they will engage in combat."

The crowd of women watching the fight, who'd already begun to stream out of the arena exits, began to panic. Lady Macbetha's voice continued to speak over them, "When the great Slugs battle, our entire civilization here will suffer; much of the place we call home will be destroyed...

"But fear not! Do not panic! We must immediately get to our ships and evacuate this place. There is plenty of time. We will then fly to a safe distance to watch the titanic duel. Once it is finished, we will return to rebuild our homes within the victor. But in the meantime, while we are out in our ships, we shall strike at the Octopus-Men, whose flying saucers can be seen fleeing this Slug even now. We shall find great victory in the face of disaster, my girls! And ultimately, we shall have our revenge upon the men of Earth!"

The situation in the arena's bleachers had degenerated into bedlam. A secret entrance in the floor of the arena opened up and Jane and Zelda appeared, calling the two men over. Old Tug held his ground, gripping the spiked bat, but

Dirk waved for him to come along. Reluctantly, the old man followed.

The two of them jumped down into the hallway where the women were, and Dirk saw that he was again at a sub-level crossroads room intersecting a number of different tunnels.

"Lady Macbetha often spoke of the disgrace of old age, but you sir, are amazing!" Jane said.

Zelda nodded. "Now we still need to retrieve your other friend from the Chamber, if it is not too late. And there is also the matter of your scientist, Ms. Bloodsky."

"Yes," Dirk spoke up. "And I still don't have my—"

"Hand, yes of course," Zelda said. With a smile, she stuck his right hand back onto his incomplete arm. It was still holding Zap Gun. Dirk felt great to be nearly complete again. "Now come, we must get to the Chamber before it lifts off. We'll get there faster by boat."

"Lifts off?" said Tug.

"By boat?" said Dirk.

"Yes," Jane said impatiently as the four of them ran off again through the network of corridors. "The Chamber itself is inside of a Flying Saucer that had wedged itself into a deep fold of the Slug's skin. Lady Macbetha's Court is also merely a room inside of another Flying Saucer."

"The boats are through here," Lady-Princess Zelda chose a spot on the corridor wall, seemingly at random, and dug her way through it. The three of them followed, and found themselves coming out through the wall onto a ledge of tissue, overlooking a fast-moving river of viscous, blue fluid. A number of organic-looking, brownish capsules lay strewn about on the bank where they stood, tied to shore by thin, vein-covered ropes.

"Into a boat! Quickly!" Zelda cried, and moved through the outer skin and into one of the capsules; the fleshy wall resealed itself immediately after she'd passed through it.

"I was afraid she was going to do that," Dirk said, and followed after her, ignoring the revulsion he felt. Inside, he could see out in all directions through the tan shell of the capsule. Once Tug got in with a grimace, Jane severed its tendon-like tie-line, kicked the boat off, and jumped in through the membrane. They were soon being pulled by the fast current, through one the Slug's huge arteries.

It was cramped inside of the capsule, but watertight. There was nowhere to sit, so the four of them sat nestled together at what was usually the bottom of the vessel. It skipped along in the water at alarming speeds, occasionally bumping a wall here, a column of galactic cholesterol there, and various unknown objects all throughout the large, organic pipe.

"Dirk, assuming we can even get back to our Rocket before the huge slugfest begins," Old Tug said. "Do you think we'll have time for me to fix the controls so we can take off?"

"Our women have already repaired your ship; in fact we've improved greatly upon its numerous design flaws," Zelda said. "While your rockets are quaint and old-fashioned, we would never waste a gift like that, left so conveniently right on our doorsteps."

The men made no reply. Jane suddenly said, "There's our dock!" She tore a panel of skin from the wall, and removed a hook and rope that had been concealed within. She threw them out through their boat's skin, and the hook stuck to a spot on the bank just ahead. Pulling with all of her might, refusing help from the others, she hauled their boat to the shore.

As they all emerged from the capsule onto land again, the sound of dull klaxons permeated the air.

"We're not yet too late to get into the Chamber, even if it might be too late to get your friend out," Zelda said. "We must hurry; those ringing bells mean the Chamber is preparing to launch."

They burst through a wall and found a sealed metal door. Lady-Princess Zelda waved her hand; a sequence of light patterns glowed on the door for a moment and it whisked open. They rushed in to find a huge, lavishly decorated room, every square inch of it adorned with leather, vinyl, suede, satin, velvet, and silk.

They saw Blink lying in the center of a huge circular bed, with an undulating blanket of silk covering some of his naked body. A hive of at least two dozen beautiful women, each wearing more make-up than clothing, swarmed and moved animalistically across the surface of the round bed.

"He needed rescuing?" Old Tug said, his eyes wide in awe.

"Once he has fertilized enough of the breeding women, he will be permanently drained of his lifeforce," Jane said. "No man has ever survived the Chamber, though all who come here end up posthumously as the fathers of many, many children. A man's ability is infinite in this place, even if his stamina is not."

"Blink. Blink!" Dirk called, finally getting his crewman's attention. "Come on, you have to get out of there. We're going back to the ship. Get out of that bed now."

"Oh hey there, Captain. I think I'm gonna disobey that order."

"Blink, don't make us wrestle you out of there," Dirk felt his anger rising. He also realized that had he had all of his body's proper equipment, he probably wouldn't have been able to resist jumping into the fray before him.

"Captain, anyone who pulls me out of here is going to get shot."

"Dammit man, these women will use you to death! They're draining your life away!"

"Well, since everyone has to die eventually, then this is the death I choose. Now go away. Stop distracting me."

"Mr. Blink, sir," Lady-Princess Zelda said, slipping her voice into something smoother than all of the surfaces in the Chamber, "If you come with us now, I'll personally show you pleasures that none of these breeding women are capable of."

Blink Buzzard seemed to consider this for many long seconds, unable to tear his eyes away from hers. Finally he said, "Deal. But I'm holding you to that, lady." He rose from the bed, prying away the many clutching hands grabbing at him as he put his pants back on.

"So where are we going now, gang?" Blink said, standing before them wearing only his trousers. The breeding women were all cooing him seductively to return to them, but would not leave the perimeter of the massive bed.

"Come," Zelda led and they all followed her out of the Chamber's ship through its door, back into the hallways of Slug flesh just outside of the Flying Saucer's hull. She then turned and addressed the group.

"We still have to get Dr. Bloodsky away from Lady Macbetha. And then we have to get to your ship and get off of this Slug before it fights the other giant Slug."

"Huh?" said Blink.

Dirk felt his patience burst at last, like an overwhelmed dam. "And my most important body part is still M.I.A.! I'm not leaving here until I get it back!"

"What?" Blink said, his stupid expression growing more puzzled.

"That bitch took my body apart piece by piece!" Dirk exploded, spittle flying from his mouth, his red face mere inches away from Blink's. "And I'm still not fully together yet! My left arm will still be under their control when it wakes up, and my manhood parts are still lost somewhere in this giant fucking Slug!"

"Well do you think you could live without that stuff, Dirk?" Old Tug asked. "They're telling me that this place is going to get real dangerous real soon, and personally, I'd rather not get killed looking for your meat and potatoes."

"And if we do find it, I ain't gonna be the one to pick it up. That's all I know," Blink said while slicking his hairs back into place.

Dirk slumped his head against the corridor wall, ready to tell them all to go on without him, when the Slug's voice spoke in his mind again, "Get Zelda to touch flesh me. Her mind must also be awakened to mine, Dirk."

The ground began to tremble all around them, accompanied by the deep rumblings of the Chamber's Flying Saucer's engines lifting it out of the Slug.

"We must move quickly to reach the Throne Room Flying Saucer, before it also blasts off into space," said Zelda. "That's where we'll find my mother Macbetha, Dr. Bloodsky, and quite probably Mr. Moonfire's genitals."

"Enlighten her, Dirk."

"Wait, Your Highness," Dirk said. "Give me your hand."

"Hey!" said Blink as Dirk took her bare hand in his right one and led her to the wall.

"Dirk what—" she began, but abruptly stopped speaking as he gently pressed her fingertips against the cool, flesh walls of the Slug's interior. Her eyes widened; Dirk could sense the Slug's great voice speaking to her, as if a voice was heard from far away. He knew it was telling her of its pain, of its past, of what she must do, though he couldn't understand the words it spoke in her mind.

The others all looked at him expectantly, waiting for an explanation of what it was they were seeing, why they were delaying here in the hallway.

"Don't ask," he said, shaking his head. "It's too weird to explain right now."

After about a minute, she stepped away from the wall, with a stunned expression on her face.

"My lady," Jane looked concerned, "What has happened? Are you all right?"

Zelda looked deeply into Dirk's face for a few seconds, then nodded slowly. "Yes, I'm fine. Come, we must catch my mother before she blasts off. It's not far from here."

They followed a single, winding corridor for some time, occasionally passing small clusters of Slug Women, who were all running frantically toward their own escape routes. The rumbling of departing Flying Saucers all around filled their ears. Suddenly, the entire world seemed to lurch and shift.

"The whole damn Slug is moving!" Old Tug shouted.

"Hector draws near," The Slug spoke in Dirk's mind. He could tell it was simultaneously telling Zelda as well. "I must assume a defensive position."

The hallway shivered again as Zelda led them out through a small sphincter-like opening in the side wall. They found themselves squinting and holding up their arms to shield their eyes from the brilliant lights of a Flying Saucer's lower Rocket Boosters. Both Lady Macbetha and Dr. Bloodsky stood at a railing atop the saucer, laughing down at them. Lucilla's laughter was forced and mechanical, but Lady Macbetha's was sincere and evil enough for them both.

"You were too late, males and traitors! Now I shall fly off to safety and you shall all die on the surface during the great SpaceSlug battle. And Dr.

Bloodsky's MatterBomb is very nearly completed, so once I return to the surface of the victorious Slug, I will tests its power by eliminating all of the Octopus-Men. Should it satisfy my destructive lusts, it will then be used to rid the Earth of its most foul creature: men!"

"You'll never get away with this, Quasar!" Dirk shouted.

"Oh yes I will," she gloated. "And I'll also be getting away with something else very precious to you. Something I enjoyed immensely while you slept. Though I'm sure the experience was also pleasant for you." She laughed again, and the Flying Saucer ascended out of the area in a burst of brilliant blue fire.

"They're getting away!" Jane said.

"We must get to your Rocket and launch after them, before we're caught here in the Slug battle!" Zelda said frantically.

"But what about my..." Dirk said, unable to suppress the whine in his voice. "What if she uses it as a hostage?"

"Your body parts are safe with her, Mr. Moonfire, for the time being," Zelda said. "My mother has been unable to conceive a child for over twenty-two years; I was her last daughter. Since then she has desperately tried to birth another, seeking impregnation from nearly every man brought to our Slug. Since your parts are functioning properly, even detached from your body, she will use them daily, in the hopes that you'll be able to reawaken her sleeping womb."

"But if she's barren, then Dirk's dick will never knock her up," Blink said plainly.

"Exactly," Zelda said. "It is then that she will become frustrated and either discard Dirk's pieces of flesh, or she will destroy them in her rage."

Dirk found himself unable to speak.

"Come; to your ship," Zelda said again, "We have no time to waste."

Blink, Dirk, and Tug followed the two women up a severely sloping corridor until they were forced to push themselves through another thin layer of skin at the tunnel's end. It was just before then that Dirk noticed how empty and alone his mind felt.

"Slug?" he said without speaking.

"Call me Chuck," replied the voice in his mind. He felt its presence flood through him once again. "But if you don't mind, Dirk, I'm rather busy preparing myself for colossal battle against another godlike space being."

"Right. Sorry."

"No harm done."

Chuck departed, and the emptiness of being alone in his own mind returned once again.

They burst through the membranous gate, out of the tunnel and back into the central bowl of one of the surface craters. The starry sky above them shone brilliantly with countless, moving specks; the flying saucers of the Slug Women and the Octopus-Men. Thousands of little fires bloomed amidst them as they waged deep-space dog-fights.

"There she is!" Blink shouted happily, standing on the rim of the crater. Everyone else followed him over the edge, and continued running toward the Rocket Ship, which had been parked and flipped upright close by.

The Slug Women technicians had left their ladder leaning against the Rocket's hull, leading directly to the entrance door. The five of them darted up the ladder, with Dirk and Old Tug in the rear. They both found themselves using their Zap Guns to ward off a group of savage Octopus-Men and Slug Women who'd apparently joined together in their last desperate bid to commandeer passage off of the soon-to-be turbulent Slug surface.

Once inside, they sealed the hatch, rotated the cockpit floor, and began the launch procedure without even bothering to strap themselves in. In less than a minute, their Rocket was once again flying effortlessly through the stars.

"Your mechanics did an admirable job," Old Tug said, reading his printout and nodding his approval.

A squadron of Flying Saucers waving green, octagonal flags atop their hulls shot past their Rocket, Beam guns blazing wildly. Dirk fired back at them with the Rocket's deadly Atomic Spaceray Gun, while Blink did his best to maneuver their ship between the shots and the flock of Flying Saucers.

Another squadron of a dozen identical Flying Saucers, these all wearing pink flags, suddenly appeared. This group had apparently been pursuing the squadron of green-flagged ships, but Dirk and Blink found themselves fighting their way through this wave also. The Earth Rocket finally emerged from the fray unscathed.

"Look there!" Jane pointed out the window, an expression of awe upon her face. The others looked on, but said nothing. Hector the giant SpaceSlug had arrived just before Chuck, and it had borne itself up into a threatening stance. Chuck quickly moved to match its stance. The two space behemoths sat squared off against each other for some time, the tiny battles of Women vs. Octopus-Men in Flying Saucers continued to rage all around them. Four appendages seemed to sprout from evenly spaced points along the outside each of the Slugs' bodies. Simultaneously, huge, gaping mouths formed at the upper tips of both Slug's lengths, filled with fearsome arrays of long, jagged teeth.

"Did you know they had all that?" Old Tug asked Jane, who merely shrugged in astonishment.

In the following seconds, both SpaceSlugs emitted hair-whitening roars that shook the very fabric of space. Hector lunged first, striking fiercely with its powerful jaws bared. Its attack was turned away at the last second by a parrying punch from Chuck's upper left limb.

"Come on, Chuck," Dirk said, and Lady-Princess Zelda gripped his hand to share in the thought. The two titans locked themselves together in a mighty grapple, with strikes and gnashing teeth ranging all about. When they finally shoved themselves apart, Hector let forth a stream of glowing red fire from its huge mouth, roasting much of Chuck's central torso. Zelda winced at the terrible damage being inflicted upon her home.

Finally, Chuck managed to spin itself out of the line of fire, and Hector ceased that attack. Charred pieces of Chuck's flesh drifted free of its smoldering body. Hector dove in for another strike. This time Chuck was not as swift, and Hector's two front limbs smashed hard into Chuck, folding its huge, elongated form in half.

"Look!" Jane suddenly shouted again. Dirk risked a glance to see her pointing out a different window in the cockpit; one that had no view at all of the SpaceSlug Fight. "It's Lady Macbetha's Flying Saucer!"

The others all tore their eyes from the great duel to look where Jane was pointing. They saw an ordinary-looking, pink-flagged Flying Saucer sitting idly, alone in a section of space far away from all combats.

"Is that hers?" Old Tug looked skeptical.

"Oh yes, that is my mother's ship," Zelda spoke coldly. "I'd recognize it anywhere."

Dirk looked out the other windows to see that both Slugs were tied up in another advantageless grapple again, then said, "Blink, Macbetha may be distracted by all that commotion out there. Bring us around the back of her Saucer and get us in real, real close."

"Boss, you don't intend—"

"You're damn right I intend to," Dirk said. "Now go, before we lose our distraction."

Blink nodded and began to steer them even further out, while Dirk watched Chuck strike Hector's jaw from four different angles with all four of its appendages. Hector spun away and fired another beam of fire at Chuck; this one much weaker than the first. It narrowly missed and charcoaled a small fleet of green-flagged warships.

"Chuck must be saving up her fire attack," Zelda whispered, her voice full of hope. "Hector is just wasting all of his early."

Blink had quickly steered the ship to the location Dirk had ordered; Dirk peered out the hatch window to see Macbetha's Flying Saucer, now less than ten yards away.

"She truly does seem oblivious to our presence," Dirk said, mostly to himself. Then to Blink, "Good work, my friend. But inch us closer."

Blink blew out his breath, but nudged them even closer to the Saucer.

"Closer."

The others' attention suddenly diverted from the Slug Wrestling to the events occurring right in the room with them.

"Dirk, what do you intend to do?" Old Tug said.

"I still haven't completed my mission," Dirk spoke boldly, his chin jutting as much as ever. "And I don't intend to return home less of a man than when I left."

"My god, you intend to–" said Jane.

"That's right."

"Do you want anyone to accompany you?"

"The danger will be very great," he said. "I think I should handle this alone."

Old Tug wiped sweat from his brow while Jane exhaled in relief. "Oh good," she said. "You take care of it and hurry back then."

Dirk knitted his brows for a second, then donned his Space helmet and opened the door, leading out into space. He quickly shut it again, much to the relief of his Rocket's occupants, and kicked off of its shiny hull, landing atop the Flying Saucer, which was now a mere ten feet away. He tried to grab on with his left arm as he slid down its roof, but remembered too late that Jane had sedated it. He reached out with his right just in time to keep from falling away forever.

He looked across the field of space to watch the SpaceSlugs charge at each other, kind of like two massive knights in a deep space joust.... but not really all that similar... The two massive Slugs hit hard and locked limbs yet again, struggling against each other; their heads pressed close together. The SpaceSlugs then locked their massive jaws in a furious, savage, galactic kiss.

Hector's furious scream of realized defeat could probably have been heard all the way back on Earth.

Chuck blew out its full strength of fiery breath directly into Hector's open maw, and the huge Slug's entire body glowed with the terrible blaze. Geysers of flame burst from places all over its body, as Chuck relentlessly poured more in through Hector's mouth.

Dirk turned his attention back to the surface of the Flying Saucer. He crawled around its circular top dome until he found the door. To his surprise, it opened as soon as he turned the knob.

He swung his body inside and the door swung shut again behind him. But he looked up at his surroundings, only to find himself on his ass in a hallway, with eight large robots standing over him, pointing Beam Rifles directly at him. Macbetha and Lucilla Bloodsky stood just beyond them, in a room he recognized as the throne room where she'd handed out their sentences.

"Such bravery, Dirk – for a man," Macbetha sneered. "A shame that it was all for naught. Observe out the window as my ships withdraw from their combat into holding patterns at a deep space perimeter. Observe also how the Octopus-Men's Flying Saucers already fly in droves back toward the surface of our injured, yet victorious Slug. The eight-armed fools are utterly unaware that the MatterBomb is 96% percent ready. As soon as their last ship lands on the surface, we shall fire the MatterBomb directly into the Slug. Its explosion will decimate every last Octopus-Man aboard and the Slug will finally be ours and ours alone!" She cackled with delight. "But you won't be around to see any of this, Earth*man*. Our robots are going to execute you right now." The circle of mechanical men drew tighter around him. "Though there is one thing we want you to see before you die."

She moved to a control panel and directed his attention out the window that looked upon his Rocket. "No!" he cried, but she pulled a lever and huge bolts of white lightning streaked out from the Flying Saucer and scourged the ship, all over. He could see the panicked faces of his crew inside as more electric shots caused smoke and sparks to shoot up from places all over the Rocket's hull. It listed backward and began to spin out of control, floating helplessly off into the reaches of deep space. Macbetha let up on the electric attack.

"There, we won't kill our last daughter, but we will allow her to drift and either starve or freeze to death in the depths of the galaxy. Now, for you, Captain..."

"Wait!" Dirk called out. "You can't kill me! You need me to impregnate you."

Macbetha shrugged, "Unfortunately, there are plenty of other living men in the universe. Maybe we'll fish that nubile little man out of your dead Rocket there and give him a try. I don't need your parts badly enough to keep you alive. Now robots, it's time for Mr. Moonfire–"

"Wait!" Dirk's mind searched. "You said you wanted revenge against the men of Earth. Why?"

Lady Macbetha rolled her eyes and snorted. "Why not? The toilet seat, war, guns, rape, bad pornography, oppression of our right to vote, the fact that you never have to go through pregnancy or PMS, oppression of our personal freedoms, Wayne Newton; the reasons are too numerous to list!

"Now, Dirk Moonfire, no more stall tactics; it's time to die. Any last requests?" She slapped her forehead in disgust just as she said it.

"Yes! Yes, I do have a last request!"

"Well, what is it?"

"I, er..." Dirk's mind raced frantically. Macbetha rolled her eyes again.

"Robots, aim your weapons."

"I want to kiss Dr. Bloodsky; that's my final request," Dirk spoke up quickly.

Even through her mind control, Lucilla Bloodsky looked surprised.

"That's it?" Macbetha asked.

"That's it. One kiss, anywhere on her body. Then your robots can Zap me."

"Oh all right," Lady Macbetha sighed. "One kiss. Get on with it then."

Dirk approached Lucilla Bloodsky, his chest heaving. She held him in her cold, scientific gaze as he approached; Dirk found himself struck for the first time by her beauty. "Earth girls are still the best," he murmured and bent to his knees, gently lifted the hem of her short Slug Woman skirt. Everyone made surprised noises, even the robots.

A few inches up upon her thigh, he found the Mind Control garter.

"What do you—" Macbetha began behind him. With held breath, he tore the garter away from her leg with his teeth, snapping the elastic inside. The fabric brushed against his face as he pulled it off of her. Knowing he had mere seconds to spare, he spat the band of fabric out at Lady Macbetha.

She jumped back and two robot guards dove in front of her, catching the garter just as it exploded. One of the robots was blown to bits, but the other was slammed hard into two other guards standing nearby. The three of them all fell to the floor in a hail of metal pieces. "Kill them both!" Macbetha screamed as she ran off into the throne room, disappearing behind the curtains next to the great bronze stairway.

The remaining four robots attempting to fire their Ray Guns at Dirk and Lucilla, but he jumped on top of her just in time to dodge their fire. Their shots ricocheted wildly off the walls, eventually hitting each of the other guard robots. All four of them toppled to the ground in immobile heaps of scrap. Both Dirk and Lucilla Bloodsky rose to their feet.

"Are you OK, Dr. Bloodsky?" he asked.

She nodded and said, "Please call me, Lucilla."

"OK Lucilla. We have to stop Lady Macbetha before she hurts my—"

"Before she uses the MatterBomb!"

"Well yes, that too."

"It's not ready for use yet! If she fires it there, it will destroy that poor SpaceSlug along with all of those Octopus-People."

"You bested the four guard robots; very impressive," they both looked up to see the blonde and redheaded Slug Women – Jane's former colleagues – standing at the foot of the stairs. "But now are you ready for us to double-team you?"

"So you bitches survived the hallway collapse back on the Slug, eh?" Dirk smirked. "Lucilla, stand back. I'll handle them."

"You will?" Dr. Bloodsky looked at him dubiously, but then said. "Well ok. You handle them then; I'll be right back." She ran off and left Dirk to face the two women, who began a flanking approach toward him. He got into a defensive posture, ready for when they would move in for a simultaneous strike.

He was caught off guard by both attacks, and suddenly found himself down on the ground with throbbing pains in his ankle and his shoulder.

The two women moved far too quickly for him, when he tried to get to his feet, they pummeled him to the ground again. This time they did not let up their assault. He curled up into a ball and continued to suffer their beatings for what felt like ages until finally, he was vaguely aware of Lady Macbetha's returned voice. "That's enough, girls. Prop him up; he's survived this long, he might as well witness our moment of glory."

The blonde and the redhead dragged him to his feet. He could see that Lady Macbetha had escorted Lucilla back into the throne room at gunpoint, but now shoved her off toward Dirk and his two captors. He noticed for the first time that Lucilla was holding something fleshy in her hands.

"I thought I'd detected an odd, pleasant feeling while I was getting my ass kicked!" he whispered in astonishment. "Oh thank you thank you thank you!" She smiled at him.

Macbetha spoke again as she wheeled a control table directly in front of her throne, then took the seat. "The MatterBomb is right here on this Flying Saucer, loaded into the torpedo bay. The last few Octopus-Men ships are fast approaching the Slug; it will soon be time to demonstrate the awesome destructive power we now wield, thanks to Dr. Bloodsky."

As if on cue, Lucilla Bloodsky punched the redhead to Dirk's left squarely in the face, knocking her down. Lucilla's swift kick across her jaw was enough to knock her unconscious. Dirk looked on in stunned amazement as Lucilla stepped around him and swept the blonde's feet out from under her. The blonde's head hit the floor hard, and she too was knocked out.

Macbetha flipped a large red switch on her control panel and shouted, "Damn you Earthlings! But you're still too late to stop the MatterBomb! We've begun the launch sequence; there's no way to stop it from shooting out of the torpedo bay in 10 seconds from now! Nine seconds..."

"Quick Dirk!" Lucilla said frantically, taking his hand in her free one and running. "To the Saucer's exit hatch!"

"But we can't just leap out into space, Lucilla," Dirk said, allowing himself to be led. "That's certain death!"

"So is staying in here," she handed him his final, detached body parts and drew a small box from her pocket. It had an antenna, a single red button in its center, and the words, "MATTERBOMB AUTO-DETONATOR" stenciled upon it. "I'm going to explode the bomb before it even leaves the torpedo bay. And even though I invented the evil bomb, I'd rather not be killed by it. That's far too clichéd a manner in which for me to die."

He shrugged and fit his genitals into place inside his toga, glad to be whole again, even as he rushed toward his own death. In mere seconds, they reached the same hatchway door through which he'd entered the ship a short while earlier.

"Five...four... three..." Macbetha's voice was edged with maniacal glee.

Lucilla pushed the red button on the detonator and opened the Saucer's exit door, all in less than a second. She kissed Dirk quickly on the lips and leapt out into the black. Dirk followed directly after her with a wild shout.

The explosion of the Flying Saucer was tremendous.

Dirk and Lucilla's bodies hurtled across the void of deep-space, propelled by the massive blast of the MatterBomb. He noticed that control of his wildly flailing left arm was back; it had returned just after Macbetha's Flying Saucer blew up.

Dirk closed his eyes, bracing for death as his body drifted at ludicrous speed across the deadly void of space. But he was suddenly surprised as he impacted into the surface of something; something sort of soft and squishy.

He opened his eyes to see that a colossal arm had reached out to catch him and Lucilla before they could float away across the light-years. He inhaled and realized he was in a contained, breathable atmosphere again.

"Chuck!" he called out in joyous disbelief. Lucilla looked at him and their surroundings with wide-eyed amazement. "Chuck, you beautiful SpaceSlug! I could kiss you!" And he did just that, fell to his knees and kissed the foamy soil upon which he stood. "No, thank you, Dirk," the Slug's voice spoke again within his mind. "I might not have survived if it hadn't been for your help."

The massive arm swung them inward, and deposited them at a place near the center of its torso. Much of the landscape here was scorched, but Dirk jumped up for joy when he saw that Chuck had dropped them on his belly, right next to the place where his beaten and battered Rocket Ship had landed. Old Tug, Blink, Zelda, and Jane all stood outside of it, running cheerfully toward them.

"Oh, I thought I'd never see you guys or that beautiful Rocket Ship again!" Dirk wept happily. The six of them joined in a group embrace. After a few emotional moments, they withdrew slightly into a tight circle, arms still locked. They all smiled back and forth at one another.

"How bad is the ship?" Dirk asked.

"Pretty bad," Old Tug said in his gravelly voice. "Most of the circuitry was completely fried by that electrical attack."

"But it's nothing that my technicians can't handle," Zelda said proudly.

"*Your* technicians?" Dirk said.

"Yes," Zelda said. "Now that my mother's dead, I will take over as ruler of the Slug Women. But there will be a number of changes during my reign. First, we will cease our plans to destroy the men of Earth. But second, and most importantly, we will draft a truce with the Octopus-Men. Our two peoples will find a way to live harmoniously here, in a way that benefits all of us, including Chuck."

"Do you think you can convince your women and the Octopus-Men to end the war, Lady Zelda?" Blink asked, his arm around her waist.

"I can only try," she replied. "I know it is the correct thing to do, so therefore it is the only thing I can do."

"So will we be able to return to Earth tonight?" Lucilla spoke up. "I'm anxious to get home again. I miss my planet, and my little house on it."

"The damage to Dirk's Rocket will take about a week for us to fix completely," Lady Zelda replied. "But if you are in a hurry, we can escort you back home tonight in a Flying Saucer."

"This is my home too," Dirk said, winking at Zelda. Lucilla looked at him; he slipped his arm around her waist. "What do you think?" he said to her. "Want to fly back to Earth tonight and face the press? Or maybe stay here for a week and enjoy the scenery the Slug has to offer?"

She smiled and kissed him.

"I think I know her answer," Blink said while everyone laughed. "Now Lady Zelda, I seem to recall a certain promise you made…"

"Which I fully intend to fulfill, even though my kingdom has been badly damaged from the slug battle," she said. "Come, let us take our leave of your friends; I would not wish to begin my reign as a liar." The two of them walked off toward the nearest crater.

"Let's go, Captain Moonfire," Lucilla said to Dirk, "and make sure that you've had everything put back together correctly." She winked at him, and they walked off after Blink and Zelda.

Old Tug and Jane merely looked at each other and shrugged. "Don't even think about it," she smiled, and they followed after Dirk and Lucilla, holding hands. Above them, a small fleet of Flying Saucers whooshed by, bearing no flags at all...

...and you could barely see the strings that held them up.

Scattered, smothered and covered

No, that's the only way they come.

You got two options, champ: take it or leave it. Ok, and toast or biscuit? Sorry, we're out of biscuits. Now that I think of it, we're a bit shy on toast. Tell ya what, how about some extra browns? What are they smothered with? Now I can't tell you that, sport — family secret recipe.

Ok, here's another splash, but don't get carried away; this is strong stuff. The dead aren't real choosey when it comes to Joe, as long as it's hot and strong. You ain't going to find this stuff in Seattle. But then again, that Seattle crap can't pick you up like this will.

Yeah I know, it warms the cockles. Which is just what I need, a diner full of warm cockles.

Cultural Clashes in Cádiz

by Jetse de Vries

Prologue: In the Grotto of the Daring Deeds

In a grotto somewhere between *Sierra Bermeja* and *Serrania de Ronda*, shadows dance across the wall of the fire-lit cave like haunted spirits fleeing from enlightenment. Two men, years apart but still close, sit next to the fire. If not for the age difference they could be identical twins. Sleek black hair, pointy brows, prominent noses and thin lips. But twins they are not, neither father and son nor clones. The young one sprouts a full beard while the old one is clean-shaven.

"Nice beard, Leonard two."

"Indispensable for an apprentice of the Sufi Path."

"Apparently you managed to convince the holy man to go on a new quest?"

"It wasn't easy. When I arrived I found that he was dying. It took all my skills and skullduggery to visit him before they put him on his deathbed. Intestinal cancer was finishing him off. The nanos could barely save him. The damage already done was so great that he has ten more years, tops."

"Enough to play his part in our grand scheme. Was it hard to inspire him?"

"After some theater they believed I was Allah's tool miraculously saving the great mystic for his last pilgrimage. The man himself was a lot more difficult to fool, though. I needed several tries with the 3D equipment to get the vision he needed right. It was still harder to convince him to let me be his apprentice."

I

In the Hall of the Moorish King

Muhamad I Al-Ghalib, King of Gharnata, mentally shakes his head as the two visitors enter his residence. Outwardly he reveals nothing of his slight bafflement, as his welcoming smile is warm and inviting, however hard it is not to smirk. The credentials of his guests look authentic enough, it is more their appearance that defies convention.

The first nobleman, Baron Kirkinnison, is not too bad. His long, gray hair and pointed goatee could have given him the aura of a distinguished gentleman. But his dandy dress spoils much of that effect. The clothing is fine enough; it is all that ornamentation dragging him down. Some restraint would do wonders. Too much frills and frippery, pompous patterns embroidered everywhere, even on his boots. On him, though, at least most of the colors match.

Compared to his younger companion he is a paragon of moderation. Baron Whattage rises up from his deep bow and as his curly, blond locks fall on his shoulders the radiant smile under his curled up moustache is grossly outshined by the screaming, iridescent and intertwined color combinations on his trousers and shirt. Apart from the incompatible compositions they share another symmetry: both are tight at the waist and become very wide at the limbs. Trouser legs wavering out like a Bedouin's tent, shirtsleeves like a wind-tattered turban unwinding. Oh how he wished he hadn't asked him to take off his shining, deep purple overcoat. It was tolerable compared to what was lurking beneath.

Normally he wouldn't have wasted his time with such eccentric lordships from this cold, northerly country but they offer trade and any new source of income is very welcome indeed.

The building of his beloved Alhambra is draining his funds enough as it is, then there is the ongoing struggle with the Almohads trying to regain the dominance they lost to his Nasrid dynasty. And last – but certainly not least – the problem of fighting off Ferdinand III and his zealous Christians hell bent on their *Reconquista*. His decision to redirect the regiment at Cádiz to defend Seville against Ferdinand's furious attack was a two-cutting sword: it saved Seville but it lost Cádiz.

In a perfect world he would reconcile with the Almohads, hold off the Christian hordes and concentrate on the construction of his glorious citadel, his personal palace with the majestic courtyard and a grand reception room, the Hall of the Ambassadors, where lesser officials could deal with clowns like these two.

In the real world, though, he is forced to deal with the lesser devil to get the greater evil off his back. Clowns all right, but rich clowns, so he must pay attention.

"Welcome, dear gentlemen from the north. I understand you seek trade with our humble kingdom?"

"Indeed we do, your highness. We are interested in all kinds of art objects that originate from your culture, like your elegant pottery, your intricate silk tapestries and your finely decorated glassware."

To Al-Ghalib's dismay, it is Baron Whattage that answers. As he speaks, his hands wave, his feet shuffle, he uses his whole body to emphasize his points. At the same time, the crazy patterns on his clothes move as well. Paradoxical pain: eye-watering effects that are impossible to ignore. Dancing designs with a hypnotic hue. Even Yul, his most stoic guard, has trouble keeping his face straight.

"Our art objects? It seems you gentlemen have no lack of – well – ways to express yourselves."

"We are not really representative – in the artistic sense – of our people. We are only a small minority, the avant-garde. In our middle class, at the moment, arabesques are all the rage. However, due to unfortunate circumstances like the Crusades and the *Reconquista* here in Spain, our access to these articles is severely limited."

"Precisely what I'm wondering, my dear lords. Relations between our cultures are not exactly top notch, as you are well aware. Your monarchs Richard I the Lion-Hearted and John I, for example..."

"True, but these were despots that have ignored the will of the common man. Now with our hard-fought Magna Carta we – the people – are able to approach you directly. You are not our true enemy, the despicable French frogs and those Viking bastards are. The English people never had any fight with you."

"Do I hear this right: due to this Magna Carta you can trade with us without the implicit consent of your ruler?"

"Correct. Henry III has confirmed our Great Charter. This gives us the liberty to trade with anyone we choose."

"Interesting. Now how do you gentlemen think to pay for these precious articles of our cultural heritage, these superb examples of our Moorish craftsmanship?"

"Our English money, or, if this is inconvenient, gold. Or maybe you would be interested in weapon deliveries?"

"Weapons? Excuse me, but Christians delivering arms to Muslims? Your king might grant you the liberty of trade but this will certainly not please him."

"Discreet deliveries. Armaments purely for self-defense. After all, these overzealous Spaniards might just destroy the fine artifacts we seek. Just a deterrent to maintain the status quo."

"These proposals are...interesting. Would you gentlemen be my guests for the night while I confer with my advisors?"

"We will be delighted. On behalf of Baron Kirkinnison and myself, I hope the night brings you peace and wisdom."

"Thank you. I hope you will enjoy your stay here. Ahmed and Yassar, show our guests to their quarters."

In their lush guest rooms, Watt and Krikksen evaluate the day's proceedings. After ensuring nobody is overhearing them, Krikksen opens the discussion.

"Not bad. Still, weren't you just a little – ahem – overdressed?"

"Overdressed? Impossible. No such word in my dictionary. Anyway, was I not supposed to divert the attention while you scanned the place?"

"Sure. His eminence's guards had enough trouble keeping the tears from their eyes to watch my circumspect self. They now probably think all English are crazy."

"Not crazy, only somewhat eccentric. Did you find anything?"

"Most certainly. Micromikes and spycams all over the place. Not top of the line in our timeline, though. So they all had several spontaneous blackouts."

"Aha, our quarry is active here. I've always wondered why they go to such strange places, like undiscovered Americas, Big Brotherish governments and these Dark Middle Ages. Why not hide in the 'Rio Carnival forever'-timeline?"

"We'd never find him. Even your most garish outfits are normal there."

"Unimportant. Think of all the time we could spend just searching."

In the Grotto of the Daring Deeds, part two

The conversation in the cage continues. After the younger man has told about his pilgrimage with the Sufi Master from Damascus back to the Iberian Peninsula, it is time for the older one to report about events in Spain.

"Ferdinand's *Reconquista* almost got too much steam. With all my diplomatic and intriguing skills I was able to let him mount an attack on Seville before he was ready for it. The siege failed, by a hair's breadth. Frustrated, he marched up to Cádiz and took the city by surprise, or so he thinks."

"So you've finally decided to make Cádiz the center of action. Why not

Seville, like we originally planned?"

"A hunch. Its location is better: a seaport almost right on the border of Africa and Europe. Also the place where the next discovery of the new world is launched."

"How did you fare in Barcelona?"

"Fine. Peter Nolasco is just the right man to approach Ferdinand, I think. And old Ferdinand needs quite some softening up, believe me."

"Was Saint Peter difficult to convince? I had quite some trouble with Ibn al'Arabi."

"Peter Nolasco needed just a small push. An Unbloody Mary was enough for him to make his way to Cádiz."

"You still long for the alcoholic pleasures of your Big Apple days, I see."

"You know my drinking wasn't for fun. The real stuff, like single malts and cognac, still have to be invented, let alone cold beer. Only some of the wines are tolerable here. As an apprentice of the Sufi Path, you abhor alcohol, of course."

"I don't miss it, never getting the taste for it like you did. That's why I needed to go to Damascus."

"A minor reason. Mostly I believe that my cynicism would make it impossible to keep a straight face for all those years with the Muslim mystic."

"Quite true. Even I had trouble keeping up the charade. Still the pantheistic philosopher is as pure as they come. He constantly doubts his own wisdom; he's a lot more flexible than you think, even at his advanced age. And a charisma that is almost tangible."

"You're still under his spell."

"Just as much as you're an alcoholic, not really. I intensely enjoy his lessons, yet I try not to be overwhelmed by them."

"Balancing on the edge of insight and introversion. Even now you think this makes sense, our mad scheme?"

"I do, more than ever. Maybe I caught some holy fire, you know. But how about you, do you still think it worthwhile?"

The older Leonard's face distorts in a painful grimace. "How dare you ask? It may be much longer ago for me, but I still see her face through tons of burning rubble. I didn't invest so much to go back now. Also, contrary to my superficial sarcasm, I do hope. Now, the timing is everything. It will be another five hundred years before the dates match so perfectly again."

II

The Sub-Minimal Men

Early February 1247, *Anno Domini*, two lonely horseman ride over a dusty plain towards the coastal city of Cádiz. While most of Europe is still embraced in the cold grip of a severe winter, in the province of Andalucía the temperature reaches a balmy 21-centigrade.

The riders proceed a bit awkwardly, somewhat from lack of experience but also from apprehension, of not knowing what to expect. They're both young and longhaired, the blond one beardless, the dark-haired one sprouting some random tufts of facial hair. To break the uneasy silence, the fair one starts to speak.

"So these are the Dark Middle Ages? The sun's so bright it hurts my eyes."

"Dark as in uncivilized, you know."

"As opposed to our time being civilized?"

"I guess so. Why?"

"This guy we're supposed to trace, this Leonard Yomin..."

"What's with him?"

"I don't understand why we're after him. He's not the criminal type."

"He illegally used the Trans-Timeline-Transporter and disappeared into this worldline."

"OK, so he used the triple-T. But he hasn't done anything illegal before that. No criminal record, on the contrary: a PhD in physics and an M.Sc. in applied electronics. He applied for a job in our research department. They were on the brink of hiring him when he – well – disappeared."

"You know the rap: any person trespassing without permission into an uncontaminated worldline can potentially change the course of that world's history: C.I.P.-violation of the second degree."

"But what can a single guy do in times like these? The mass readings of the triple-T showed that he arrived here with his clothes and barely anything else."

"His knowledge. Unleashing technologies in times where the people are not ready for them can have catastrophic consequences."

"According to theory. But I very much doubt it. Take Leonardo da Vinci, even such a genius hardly made a dent in our history's course."

"Come on, Watt. I didn't make the Causality Interference Policy. And the

CIP is officially part of the law we must try to uphold."

"OK, Krikksen. But it doesn't mean I need to agree all the way with it."

Having voiced his misgivings, the blond horseman takes a more relaxed position. He pulls his red, felt hat over his eyes, shading them from the midday sun and sticks one hand deep in the pocket of his purple silk trousers. Still, not all unease has left his mind, far from it.

"How are we supposed to find him? The locator is only absolutely accurate as to which worldline, but it has an error margin of fifty kilometers and five years."

"You know the lessons: look for behavior, tools, policies, ideas, almost anything incompatible with the period."

"In these Dark Middle Ages? You know: dark as in almost no historical records."

"How would I know? It's only our first assignment. I guess we have to learn along the way."

"Then why Cádiz? There's Xerez, too, in the 50k circle."

"Intuition. And it's much more ancient, more interesting. So I say we try there first."

Then the dark-haired rider sweeps his left hand over the fabric of his bright green coat in a dismissive gesture, ending the argument. Watching his attire, other questions rise in his mind.

"You're sure our clothes are not too gaudy?"

"No problem, we're from Flanders, aren't we?"

"Flanders?"

"*Awel zunne*, the brightest and most flamboyant dressers of the Middle Ages."

"I thought we were supposed to be British merchants, searching for new markets."

"The English of that time? Way too dull. No, I decided we're from Brugge, West Flanders, an upcoming emporium of the Hanseatic League. A virtual monopoly on English wool, lace and its people dressing up like there's no tomorrow, it's our perfect cover."

Surprised by his colleague's research, Krikksen cannot argue with that. After a few hours, as they reach the gates of Cádiz, he urges Watt to announce them: "You have worked out our cover, after all."

The guards at the gate seem at least as bewildered as Watt and Krikksen at their mutual sights.

"These guys don't look like Moors at all!"

"What do we know? Talk to them anyway."

While Watt talks to the guards in what he hopes to be fluent Arabic, their jaws, that were hanging wide open, clap decidedly shut and their arms are raised threateningly. This forces Watt to take another approach, quickly.

"Allee, hombre, tu es Espagnol?"

This gives a more positive reaction. Watt excuses himself: "Sorry, *signores*, but I thought this beautiful city was still in the hands of the Moors."

"No, stranger, the *Reconquista* has claimed this city as well."

"My, my, things move fast in this year of our Lord 1252, don't they?"

"1252? But it is 1247!"

"Slip of the tongue, a joke. We from Flanders make little jests all the time. Therefore, let me introduce us: Duke Watterstraal and my companion Duke Krikkeman, or *Manneke Krik*, as our beloved people of the town of Brugge call him. In our function as representatives of the Hanseatic League we like to talk with the mayor of this major port."

The Imperfect Ghost

In the eighth lunar month of the Islamic year 644, an old, holy man returns to his native land. After his long pilgrimage in the Orient, Ibn al'Arabi wanted to spend his last days in Damascus in peaceful contemplation, teaching and writing. After finishing his masterpiece: *Fusus al-hakim* ("The Bezels of Wisdom") he was ready to take up his role in the afterlife.

But Allah decided he was not ready yet. A mysterious stranger saved him from the brink of death. Shortly after that he had a series of visions, the most intense since the revelations in Murcia fifty years ago that set him on his famous pilgrimage. This time, though, they instructed him to go back to his land of birth, incognito, humble and as an emissary of peace.

The first vision was strange. She didn't look quite as he remembered her, some of her features were all wrong. In Mecca she was so much more vibrant and enchanting, not the static, still picture he was seeing now. It was almost as if Allah was sending his message to the wrong receiver. But such a thing is impossible, indeed, unthinkable. So it must be his own mind that was failing there, he was not ready to receive the divine revelation.

The second vision was somewhat clearer: her eyes had the twinkle he fondly remembered and her beauty was like the one he celebrated in his *Tarjuman al-ashwaq* ("The Interpreter of Desires"). It showed him that all is Allah and Allah is all. But then again, the way she addressed him was wrong:

all cool, impassive and indifferent, not the sultry voice that sparkled all his passion.

It was with the third vision that he finally understood. Now she was perfect in all her beauty, now she embodied the eternal *sophia* that had guided him all his life, now she spoke with the sensual whisper of the muse that set his heart afire.

The power of the vision was so great that it swept him away, both literally and figuratively. She arose from a circle of light. Her words were perfect poetry, the kind he tried so hard to capture in the *Tarjuman*. As in "Expelled from Allah's Garden":

In a dream, wild
I saw a serene sight
An angel smiled
In the red morning light

Carved in stone
The circle spoke
Her face shone
The spell broke
And I froze in fear

Lightning was hurled
Down, in a bolt
As her lips curled
Breaking the mold
And I fell as a tear

From her eyes of gold
While the vision unfurled
The eyes that hold
All the pain in the world
More than I could bear

Innocence died
In a vision of fright
An angel cried
At the fall of night

The divine commandment was unequivocal: "Remember, always, Ibn al'Arabi that Allah is love. There is too much violence in our world. Two religions that have the same prophets but one are fighting each other to the death. This is not *sophia*, this is madness. You will travel to the place where the religions are closest, the place you were born. There you will approach your local leader, Muhamad Al-Ghalib and tell him that peace and a mutual understanding between the religions is Allah's will because in truth, these are but two sides of the same coin, different aspects from all that is real, all that is good, all that is, Allah."

So he set on his way, with a new apprentice, the strange youngster apparently sent by Allah to save his life. Ibn al'Arabi is the first to admit that he would never have made it back to Andalucía without him. Unquestionably, the young man is the smartest apprentice he has ever had. On the other hand, he can come up with questions that are much too deep and unsettling to come from such an untrained mind. This strange apprentice tries very hard to understand his master, yet the master sometimes wonders if the apprentice truly *believes*.

On the surface, the young man served him well and got them to the Iberian Peninsula. Below that, Ibn al'Arabi has his doubts. Their discussions are among the wisest he has had, better than most he had with his – supposed – equals. Which made him extra suspicious: it should not be possible. This Yo'min Le'enard, sometimes he seems like Allah's chosen one to guide him in his last pilgrimage, sometimes he seems like the instrument of evil to test his faith.

In the end, though, Ibn al'Arabi can only do what he must. Allah's will is inscrutable, and he can only try to serve him with the best of his abilities. They are approaching Gharnata and Yo'min will present their credentials to Muhamad Al-Ghalib's guards. Maybe things will clear up after he talks with the Moorish king, but somehow the wizened Muslim mystic doubts that.

III

Second Variety?

Cádiz! One of the oldest cities in Europe. Also one of the most picturesque, with sights subtle and enchanting, the city's charms creeping up on you slowly but inexorably. White mosques with bright-colored domes between humble houses, elegant in their simplicity. The pathway on the city's bulwark doubles as a beautiful promenade, overlooking the crowded center. A center where narrow alleys zigzag through dense conglomerations, leading to prominent plazas, broad main streets and well-cultured parks.

Watt and Krikksen walk these alluring alleys. Their horses, after having their shoes renewed by the town's blacksmith – a guy so big and fat that he might be able to lift them – are now enjoying a well-deserved rest in the city's stables. As usual, their unusual outfits draw plenty of attention. Seemingly oblivious, they plow through the thickening crowd, cool outward, gleeful inward. This bustling, vibrant city is quite contrary to the dark, stagnant streets of perdition they were mentally prepared for.

Their light mood would be disturbed if they knew who was watching them, quiet and astonished. Two gentlemen that, by an unprecedented act of will, look only slightly conspicuous.

"By all Jerry's lost picks, that's us!"

"Younger versions of us. Did we really dress like that?"

"I guess we did. Mind you, my junior's bright yellow overcoat matches nicely with those purple tights."

"But those ultramarine bells on his megapink boots are not exactly *ne plus ultra*."

"Really? Anyway, luckily we're incognito so they don't notice us."

"OK, Watt, let's go in this tavern and discuss this complication."

"Right. And some wine to ease the shock."

The older Watt and Krikksen enter the inn that is filled with merry people enthusiastically discussing preparations for certain festivities. They tactfully seat themselves at a corner table near the back entrance with a good view of the front door, just in case. After the waiter has brought them a carafe of the local *Jerez* they begin to talk business, with Krikksen being concise and Watt wasting the most words.

"Those junior versions of us must come from a near-identical timeline with TTT-capacity. Would they be after the same quarry?"

"Probably."

"But the chances of that happening are infinitesimal. Did they chase their prey to the wrong worldline?"

"Unlikely."

"Unlikely? Have you forgotten how many mistakes we made when we were young?"

"No. But our equipment – and theirs must be equivalent – never set us in the wrong world."

"True. Then what are they doing here? Going after another guy?"

"No."

"No? How can we be tracing the same guy? We're from another worldline, fergarciasakes!"

"Look, Watt. We have fingerprints, iris scan, DNA-sequence and exact age of our quarry. If theirs has exactly the same characteristics, which is so unlikely as to be well-nigh impossible, for all purposes he *is* our quarry."

"I get you. He's the same guy, but from their worldline."

"Right. So probably also somewhat less devious, less experienced as our quarry."

"Aha. Easier to trace."

"And he might lead us to our quarry. I suspect our man – who after all managed to fabricate his own TTT, a feat unparalleled in the Multiverse – picked up or contacted our juniors' quarry from his worldline."

"Reinforcements from a parallel Universe. So we can cooperate with our juniors? We're the best mentors they could wish for."

"Unfortunately not. I checked the rules: In the extremely unlikely event of meeting fellow agents from a near-identical timeline, keep your mutual distance. In the General Multiverse Treaty it was decided that each worldline in possession of TTT-equipment must take care of its own renegades. Otherwise we'll never stop working, I guess."

"A shame. Imagine the flamboyance of my youth combined with the experience of my superior years..."

"I think no parallel world is quite ready for that."

'Reconquista, Ferdinand!' said the Hailmaryman

Ferdinand III, king of Castile and Leon, is talking with his best spy. He doesn't like what he's hearing but this is one of the qualities that make this man so valuable: he does not twist the truth in order to please his majesty. He looks like the kind of half-breed that might pass unnoticed in both camps: his heavy brow, prominent nose and slight olive skin represent a Moorish kinship; his fine moustache, noble mouth and the resolute yet impertinent set of his eyes betray a Spanish ancestry. Léon's recommendations would have imprisoned a lesser informant, just for infuriating the king.

"It might be advisable to make a temporary truce. The failed siege of Seville has drained your funds and the Knights Templar are – understandably – reluctant to finance a new military adventure."

"A truce? No way, we must crush the infidels. Drive them from our homeland!"

"Unfortunately, these infidels are not so easily crushed. Some time off to regain our strength would surely be in order."

"Do you realise time is something I am running out of? We must push on, Córdoba, Jaén and Cádiz have returned to the mother country, Seville must follow!"

Léon's big Adam's apple bobs slightly as if swallowing a sigh. "With Córdoba and Jaén we were better prepared and we profited from the internal struggle between the Almohad and Nasrid dynasties. We weren't so lucky last time."

"Luck's got nothing to do with it. We are God's chosen carrying through his *Reconquista*–"

"Of course. As long as God's hand is helped by fresh armaments from the Knights Templar, superior intelligence and other convenient circumstances. At Seville those were not forthcoming."

Sometimes Ferdinand wishes to dispose of this strange man, this illicit informer with his impious mouth. But, blasphemous as he might seem, his information is so valuable as to be quite indispensable.

"So you admit that superior intelligence, your department, was lacking as well."

"I am sorry, your highness, but even I cannot go in and out of a thoroughly besieged city. Furthermore, I advised you against moving to Seville too soon."

"True. However I cannot suppress the feeling that we were *this* close to taking the city, several times." The distance between Ferdinand's thumb and forefinger is barely enough to hold the thinnest of papers.

"Close, but not close enough. However, the moment I found out that the Moors had withdrawn their regiment at Cádiz you knew the city was there for the taking, like an overripe pomegranate."

"A minor victory after a devastating defeat. The recapture of Seville would be the crown on my *Reconquista* campaign, the reward for my pious life."

"Sire, I am as disappointed as you are. Yet the ways of the Lord are inscrutable. It may still happen if we act prudent and wise."

"And you think negotiations are the answer? Heed to the heathens?"

"For the moment, yes. To the best of my knowledge, Al-Ghalib has reconciled with the Almohads and is now in the process of assembling a force to recapture Cádiz. He seems to have found a source of new armaments."

"Let him come with his army, we will slay them at the gates of this God-given city."

"It would be more advisable to avoid battle while we lick our wounds. I would even say: surprise him with a peace offer."

"A peace offer? Me, Ferdinand, the leader of the *Reconquista*? Are you out of your mind?"

"A temporary truce, of course, until the time is ripe for the conquest of Seville. Lull them to sleep in the meantime. Now is the perfect moment for a ceasefire. Did you know that this year Lent starts on exactly the same day as their fasting period, the *Ramadan*?"

"Do they fast as well?"

"Certainly. Only a lunar month instead of our 40 days, but even so. We could propose a truce during that period to begin with, and – to show our good intentions – invite a delegation of them to join in the *Carnival* celebrations."

"Not only make peace but party with them as well? Why not give Al-Ghalib my daughter as a bride, too!"

"Of course not. But we must play this well. Al-Ghalib will see through a half-hearted peace proposal. An official invitation to one of our most important festivities though, is an offer he can't refuse. It will delay his war plans and give us breathing space."

"You are very devious indeed. Still you must also know how I hate to deal directly with the infidels."

"Then don't do the proposal yourself. Send an emissary."

"I need to think about this crazy proposal of yours. Dismissed."

Even more stealthily than he came in, the strange spy makes his exit, leaving Ferdinand alone with his thoughts. He is getting old. He feels it in his heart and in his bones but mostly in his head. He's had a hard life. Fighting his father over the legacy of Leon. Fighting the Moors to reconquer Spain. Fighting his first wife Beatrice over the stupidest of things.

Not that he ever married for love. Politics prevail; marrying the daughter of the Holy Roman emperor seemed a good idea at the time. However, when Frederick II's attempt at reconciliation with the new Holy Father backfired it muddled things up considerably. Through all their fights, though, she did give him an heir, their son Alfonso, before she died. Now his second marriage is turning sour, too.

Still, it would all be worthwhile if he could have put the crown on his military campaign. After the fall of Jaén Seville seemed ready for the taking. Conquering Seville would have been the pinnacle of the *Reconquista*. Al-Ghalib would have become his vassal. More importantly: it would have been a sure ticket to sainthood. His ultimate prize: to be canonized, to be named *San Fernando*, to be remembered forever, maybe even have his own feast day.

But he failed. He put all his effort in the long siege and every time he thought he'd make a breakthrough something happened. New armaments arriving too late or not at all. An outburst of dysentery in his troops just when they were ready to bring down the main gates. Much more resistance than he had expected (the Cádiz regiment, undoubtedly).

The swift conquest of Cádiz was small consolation after the failed siege of Seville. Worsened by this report of the Moors preparing to retake the city from him. His disturbing thoughts are interrupted by an announcement of his master of protocol.

"Peter Nolasco of the Mercedarians requesting an audience."

Peter Nolasco, the famous ransomer and exemplary priest. What is he doing in Cádiz? Intrigued, Ferdinand immediately grants the request.

"Welcome, Father. What brings such an esteemed man to this humble city?"

"Thank you, sire, for granting me this audience. In all honesty, just between us: I had a vision of the Blessed Virgin Mary instructing me to go here."

"By the Father, the Son and the Holy Ghost," Ferdinand exclaims as he crosses himself. "We only recovered the city a few days ago. Only God would know..."

"As He indeed does, your majesty. I am only a minor player in His Grand Chess Game, yet He moved me very timely, as you astutely realise."

"Mysterious are the ways of the Lord. Did the Mother of the Immaculate Conception tell you why?"

"Only that things would become clear at the right time, your highness. She said my negotiating skills would be required."

"It has always been my belief that my humble role was to lead the *Reconquista*. It has driven me all my life, a holy fire burning within me. In my hubris I thought it would bring me sainthood—" The words escape Ferdinand's mouth before he can stop them. But instead of rebuking him, Peter Nolasco shows understanding.

"There are other ways to sainthood, your majesty. Last year I had the honor of visiting the Holy Father in Lyon. In a private moment, he conceded to me that he was – at times – getting weary of all the increasing troubles in our world. For the eyes of the world he needs to support the *Reconquista*, but inwardly he yearns for peace."

"But His Holiness surely has other things on his mind, his conflict with Frederick II, the liberation of the Holy Land, the advance of the Mongols..."

"All too true, your majesty, but his peaceful intentions are clear. He has sent a mission to the Great Khan, led by Giovanni Carpini; he is attempting ecumenical union with the Eastern Church. He implied that my meager efforts might find a rightful reward in due time."

"So he knew of your ransoming of our imprisoned fellow Christians?"

"Indeed he did. Even in these dire times, he keeps track of his lesser dignitaries. So be assured he has not lost sight of you and your sacrifices for the church. Quite possibly a temporary change of policy might be sensible."

"I was just considering such a thing, to be honest. But my reputation as zealous leader of the Reconquista hardly makes me the right negotiator."

"I can be your emissary to the Moors, your highness. I have negotiated with them before, they know I am true to my word."

"What you say makes a lot of sense. By the way, did you know that the Moors' fasting period, called *Ramadan*, exactly coincides with Lent this year?"

IV

The Flame of the Dancer and the Free

Festivities brighten up the promenades of Cádiz. In fact the whole city has turned into one big festival: everybody is disguised, dressed up in their most colorful outfits or even in costumes prepared specially for the occasion. People are not the only ones that have changed. From the vibrant sails and lively flags of the ships in the harbor to the extra ornaments of the main gate of the thin peninsula: even the smallest lane has become a grand decoration street.

Those streets seem to hold more than meets the eye. The streets are filled with people, partying like there is no tomorrow. The streets are filled with sounds: shouts, happy banter, cheering chants and merry music. The streets are filled with swirling clouds of confetti, wild waving banderoles and the clattering of the richly assorted small sweets thrown everywhere. The streets are filled with atmosphere, with vibrancy, with a special quality, that indefinable extra that gives a city its character. Even then the streets are not completely filled: there still is the resonance of expectation, of yet another gap to be filled.

The younger Watt and Krikksen walk through these streets, for once hardly standing out and enjoying every minute of it. They absorb the anticipation in the air and radiate it back, amplified. Then they hear a strange overtone in the invigorating noise, something not really disharmonic but still in discord with the general racket yet with a harmony of itself. Somebody singing a solitary chant of sadness and sorrow, using only a single phrase.

"AyeAyeAyeAyeAyeAyeAyeAyeAyeAyeAyeAyeAye!"

It is Jorge José Jesus Juan Guadalajara, the acknowledged master of the *cante jondo*, the tremendous tenor of the profound sound. He started as a classical chanter of the *grande cante*, singing about death, anguish, despair and religion. But as the expressive power of his voice grew, he evolved beyond the need to use actual words. Pain breathes from the timbre of his voice, anguish gushes from the subtle shades of his sighs, despair is denominated by the depth of his desire and his religious fervor is emanated by the exaltation of his exhalations.

"AyeAyeAyeAyeAyeAyeAyeAyeAyeAyeAyeAyeAye!"

To the untrained ear it may sound like one long litany of lamentations, but to the connoisseurs of the curtailed cry, the aficionados of the accentuated aye it is both fresh *panne* from the oven and pure *manna* from heaven, a feast for the senses and the spirit. Each single "Aye" echoes with its own inflection, each incantation with its own intonation. Every delicate permutation emphasizing another strain of suffering.

Although his incessant intensities are quite in contrast to the general mood, the festive spirit has risen to such heights that it easily tolerates, almost incorporates this distinct voice. Jorge climbs the stair of an elevation in the plaza so that his voice can carry further over the heads of all the partygoers. A circle of admirers gathers around the plaza's plateau, followed by more people, clapping their hands in approval and encouragement. In its enthusiasm, the crowd cheers:

"*Viva el cantator!*"

Watt and Krikksen begin to appreciate it, too.

"Do you hear that? Heavy stuff, man!"

"Far out. Down in the dumps to the nth degree."

"He makes the blues sound like the wailings of a lovesick puppy."

"And listen how he interacts with the crowd's clapping, the guy can improvise as well."

"I wanna chip in. Hey *hombre*," Krikksen says to a bystander carrying a guitar on his back, "Can I borrow your *guitarra* for a moment?"

"*Aye, Los Flamandos locos*," the spectator says, "Be my guest."

Strapping the guitar on, Krikksen walks up the rise and strikes a sustained chord. He tries several others until he finds one that complements the sad singer's cantations. The enthusiastic crowd applauds their jam session. Krikksen plays on, calling up every inch of restraint not to drift off into Jerry Garcia territory. Instead, he focuses on the rhythm clapped by the audience and adapts his riff churning around that. The crowd goes crazy:

"*Lo Flamando poco-loco.*"

"*Viva el guitarrero!*"

In the meantime, the Moorish party delegation has gathered near this happening. Breath-taking belly dancers, fakirs performing freakish acts like laying on a bed of nails, eating fire and spitting flames, expert jugglers keeping up an amazing amount of multihued balls, acrobats forming human pyramids, the lot. While the Spanish clap their rhythm with their hands, the Moors appear to have a special instrument for that: two handheld, hollowed-out pieces of hardwood. They are tied together with a chord; the chord is secured to the thumb while the fingers clap the pieces together, creating a rapid drumming sound, dry and penetrating. These pear-shaped clappers closely resemble big chestnuts so the crowd, going bonkers and bananas, shouts:

"*Viva los castaños!*"

Then Watt cannot refrain himself anymore and he storms the temporary stage with three great strides and a big jump. A fanatical free-time tap dancer, he raps out a rhythm of his own with his heavy boots on the plateau's marble floor. While his arms and upper body move with economy and grace, his dazzling legwork and intricate steps, accompanied by the clicking foot music set the crowd on fire:

"*Lo Flamando todo-loco.*"

"*Viva el zapateador!*"

Now one of the Moorish belly dancers hurtles herself forward through the crowd and completes the spectacle. She joins Watt in his feverish tap dance, matching her belly dance with Watt's performance in a weird yet elegant way. Circling each other, each seemingly in a gracious orbit of their own. Her hips and abdomen swing in a pulsating, quintessential Arabic cadence that is complementary at the same time, while her hands wave enchanting patterns hypnotizing everyone. Her dark eyes radiate passion and fire, of which not the least part is aimed at her strange, flamboyant dance partner. His feet keep up their blurring movements while his torso remains almost still. He acts cool and controlled; but his longing glances her way betray something else. The crowd, if not already there, goes completely apeshit:

"*Viva el bailarín!*"

Music and dance at the fringes of cultures, a spontaneous combustion of just the right ingredients: of passion and fire, wonder and desire; of poetry and madness, party and sadness; of dancing on strings, flying without wings. The lighting of a new flame, started by Spanish effusiveness, catalyzed by Flemish absurdity, harmonizing with Moorish élan.

"*AyeAyeAye,*" as some astute Spaniard would put it, "*flamma, flamando, flamenco!*"

So everybody is completely crazy, but what do you expect: it is *Carnival*!

Reasons to be Gleeful, part three

Just as Muhamad Al-Ghalib thought he had seen it all, another unexpected visitor announces himself at his court. As if things weren't spinning out of his control already. First those queer English barons proposing – of all things – arms in the form of trade, then the sudden arrival of the great master of the Sufi Path, Ibn al'Arabi with a strange, sly apprentice. Enter Peter Nolasco, the Christian ransomer. Do these people not realise he's trying to build the Alhambra, here?

It seems like the world is slowly going crazy. But, whatever happens, let it not be said that the king of the Moors is not a man of the world, reasonable and hospitable. He can always get mad, or even, later. Al-Ghalib signals his master of protocol to let the visitor in.

"Welcome, dear father, in my humble house. What tidings do you bring?" Al-Ghalib says in passable Spanish.

"Glad tidings, your majesty." Peter Nolasco answers in understandable Arabic, "Peace proposals from king Ferdinand."

"Peace proposals?" Al-Ghalib says, stunned, "From the fierce warrior of the *Reconquista*, the zealous leader that has foresworn to drive us heretics from his homeland?"

"Well, peace proposals is somewhat overstating it, but I am fully authorized by the kingdom of Castile and Leon to negotiate a temporary truce between the two parties."

A cease-fire to cement the standoff, Al-Ghalib thinks, *that's more like my esteemed, scheming opponent.* Out loud, he says:

"How do I know you are not setting me up?"

"I know this may sound strange to you, your majesty, but I assure you our intentions are sincere. Allow me to explain.

"First: did you know that our Christian fasting period, Lent, begins on exactly the same day as your fasting period, the Ramadan, this year? Some would say this is pure chance, but I do not believe that. I believe this was preordained, a subtle sign from above to change our policies.

"Therefore we propose to keep the truce at least until the end of Lent, or longer if both sides so agree.

"Furthermore, to prove our good intentions, I have an official invitation for a delegation from your side to join or pre-Lent celebrations called *Carnival*."

After Peter Nolasco has been led to the guest quarters, Al Ghalib muses about this new development. There have been more lulls in their fight over the decades; this is just the first time they are trying to make it official. Of course, the party that is first ready to strike again will break it, but for now, it's not a bad preposition.

It gives him time to see if these Englishmen were serious with their weird proposals. Even if they're not, he could use the time to reconcile with the Almohads. After the bloody siege of Seville they should now realise that the two dynasties must stand together against the Christian coalition if we want to remain on the Iberian Peninsula.

With Ibn al'Arabi preaching love, peace and harmony in every mosque and on every street corner of Gharnata, a temporary truce will meet with approval amongst his people.

Also, Ferdinand is probably licking his wounds, as well. The Knights Templar will not be overjoyed with the failed attack on Seville so Ferdinand might be short of funds, too. Best to put up with the charade and send a party delegation to their celebrations.

Those barbarians. Don't they know you're supposed to party *after* the fasting?

V

Juggologic

On the second day of Carnival, the Moorish party delegation sets out again to participate in this crazy festival. Yul, the chief of the – disguised – security party guarding the artists and most specifically the belly dancers, fiddles around a bit. His mood is fine but not quite perfect. He enjoys the celebrations of these crazy Spaniard Christians that party before the fasting. A Muslim celebrates after the abstinence, and then only for one day. OK, their Lent is ten days longer then our Ramadan, but feasting for four days? One Spaniard told him one day of feasting for every ten days of fasting, so there is some logic there. Somehow it makes sense to stuff yourself before the fasting. They just do it a bit excessively.

He likes the Carnival well enough; his problem is that he wants to join in, if only for a little while, instead of constantly being on guard for the belly dancers. Get into the spirit of the thing. As a young boy, he loved to juggle. He was of the 'juggling 9 or dropping 10' kind, being quite good, but not top notch. On a good day he could keep up ten balls. Amateurish, compared to the amount the best jugglers nowadays throw around, let alone the patterns they make with them. It both astonishes and frustrates him and it doesn't cease to amaze the Spaniards either.

Little boys grow big and Yul grew very big indeed. As tall as the tallest of the troupe, but easily twice as broad, Yul is a giant among the Moors. While he still likes to think of himself as Yul the Juggler, with those big muscles rippling under his olive skin and his prominent bald-shaven head, the belly dancers soon called him Yul the Stunner. The weight lifting tricks he did soon bored him witless, made him feel like Yul the Struggler. The offer to join Al-Ghalib's palace guard was quite welcome. His imposing physique, sharp eyes and quick wit eventually got him promoted to chief. Now this assignment brings a temporary reunion with his old troupe.

A happy reunion, not in the least enhanced by the circumstances. Things are great; Yul just wishes he could make them perfect. The atmosphere is there, the Spaniards even allow the troupe and his men to walk over the bulwark surrounding the city, so that they are even more visible to the city's partygoers. Such a complete trust, they even haven't bothered to remove the cannons and the piles of cannonballs. Then – standing on this ton of bricks – inspiration hits him.

He moves to a heap of cannonballs, a pile of ten stacked up like a triangular pyramid. He takes the top one in his huge right hand, weighs it and nods to himself. Not quite as heavy as he feared. He throws it high in the air, quickly takes a second and a third and before anyone realizes what happens Yul is juggling three cannonballs.

As the rest begin to gaze in astonishment, Yul thinks that this is a lot easier than he thought. He calls out to one of his men:

"Yassar! Give me one more!"

The sight of his stoic boss going crazy paralyzes Yassar, but only shortly, as he remembers the penalty for disobedience. Then, acting as if it's the most normal thing in the world, he walks over to the cannonball pile. A startled expression lights his face for the shortest moment, then he huffs and puffs as he lifts a cannon ball and hands it to his chief.

Juggling four, Yul wants more.

"One more!"

The stunned Yassar hands over another to Yul the Stunner.

"One more!"

Six still doesn't finish Yul's fix.

"One more!"

Seven, not enough to be in heaven.

"One more!"

Eight, hand of sleight, can he take the weight?

"One more!"

Nine, a smile breaks through his contorted concentration, he feels fine.

"One more!"

Then, in a final tour de force, Yul is juggling all ten. In the meantime, a big crowd has gathered before the defensive harbor wall and is cheering Yul on. At first, only a few of the festive crowd noticed the spectacle and with a big "Oh!" draw the attention of their friends. These cry in surprise: "Aye!" and, soon after that, in appreciation: "El Joculatore!"

The cries, shouted almost simultaneously but in disharmony, mix, mingle and warble.

"*Oh!*"

"*Aye!*"

"*El joculatore!*"

"*Oh—El—Aye—joculatore!*"

"*O—L—ye—olate!*"

"*OLE—ole—olé!*"

A new yell is born. Yul keeps juggling, seemingly effortless. The master jugglers of the troupe gaze in astonishment. The belly dancers, though, seize the opportunity and start dancing in a big circle around Yul. The crowd freaks out and the cries of *olé* echo around the whole city.

"Olé, olé, olé!"

But even the inhumanly strong Yul can't keep this up for long so after his ten minutes in the spotlight he calls his assistant again:

"Yassar, take one!"

One by one, the cannonballs are put back in their triangular pile, among loud cheers from the mesmerized masses. Still, Yul figures the moment is not yet perfect. Ten long minutes of limelight is good, but somehow they cry out for more. The veiled girls keep up their hypnotic dance and Yul knows exactly how to end with a bang.

He calls up three petite dancers he still knows from his touring days and asks them to dance right in front of him.

"Keep facing the crowd," he whispers loudly over the excited din as they comply, "and whatever happens, trust me."

The girls look small against the huge Yul, who holds up his long arms and claps his hands above his head to fire up the crowd further. He is answered by a rising roar of rhythmic applause, clapping hands, snapping fingers and clicking *castañets*.

A naughty gleam appears in Yul's eyes as his huge hands go down, grip the waist of the first girl and throw her up, high in the air. Her slightly shocked shout is hardly heard as in blurring speed the other two follow suit. Their surprised cries turn into screams of delight as they realize what the multitude must be seeing: Yul the Stunner is juggling belly dancers!

The girls, hardened performers under their fragile looks, start swinging their bellies as they swoop through the air in slow arches. Yul has no time to smile as this is hard labor, taxing him to the max. Then again, nobody notices the beads of sweat on his head and body as all eyes are on the graceful girls who milk the moment for all its worth. A performance to burn itself in the collective unconsciousness, an act to never forget.

Knowing the limits of his strength, Yul puts the girls down one by one. Any small glitch from his side is expertly covered up in the athletic way the acrobatic dancers land on their feet and dance on as if nothing happened.

The crowd goes berserk, barking mad, over the top and completely knockout. Yul bows to the astounded audience, bathes in the bottomless admiration and thinks: 'if this isn't fifteen minutes of fame than I am a pudding of poodle poo.' Knowing that stopping at the very peak of his performance is the best timing he retreats behind the ranks of his security staff. Only Jeffe Garreta, the Spanish defense *commandante*, also celebrating Carnival and oléing with the jolliest of them, would understand the wink that is exchanged between Yul and his assistant Yassar: the cannonballs on display were lightweight dummies exhibited to hide the actual lack of ammunition.

But what the heck, who cares, it's *Carnival*!

Empty Illustrations

Granada, or Gharnata as its Moorish inhabitants call it, bathes in the sun's radiance, light so pure it seems like light from light. In this light its many mosques look whiter than white, so white as to induce headaches in some. On the other side of the Darro River the *Generalife* and the building of the *Alhambra*, the old and the new palace for the sultans, stare down at the *Albayzin* quarter.

In one of its narrow, cobbled streets, walking between the red-bricked *cármenes*, Sufi Master Ibn al'Arabi and his apprentice Yo'min Le'enard are discussing both spiritual and earthly matters.

"Apprentice, I keep wondering: how strong is your belief, how strong is the *tahwid* within you?"

"Master, I witness that there is no deity but God."

"Don't give me the answer by the book, tell me what you feel."

"Allah loves us and we love him."

"There is no doubt in your heart?"

"Master, there is uncertainty lingering in my mind. My heart believes with passion and fire, yet the seeds of doubt are difficult to expel from my mind."

"Other masters would have purged you for less, my wayward son. Now why do you doubt?"

"It is all the fighting. The Crusades, the *Reconquista* and those rumors of a fierce race from the East heading for the Holy City of Jerusalem. My mind wonders why a God that loves his people would allow all those wars."

"Watch your hubris, apprentice. No mere human can understand the mind of God."

"Forgive me, master. I just wished I could do more to convince people that love and peace are wiser than war and hatred."

"It is your inclination towards action. Disregard the unruliness of youth and adopt a more meditative attitude. Develop your inner life."

"I try. Yet as you teach me, should I not try to teach even the smallest of wisdoms to the common man?"

"I sense an innate need in you to change reality, if only by the littlest of bits. Certainly you should know that only Allah is capable of this."

"But Master, is it not that God and creation are two different aspects of reality, but two sides of the same coin?"

"*Wahdat al-wuhjud*: depending on each other and reflecting each other. You remember my lessons well."

"So if we see an aspect of Allah mirrored in reality, should we not act upon it?"

"Are you saying that you have received *Dhawq*, a direct taste of divine truth?"

"No, master, perish the thought. I am but a humble apprentice that has still so much to learn. It's just that some signs are so clear, so straightforward that they seem undeniable."

"Such as?"

"Well, first there is your return to your native land. Then the conjunction of Ramadan and Lent, the peace proposal from the Christians and their invitation to join their pre-fasting celebrations. Shouldn't we go too, master?"

"A humble Sufi mystic and his – supposedly – humbler servant? What can we do there?"

"I don't know, why not just be there? After all, didn't you teach me that it was the prophet Mohammed who brought peace in his war-torn Arabia?"

"Apprentice, sometimes you seem wise beyond your years. Still, I think you are far from attaining *Ikhlas*."

"I try to learn, Master, very hard. I attempt to incorporate everything my senses give me, pick up on our science, yet there is no overall picture arising from that growing body of knowledge."

"Science alone is not enough. Intuitive knowledge is needed to reach beyond science, to receive illumination to which reason has no access."

"I hope that someday I will attain such an insight."

"You may, or you may not. *Inshallah*. Just don't forget to love."

"Love?"

"Love is more important than knowledge."

"Yes, but is it alone enough to conquer all?"

"What do you mean by that, Yo'min Le'enard?"

"Nothing master, just my ignorance babbling."

VI

Carriage Cars in Spain

Big, fat Pedro Martes, the blacksmith, is jealous. Jealous of this big, strong Moor that stole the show yesterday. He, big, fat Pedro Martes is the strongest man in town. However, after the crazy stunts of this bald Moor, everybody seems to have forgotten. Even his best friends were teasing him. "Are you now going to juggle horseshoes before you put them on, Pedro?" one said, followed by: "No, they're too hot. He'll throw the horse in the air and let it land exactly on the new horseshoes!" as another said: "And for good customers he'll balance the anvil on his nose!"

Normally, Pedro can take a joke. But this is too much, his honor is at stake. He must do something. He must think of something. He must pull off some crazy stunt, if only to re-establish his self-esteem. He mentioned this to his friends, and, after their laughter had died down and they started to think, they agreed. All very nice, these Moorish spectacles, but we Spaniards will not be outdone. So Pedro has the muscles and we must provide the brains. Athletics is not his strongest point but he is indeed very, very strong. Eventually they came up with something, then had to work through half the night to prepare it. But hey, with *Carnival* this is all in a day's work.

Today the traditional tug of war is held. Quite boring, actually, as Pedro's team always wins. Therefore, it is postponed until tomorrow while something else has been put on the agenda.

In the middle of the main street five carriages have been lined up after each other. The carriages are big rectangular ones, normally used to carry goods. The horses pulling them are absent. Strangely, the wooden shafts of the aft wagons are fixed to the back of the carriage before them. Furthermore, there are no horses anywhere to be seen.

Empty carriages alone, though, are a boring sight. Therefore, Pedro's friends walk through the gathered crowd and ask the people with the most extravagant, most outré outfits to display themselves on the wagons. Not forgetting their guests, they ask the most flamboyant of the Moorish party delegation to congregate on the middle carriage.

The audience, puzzled and curious as to what is going on, watches in relative quiet at first but becomes more involved as they see who is climbing the carriages. The more colorful the costume, the dandier the disguise, the louder the cheers of the crowd. Nor do they always agree with every choice

Pedro's compadres make: a bad choice is booed away and personal favorites are put forward that – if the partying masses make enough approving noise – are allowed to mount one of the carriages.

Then, as all the carriages are filled with the prettiest peacocks, bodacious belladonnas and exhaustive ensembles, the door of a nearby building opens. From it big, fat Pedro comes out wearing an outfit that some ladies would definitely consider kinky. However, the black leather body gear and collar serve another purpose: his friends rig it up with the pulling shaft of the front carriage. After they have made sure that everything is connected nice, tight and double secure they leave the show up to Pedro.

By then even the most dim-witted suspects what's going on. Not a contest between two live teams, but a contest of wills between a man and inertia, with resistance thrown in for good measure. No tug of war of man against man, but raw foot'n'guts against stagnancy found awry. A treat of traction and immense introspection.

Surely this is impossible? What normally requires a couple of horses cannot be done by a single man. Pedro seems to think otherwise. The crowd becomes silent as he takes a very deep breath and concentrates.

His eyes glaze over and acquire that certain look. It's a distinctive quality that can evoke magic. It's the kind of gleam and the way these eyes are set that, if you see it in a dark, lonely one-way street, makes you do things you thought impossible before. Like vertical wall climbing. Like setting a new world record for the 100-meter sprint. The way they look right now would probably make you fly.

Then he throws himself forward, utters a mighty moan and pulls, pulls, pulls with every tense muscle in his big body. The gathered people cannot hold their silence any longer and start cheering Pedro on.

"*Olé, Pedro, olé!*"

Hardly heard above the crowd's noise something's creaking, is that his muscles or something else? The creaking continues and the foremost carriage makes the slightest of movements, seems to gain a minimal momentum before it stops with a clack.

"*Pedro es loco!*"

Some of the people shout as they cannot see Pedro pulling it off. However, Pedro is barely warming up. Now the first two carriages seem to move slightly as the slack between them is tautened. The creaking increases until it is stopped by a second clack.

"*Pedro motivo!*"

Others cry as they see the almost imperceptible movements. Pedro is increasing his effort, deep down there's some reserves left. Three carriages now emit a triple squeak; the exhibited exemplars of deft disguisers on those quickly shift their feet in order not to lose their balance when the next clack announces itself.

"*Olé, Pedro es loco!*"

Shouted this time with an admiring edge as four cars crunch through the gravel of the street. When the fourth and final clack tries to disturb the equilibrium of the cars' perplexed passengers some decide that, since they're shifting anyway, they might as well start dancing.

"*Olé, Pedro motivo!*"

Now Pedro really has to give it all he's got. Tapping all his reservoirs, physical, mental and metaphysical if need be. He's almost there; he has to do it, even if it will rip the tendons off his bones. The way he looks now, with every muscle almost bulging out of his skin, with his eyes focused on an imaginary opponent that needs to be crushed at all cost, with a grimace that says he will not be stopped by anything, would make any prospective wrestling candidate facing him long for lesser dangers like a stampede of bulls or an attacking Mongolian horde.

"*Pedro es loco! Motivo! Olé!*"

The crowd can't believe it: the madman is moving. The five carriages creak, groan, squeak and sputter as if protesting, but they move. Slowly, ever so slowly, but they're moving. The occupants of the carriages begin to dance wildly; the chanting hordes begin to shout hoarsely:

"*Pedro es loco motivo! Pedro el loco-motivo! Pedro el locomotivo!*"

The madman is moving. Strangely, he finds that as he gains speed he needs less effort to keep the cars moving. The train of carriages moves, not fast, more like a row of barges floating past, but they *are* moving. Eventually he settles on a walking speed that he can keep up for quite some time and begins to make his triumphant tour through the city, tugging a complete spirited party in his wake.

Everybody loves it, bathes in it, in the spirit of celebration, everybody on the carriages slowly floating by a celebrity for a day, with Pedro as their driving force. Again, the festivities reach an unprecedented peak, another pinnacle in the permutation of the people's party. You might wonder where it will all lead to, eventually. But hey! It is *Carnival*!

We Anticipate Events Otherwise

In an inconspicuous apartment somewhere in the center of Cádiz, an apprentice of the Sufi Path and an undercover agent of the kingdom of Castile and Leon have an animated discussion. The strange language they speak is almost lost in the noise rising from the celebrating crowd in the streets outside.

"Was it wise to let the older Watt and Krikksen find out about your presence here? You could have taken away the obsolete equipment from their timeline. They probably wouldn't have detected your improved gadgets." The young one says.

"Of course not. My self-designed, superior equipment was picking up their detectors as they detected the decoys." The old one answers.

"You could have noticed them without drawing their attention to the decoys."

"Being invisible and impossible to catch will only make my case more interesting. It would become a real challenge and then Interpol would send their best men, use their best equipment. No, it's better to be seen and then seemingly escape arrest by what seems sheer luck."

"But that will work only for so long. As soon as they find how great our impact on events really is, they will come in force."

"True. Therefore we have to take the agency that is most eager to get me out of action."

"How do you want to do that?"

"Easy, I will let them catch me."

"What?"

"I will lead them to the other grotto, the one where I disintegrated the triple-T vehicle. They will see its debris and pick up the residual radiation and subsequently believe that I have been stuck here all these years."

"But our mission..."

"Will be carried on by you and by the reinforcements that will arrive after I've been arrested and Watt and Krikksen will be safely gone. With the next Leonard you can move to the second phase."

"But you are the spiritual father of our grand scheme. Other versions of you have thought about it, but only you went far enough to start it."

"Unfortunately, I can't finish it. Don't act so shocked. You know this project is larger than one single lifetime."

"I just hoped you'd remain here a bit longer, if only to assure things go well."

"We can only push things so far. At a certain moment they should gain their own momentum."

VII

Beyond Lies the Hub

Even through their constant partying, some people can't help but wonder. One day this great Moor bedazzles everybody; the next day big, fat Pedro steals the show. Now who is the strongest? Wasn't the traditional tug of war postponed until today? Well, you know, couldn't those two...?

The notion occurred to more people, not in the least to Pedro and Yul themselves. Last evening, after Pedro had finished his tour through the streets, Yul was one of the first to congratulate him with his incredible feat. Pedro, happy that he had proved himself, accepted the compliment with a big smile. Now that he has shown the whole town not to forget their big blacksmith, a load had been lifted from his shoulders.

Then the two giants looked each other straight in the eyes with a respectful, yet also a taxing gaze. They hardly needed the interpreter to know what they wanted to do the next day. Not unsurprisingly, the interpreter was the young Watt, whose curiosity keeps him from keeping any cats at all. He ended up negotiating how the two giants wanted to test each other's strength, a friendly exchange throughout if only for the way this frenetic Flemish guy translated everything with mouth, hands and feet. Krikksen interfered only minimally, injecting tiny slices of sanity in the exchange.

Naturally, they ended up as referees. They're from Flanders, neutral, objective and mad as two hatters, complete with white rabbits, cheesy smiles and looking glasses. How much closer to perfection can you get?

So, on the last day of *Carnival*, there is the big match of Yul versus Pedro. It is one in three different rounds.

First round: weightlifting.

Since both Yul and Pedro had no problem with lifting the city's special rock, the manhood stone of Cádiz, something had to be improvised. So they took a strong, wooden box from Pedro's shop, put a thick rope under and around it, filled it with his heaviest tools and added horseshoes until both giants started having trouble lifting the box. Their faces become red, cheeks blow up as they huff and puff and muscles swell to bursting point.

Although with increasing difficulty, both men can still lift the box and keep it up for the required three seconds. After every round, one more horseshoe is added. At a certain moment, Yul grabs the rope, lifts and lifts, there is some extra strength left in his arms but somehow his legs can't keep up. Try as he might, the weight doesn't leave the ground.

Then it's Pedro's turn. His technique is different: instead of bending over and keeping his legs straight, Pedro sags through his knees and keeps his back and arms straight. With him it's the other way around: his thick legs have some power to spare, it's his arms that are stretched to their limits. His arm muscles feel like snapping, but they hold. Barely, and very shortly. But enough to lift the weight from the ground for the required three seconds. Then he drops the load and jumps up in triumph. The first to congratulate him is Yul.

Second round: arm wrestling.

For this, the big conference table of the town hall is placed on the staged elevation in the central plaza, ensuring all onlookers a good view. The big chairs from the same place are barely large enough to seat the two giants. In a confrontation like this, it is vitally important that the arms of both wrestlers are placed in so equal a position as is possible in order to prevent that one has an unfair advantage over the other. Watt, flamboyant referee *par excellence* makes quite a show of positioning those two pillars of power. Jumping around both contestants like a living honey statue trying to evade a horde of imaginary bees he looks at both arms from every possible angle, making small adjustments in their positions. Then, in a final *coup de théâtre*, he jumps on the table, does a fast tap dance shuffle as if to ensure it is solid enough and takes a look down exactly above the gripping hands. Moving his head up and down first, as if to ascertain he's seen it right. His arms rise, his hands make a wriggling motion like he still hasn't made his mind up but then his two thumbs are up and he smiles from ear to ear. The crowd cheers appreciatively at this clownish performance and laughs out loud as he makes a backwards somersault from the table to the ground.

Yul and Pedro repress their amusement because the struggle is near. "On my count of four!" Watt shouts for all to hear and counts down: "ONE, TWO, THREE, FOUR," and the battle is on.

With a teeth-grinding grunt, not unlike that of a bull that has just noticed a waving red flag, Pedro charges with all his might. Yul's arm bends back under this onslaught, but only about a hand width. Pedro pushes on, roaring, cheered on by his supporters. Yet Yul holds on. Sweat breaks on his brow, his muscles begin to tremble, but he holds on.

For a while it seems only a matter of time before Yul will succumb under Pedro's ferocious attack. However, the longer it takes for Pedro's onrushing opening to gain the upper hand, the more he gets into trouble. Yul is by then not the only one sweating profusely.

Inexorably, the tide turns and Yul slowly pushes Pedro's arm back in the upright position. For the longest of moments, both arms remain there. A collective sigh of disappointment escapes Pedro's Spanish fans as Yul is pushing his arm down, ever so slow, ever so relentless. The Moorish delegation starts making the most noise, the sound rising to a small crescendo as Pedro's hand touches the table. Now it's Yul's turn to jump up in triumph and reciprocating the previous sportsmanlike gesture Pedro is the first to congratulate him.

Third and last round: tug of war (finally!)

The action moves to the elongated sand pit where the traditional tug of war is normally held. Watt and Krikksen draw a thick line in the sand, take ten paces from it and position the opponents on the respective spots.

Pedro lashes the thick rope once around his big belly, grips it in his ham-sized fists and plants his feet very firmly in the sandy ground. Yul swings one loop around his waist as well, winds an extra loop around his right arm and squeezes the multi-corded cable tight. While the two giants hold the thick rope loosely taut, Watt attaches a red ribbon in the exact middle between the two opponents, right above the line in the sand.

After approving his handiwork, he steps back and signals the two colossi to stand ready. He takes his hat off, holds it out before him, watches if both rivals are truly ready and waves the blazing purple, yellow-ribboned headgear down in a sweeping gesture.

The giants pull. The red ribbon keeps hovering over the dividing line. Just as it seems to move in one direction it goes right back again. With no one getting a clear edge, the two giants dig themselves deeper in the sand and double their efforts. In what must be a first in the history of Carnival in Cádiz the whole city is silent and only the struggling moans of the massive opponents are heard.

Soundlessly, incredibly, with the separated halves furiously lashing back the thick rope rips apart. Both Pedro and Yul fall back in the sand with a dry thud. The silence remains as nobody can quite believe what they've just seen.

"How can such a thick rope break?" Krikksen whispers, dazed and confused. "Whole groups use it for tug of war. I mean: they're strong, but that strong?"

"I wouldn't know," Watt adds nonchalantly, juggling his pencil-thin laser cutter. "I really wouldn't."

Krikksen rolls his eyes, then quickly swallows what threatens to become a laughing fit.

"OK," he shouts to the confused crowd, that feel the irresistible urge to crack up as well. "Equal. A draw. It's a draw!"

For the longest moment, both giants remain down. Then it seems they have trouble getting up. Slowly it is dawning on everyone: both men are trying to suppress their sniggers but fail hopelessly. Almost simultaneously they burst out laughing, Yul sounding like a neighing horse with hiccups, Pedro uttering a deep belly laugh with infrasonic overtones. The tension breaks and everybody shares in the hilarity.

Finally, the two giants rise from their pits, walk towards each other and embrace, while tears of laughter roll down their cheeks. The roar of approval that this invokes shakes the walls encircling the city of Cádiz to their very foundations. By the way, did anyone mention it is *Carnival*?

The rest of the afternoon is celebrated with a spontaneous street procession. Pedro's friends hurriedly improvise carriage-pulling gear for Yul. The two gigantic friends are pulling together the same five cars Pedro led through the town yesterday alone, but hey, haven't they worked hard enough as it is?

The cars are filled with a colorful lot once more: this floating procession, this flotilla of flower power *avant la lettre* is such a success that it may become a tradition.

Of course, on the middle car Watt and the Moorish belly dancer are dancing, again. Krikksen is churning out appropriate riffs while Jorge José Jesus Juan Guadalajara is wailing his saddest wails, encouraged by the clapping and castañetting audience.

As the young detective and the Arabic woman encircle each other, Watt watches her face intently. Passion is smoldering behind her eyes and he'd be damned if there wasn't a big smile behind her veil.

"You crazy Flaming, my oriflamme."

"You luscious Moor, you drive me crazy."

"You mean to say you aren't already?" She says with a wink.

"I can get crazier still." Is his honest answer.

"I don't think I'm quite ready for that." She whispers.

"You never know until you try. Where can we meet?"

"We can't, my mysterious muse. I already have a meeting with destiny." At least that is what Watt thinks she's saying.

"Too bad. But I won't forget this, ever."

"Neither will I, quixotic one."

They dance on, deep into the night. They never meet again, after this fat Tuesday night, but sometimes even a small beginning is infinitely better than nothing.

In a final flash of glory, the party burns its last extravaganzas. Tomorrow is the time for fasting, of tightening belts and suppressing appetites. But who cares, tonight is still *Carnival*!

Emperor at Dusk, Vassal at Dawn

The older Watt and Krikksen decided to change tactics in Cádiz. Having seen their parallel-world younger versions they didn't visit the city's officials, as another pair of strangely clad foreigners would raise too much suspicion. After a circumspect nightly errand of mounting digicams, minimikes and tracerjets around Ferdinand's quarters they were rewarded a few days later with a very interesting conversation between the king and a very impudent spy.

Their I/spy/AI monitoring all incoming data from the remote pickups was set very sensitive so alarmed them at Ferdinand's every conversation involving politics or intrigue: discussing his choice of breakfast with a servant, every fight with his wife, just about anything. Even minding all false alarms in shifts the two detectives were getting too fatigued to even discuss setting the I/spy/AI somewhat less sensitive. Then, an overtired, apathetic Krikksen, expecting another false alarm, overheard a spirited conversation effortlessly spiking through his wall of indifference.

This was undoubtedly Leonard Yomin actively pursuing his enigmatic goal in this worldline. How hoarding Ferdinand towards a temporary truce with Al-Ghalib would serve their quarry's objective – whatever that was – baffled both detectives. Still, this conversation alone was evidence enough for Yomin's CIP-violation in this worldline. Compared to the large amount of other, similar offenses he committed, however, it was relatively minor.

In those other worldlines, parallel Universes that were nearly identical to their origin Universe, Leonard Yomin was known as under several infamous monikers as 'the whirlwind of Wall Street' or 'the annihilator of the New York Stock Exchange' or NYSE 'nihilator'. With detailed information of his home worldline, he traveled to the past in those near-identical parallel worlds and ransacked the stock markets. Tracing their man through those worlds, Watt and Krikksen, continuously hot on his trail, deduced from the increasing mass being transported with every trans-timeline jump and the vivid transactions in uncut diamonds and precious metals that Mr. Yomin was accumulating quite a capital, a treasure to dwarf the combined reserves of all European nations in these Dark Middle Ages.

With that gargantuan financial backup in mind, his machinations between the Spanish and the Moors seemed somewhat unambitious, to say the least. He could easily hire an army large enough to conquer both Christian and Moorish Spain and not stop at that, too.

On the other hand, Leonard Yomin did not appear to be the

manslaughtering kind. Chasing their prey for so long, Watt and Krikksen got a certain feel for him. The guy is sharply calculating, fast moving, slicker than an oiled eel in a grease pit, not afraid to wreak financial havoc but stops at direct physical harm. His audacious plotting might cause secondary casualties, yet Yomin is not the man to lead armies in bloody battles. His actual goal, though, remains shrouded in a veil of mystery. Through their long pursuit Watt and Krikksen have become more interested in finding his motivations than in the actual arrest.

Now, they are hot on his trail once again. Their minimikes and digicams home in on their quarry and as he eventually leaves Ferdinand's quarters one of the miniature tracerjets the detectives placed near every exit launches a minuscule radiotracer that penetrates their quarry's clothing until it unobtrusively attaches itself to his skin. This should make it easy for them to home in on their prey. During the following days, following their quarry close with the radiotracer Yomin stays in the middle of Carnival-crazy crowds making an arrest a hopeless affair. As if it's not enough that the cheerful, unrestrained way these Spaniards celebrate their Carnival conjures up all the fantastic times they had in the 'Rio Carnival forever'-timeline. Let alone the manner in which their junior versions not only join in but play a leading role in the exceeding party spirit as well.

Still, the older versions do remember how their indulgence in Rio almost ended their careers and, with a mixture of melancholy and wisdom, refrain from their worst partying tendencies and carry on with the job. Their determination is rewarded as, a few days after Carnival, their quarry is leaving town.

Leonard Yomin is heading towards the hills between the *Sierra Bermeja* and *Serrania de Ronda*. Experience and instinct keep the two detectives from arresting him out in the open. Only when Yomin stays the night in what – according to their quantum computer's best estimate – is a concealed place in the landscape do they go there and make the arrest. True, this very same tactic may have helped Yomin's escape every other time, but locating their quarry's triple-T is becoming more important, especially regarding that a junior version of him might use it after they arrest the senior one.

The end of their long chase is near when they wake the soundly sleeping Leonard Yomin in a large, very well hidden grotto with unnaturally smooth walls.

"Leonard Yomin, you are under arrest for CIP-violations of the first kind: actively trying to change the course of history in an uncontaminated worldline..."

"Guilty." A groggy Yomin answers.

"Unlawful use of TTT-equipment..."

"Not guilty. I made my own and your megalomaniac agency, in its delusions of grandeur, never made an actual law against making or using a privately made one, considering the astronomical odds that handed them their triple-T's in the first place. My advocates will successfully fight this point."

"Draining of stock markets in near-identical worldlines…"

"Never had any qualms about that. Just some more mega corporations not taking their responsibilities but bribing politicians and plundering the third world."

"The stock market is not all big, bad companies. It could be people's pension funds that you raided, as well."

"Most of which also didn't take their responsibility. They could have invested in green technologies, in ethical companies paying a fair price to the poor countries."

"Well, that's your opinion. What happened to all the wealth you accumulated?"

"Almost everything disappeared as my triple-T disintegrated. Fool that I am, I stored those in the same cave as the TTT. I was away when it happened and was forced to live on my wits and the few diamonds I had along."

"Your triple-T disintegrated? The energy released by that would have evaporated a whole mountain!"

"With yours it would. But mine had used almost all its energy with all the transworld jumps I made. You guys could recharge in our old timeline, I could not take that risk. So while I was away from this grotto, my TTT's safety system failed. It still made this grotto about ten times its original size."

Watt activates a radiation counter from his equipment bag. "Yes, Krikksen, the radiation I'm picking up here matches the characteristics of the residuals of a failed one."

"So mine is not the only one that failed?" Yomin remarks, almost smug.

"None of your business, Yomin." Krikksen says, but his heart isn't in it. "Now indulge me: why go through all this trouble for some crazy manipulations in this worldline?"

"For peace in the long run. If differences of ideology in two cultures that have almost the same basis grow so profound over long centuries it takes a mending deep into history to show them the error of their separate ways."

"Correct me if I understand this wrong: you are doing this to pave a better future in this worldline?"

"That's what I've been trying so far."

"We live in a Multiverse with an enormous amount, maybe an infinite number of parallel worlds. Why bother to save one while countless others go down the drain?"

Inadvertently Leonard Yomin thinks about his sister. Her body was never found under the enormous amount of debris that once was the WTC. He should know: he kept looking until the NYC firemen had to stop him by force. Swallowing his tears, he says: "That's an argument like saying: why save lives on a single world while thousands die every day of hunger, disease and war. No, any firefighter, emergency ward nurse or flying doctor will tell you that every life counts. So also every world counts."

The fierce glow of Leonard Yomin's expression leaves no room for contradiction. Neither do Watt and Krikksen feel the need.

"We have to arrest you anyway. Basically, you've confessed. We'll leave the ethical decisions up to the court." Krikksen says.

"Well, he'll have arranged for the best attorneys money can buy, in any case." Watt adds.

"Most probably."

"What about our junior versions partying all over town? If they're here then a junior version of Mr. Yomin will be around as well."

"Correct."

"The way our juniors are going they'll never get their quarry."

"Indeed."

"I mean, we botched up our first couple of assignments before we started getting it right. Shouldn't we just advise them a little bit?"

"You know how our beloved boss W. always insists we follow the CIP to the letter. As I told you: in this case the letter of the law states: no unnecessary interworldline contact, each wordline to his own. So we do."

"If you say so. So we leave this worldline in the hands of Leonard Yomin junior?"

"The regulations leave us no other choice."

Epilogue: the Light in the Doorway, the Leap of Faith

In the thronged streets of Cádiz, famed city of two cultures, a solitary figure merges seamlessly with the bustling mass. A pair of very sharp eyes might see a vague resemblance to Ibn al'Arabi's last apprentice. One might even imagine an indistinct likeliness to Ferdinand's mysterious advisor, the one that disappeared without a trace.

Not that anybody notices, though. Too busy. Busy bartering in the trade center between two worlds. Engaged discussing merits of both Qur'an and Bible in the spiritual haven between two religions. Manically merging artistic expressions in an ongoing attempt to improve the balance between the two traditions. Excitedly exchanging knowledge: prying Latin alchemists trying to pick up on the Arabic science of pharmacopoeia, a nascent venture in medicine. Too busy building bridges. So a single man is not singled out and future atrocities might be furtively avoided.

Lost in the crowd, he's also lost in thoughts. "Well, old Leonard thought it inevitable to let them catch him. To remove all interference before the next stage of our grand scheme. Leonard three should be arriving soon, using the new TTT Leonard one made before disintegrating the original.

"Aah, Watt and Krikksen. Nice guys, for detectives. Bickering and sly like old wives. But will they really believe that we would wreak havoc on so many stock markets only for this? Then they underestimate the scope of our scheme, the depth of our goal. What was the name of that old song?

"How Far Jerusalem."

Good to the Last Drop

All right, Sparky, here's your grub. Try not to wolf it all down too fast, that's not healthy, and you don't want to end up like these guys do you? Did you get a load of my busboy? I told him his face would stay like that, but I didn't think it would be the cholesterol that would make it happen.

I know it's good. People don't exactly come in here for the atmosphere, you know. Except for you tourists. So what brought you down this way anyway? Looking for a story, a little dirty who did who for your paper? Or maybe just for your own edification?

You don't look like the seance type, and you sure as hell ain't no Orpheus. Well, whatever — you ain't been bad company, and you seemed to keep your nose out of other people's business. Hope it was worth the trip.

But you better eat slow, and don't make a habit of this kind of slop, or you might just become a regular.

In the bad way.

Gypsies Stole My Tequila

A story of music, aging, and assorted meat bi-products.

by Adrienne Jones

Joe took extra care in his grooming ritual that morning, lingering far too long in the shower, letting the scalding water torpedo his pasty skin until he was dotted like a smallpox victim. Before the mirror, smoothing his blood-red hair into eight perfectly pointed, five-inch spikes, deciding it wasn't quite right, then combing it out and rearranging it three more times. In the bedroom, he obsessed over which animal print spandex trousers went with which army shirt; the desert or the jungle. Then there was the jacket to consider. Should it be the sleeveless denim wrought with rusted safety pins, or the multicolored vinyl? Boots. Always good for an extra ten minutes of pondering, for he owned dozens of pairs; leather, snakeskin, spiked, chained, combats, fluorescent...

None of this nonsense really mattered to Joe Blood. Not as much as one might assume in watching the meticulous primping. Joe was stalling, as he'd done every morning for the past two months. For a horrible beast now lurked beyond his bedroom, down the hall in the study, where it made its lair. And the beast would not be ignored, forcing Joe to pay it homage each morning before he could exit the apartment.

Unable to prolong his readying any longer, Joe breathed deeply, feigned a cocky sneer, and left his bedroom. He slowed his swagger in the hallway, letting his eyes examine the framed prints. He smiled at the images of himself on stage, guitar in hand, blazing lights making a halo of his former hot pink Mohican hairstyle. His eyes drifted to his old band-mates, flanking him on either side of the stage, faces pinched in anarchistic apathy. He wondered how the boys would look now, so many years later. His body tensed at the thought. Time passage was a sharp reminder of the beast. He turned his head and peered down the shadowy hallway, to where his foe waited. Stiffening his chin, he puffed out his bony, sunken chest and strutted into the study.

"Morning," Joe said with false cheeriness as he passed the beast on his way to the kitchen. The beast said nothing. It hung in its place on the wall, silent while Joe poured himself a cup of coffee and snatched his keys off the windowsill. Joe whistled a tune as he stirred his coffee, unwilling to let the beast sense his fear.

Rounding the corner with his cup, he looked up at the beast. It remained silent, pretending for the moment that it was merely a wall calendar. The month read May. Joe sourly examined the previous day's blocks, slashed in red pen. Emboldened by the calendar's silence, Joe reached out and grabbed the page, lifting it to peer at the next month, JUNE. His lip quivered. His hand trembled as he read the scribbled words on the June 19th block. *Joe's birthday*, the day proclaimed in bright green marker. Then just beneath that, *Joe dies*.

His entire gangly body shaking now, Joe let the calendar page slip from his fingers. May flopped back into place, hiding the dreaded June from his eyes. He backed away slowly, a strangled whimper starting in his throat. Tiptoeing, he set the coffee cup on his desktop, then turned and crept toward the door.

AREN'T YOU FORGETTING SOMETHING? The calendar beast called out.

Joe froze, then swiveled his body to face the beast. "Please," he said. "Not today. Can't I just skip it today? I'm feeling...a bit dodgy."

TIME WAITS FOR NO MAN!

Joe's wiry form stumbled back, hands pressing the sides of his skull in a futile attempt to block out the bellowing voice. His eyes lifted as May laughed at him, the boxy days of the month becoming teeth. The laughter angered him, but not enough to fully abate his fear. Hesitantly, he moved toward the beast, his jaw clenched. "I hate you!" he hissed as he picked up the red marking pen. "I hate you!"

May laughed. Joe dug into the day's date with the marker, stabbing it. Ink bled a spot as he dragged the pen across the day, eliminating it forever from the time he had left.

FIVE WEEKS TO GO, the deep, searing voice announced.

"Yes, thank you! I know how to fucking count!" Joe screamed at the wall calendar.

AND YOU ALSO KNOW WHAT YOU HAVE TO DO TODAY. YOU NEED TO FIND THEM. YOU'RE RUNNING OUT OF TIME.

The week of the 16th chomped at the week below as it spoke. Joe swallowed hard. "What if they've forgotten?" he asked the calendar. The days of the month smoothed out. The voice of the beast fell silent.

"Hey!" Joe shouted. "Answer me! What if they've forgotten?" The beast did not respond. "Hey!" Joe yelled again. "Answer me, you bloody—"

"Joe?"

Joe spun about at the sound of his neighbor's voice. Verne Hall was a middle-aged attorney, the kind of man who once drove expensive cars and looked down on people like Joe. But two divorces and a hearty side-helping of child support payments later, Verne had devolved to a level of loser equality. When poverty forced Verne to move into Joe's less than savory apartment complex, the single mothers had all brought cookies and casseroles to his door. Joe had brought him a tall bottle of Scotch, with a note that read, 'Hell tastes better on ice'. They'd been fast friends ever since.

"Verne. Don't you knock?"

Verne leaned into the apartment, one arm hugging the doorway. "I've been knocking. You didn't answer. Were you just yelling at your calendar?"

Joe glanced up at the silent beast, then back at Verne. He wrinkled his nose and blew out a puff of air. "No!"

"Yes you were. I saw you."

"What the hell do you want, Verne?"

"Oh, right. Your scooter. There are some kids skulking around it down on the street. They look kind of suspicious. One of them was trying to get the kickstand up."

All thoughts of the beast melted away as Joe's eyes widened in alarm. He ran for the door. "Road Bastard!"

Joe trampled down the stairs with Verne trailing behind. They looked an odd pair as they stepped onto the sidewalk, Joe in his tight, pink and black leopard trousers, camouflage tee shirt, and fluorescent orange boots; Verne in his gray business suit, burgundy tie, and black, Clark Kent eyeglasses. Joe stormed round the porch and saw three pre-teen boys in the driveway. One of them was sitting on Joe's motor-scooter, pretending to rev the gas, bouncing on the seat. Another was crouched alongside the rear tire, his dirt-stained hand reaching into the saddlebag. A third kicked the front tire.

"Hey!" Joe shouted. "I warned you little gypsies to stay away." He yanked the kid off the scooter and leaned over him. "If I catch you here again it's gonna be a sad day for your momma!"

The dirt-stained child grinned up at him defiantly. "There ain't no gypsies in America, freak. Go back to England!" The other boys laughed raucously.

"Gypsies, thieves, hooligans, missed-abortions, I catch you near Road Bastard again, I'm gonna show you a world of pain. Now piss off!"

"Who would want your stupid moped anyway!" one of the boys called out as they scampered off. "I wouldn't be seen on that pile of junk! Loser!"

Verne straightened his tie as Joe checked the condition of his scooter, brushing the seat off, examining the tires. "You off to work now, Joe?"

"Not until later," Joe said, climbing on Road Bastard and starting the engine. The motor sputtered and backfired as he revved it. "I'm off to look up some old friends. Remind 'em of a promise they made a long while back."

"Oh, that sounds nice," Verne said, stepping out of the way of the scooter. "What did they promise?"

Joe gave the scooter another blast of gas, adjusting the side mirror. He glanced up at Verne. "They promised to die with me. Have a nice day,

Verne."

Joe rode his scooter down the middle-class suburban street, checking the numbers on the identical ranch houses. Guitar sounds thrashed a chaotic beat from his stereo speakers, which had cost him more than the scooter itself. The music moved him. Normally he did not listen to Blood Blister, for dual reasons. One was that blasting his own album in public made him seem an egotistical twat. The other reason had to do with pain. Listening to Blood Blister filled him with emotions difficult to endure, reminders of good times gone, of what he was, and of how much he'd lost. But today he embraced the razor-sharp feelings the songs evoked. Today was a day of facing the past.

He sneered at the cookie-cutter homes with their neatly groomed lawns, unable to imagine Deke living in such a place. The quaint American neighborhood was distanced surprisingly close to his shoddy apartment in town, and he wondered at how it could have been so long since he'd seen Deke or Vincent. But avoidance could be an art form if executed with purpose. And three men who'd once spent every waking moment together, could easily live within a twenty-mile radius of each other and never cross paths, if that was their firm desire.

Speeding past house number fifty-seven, he was forced to circle back, then glided up the narrow driveway of the ranch. Road Bastard let out a fart as it idled near the garage, then he killed the engine. Birds chirped, filling the silence as the music ceased.

Climbing off the scooter, Joe examined the lawn, with its flagstone walk and plastic sunflowers that twirled frantically in the soft spring breeze. "This can't be the place," he muttered as he strode up the walk to the front door.

A dog barked inside the house when he rang the bell, then the sound of approaching footsteps. An attractive woman in a shimmering jogging suit pulled open the inside door, peering at him through the screen. Her dark eyes narrowed to a frown as they scanned Joe, starting at his red-spiked hair and ending at his bright orange boots.

"Ello. Deke here, then?" he asked.

The woman met his eyes through the screen. "Who? I'm sorry, who are you looking for?"

"Deke Martin. He lives here, right?"

The woman opened the screen door a wedge. "Do you mean Derek, my husband?"

Joe shrugged. "If Derek your husband is Deke the Freak Martin, then yeah. That's who I mean."

The woman frowned. "And you are?"

"Joe Blood."

Her brow smoothed and her jaw dropped. She blew a puff of air. "Joe Blood? Joe Blood from Blood Blister?"

Joe grinned and cocked his head. "Ya recognize me, then?"

"Well of course I recognize you. You look *exactly* the same." She scanned his body, her expression sour. "Why are you dressed like that?"

Joe frowned. "What ya mean?"

She stared at him for several seconds, then shook her head. "Okay. Come on in. Derek is out back."

He followed her through the house, a carpeted, floral-scented expanse of rooms, filled with gleaming wood furniture and tacky decorations. Pictures of toothy children, a girl and a boy, hung along the walls. The boy looked similar to Deke as Joe remembered him, thin-framed, flattened yellow hair, pug nose, and mischievous brown eyes. The girl looked like the mother, dark-haired and olive-skinned.

Deke's wife pulled open a sliding door and led him onto a wooden deck, which jutted onto the back lawn. An above-ground pool stood at the rear corner of the yard, and next to that, a volleyball net. To the left of the deck, a fat man lay sprawled out on a lawn chair, a beer resting on his rounded, shirtless belly. To his right was a child's wading pool, filled with ice and cans of beer. A small television sat atop a stool positioned in front of the fat man's chair, the miniature screen flashing images of uniformed football players racing down a green field.

"Derek? Someone's here to see you."

"Who the fuck is it?" the fat man snarled, his eyes glued to the set.

"It's Joe Blood," the woman said warily.

He laughed. "Yeah. Good one, Lacey. Can you bring me some chips? I'm starving."

Joe stepped around the woman and gazed at the bloated sloth in the lawn chair. His yellow hair was matted and wiry, baldness climbing the front quarters of his scalp. The man turned his head and Joe recognized Deke's brown eyes buried in the bulbous chub of his face. "Holy *Christ*, are you fat!" Joe said.

Deke's eyes widened in astonishment as he sat up, the beer can dropping onto the patio and spilling. The chair tipped and he had to grasp the sides to keep from falling over. Once he'd steadied himself, he looked up. "Joe?"

Joe walked over and grabbed a beer from the wading pool, cracking it and taking a long slug. He wiped his chin and smiled. "Hey Deke. What do ya know?"

Deke lifted himself off the chair and stepped toward Joe, his eyes registering disbelief. "Joe Blood? Is it really you?"

"I told you," the wife said, then turned and went back inside the house.

"Course it's me. Now listen, we've got to talk. It's about—"

"Whoa, whoa wait a minute!" Deke said, waving his arms in front of him. He peered into Joe's face and grinned. "I mean, holy shit, Joe. Look at you!"

"Yeah, I look great, I know. Can we talk here or should we go for a walk?"

Deke shook his head. "What are you doing here, man? I mean, I'm glad to see you but...I mean this is great, the outfit, the hair. Dude, if you're trying to mess with my head, it's working. I nearly swallowed my tongue when I saw you!"

Deke grabbed a beer from the wading pool, laughing. "Unbelievable," he said as he sat his bulky form back down in the chair. "How long has it been?"

"Since I last saw you? Seventeen years, four months and twenty-three days," Joe said. "How have you been, Deke?"

Deke took a swallow of his beer, then threw his head back and laughed. "How have I been? Where do I start? Seriously, Joe. What is this? What's going on? You doing a tribute gig or something?"

Joe sat down on the ground, resting his arms on his knees. "No gig. I just came to talk. I'm sorry to barge in unannounced, but as I said, it's important."

Deke brought the beer to his face, then lowered it again, a confused grin curving his chubby cheeks. "Come on. I mean, really. You don't seriously still dress like that."

Joe stared blankly back at him. Deke's grin dropped to a frown. "I mean, you're just messing with me, right?"

Joe reached into his trousers and pulled an envelope out, handing it to Deke. "Remember this?"

Deke looked suspiciously at the envelope, then set his beer down and took it. Reaching inside, he pulled out the stiff, tattered sheet of paper. He took in a long breath as he unfolded it. "Christ on a crutch. I remember this! We did this that night out at Anchorage Point, in the graveyard by the cliff. I can't believe you saved this!"

"You recognize your signature there?"

Deke laughed, his eyes scanning the contract. "Signed in blood. Man, this is almost creepy. I was so blasted that night!" He lowered the paper and gazed off for a moment, then looked at Joe. "Remember that thing? That shadow we thought we saw?"

"I remember," Joe said. "Right after we made the pact. We used your nail clipper to nick our fingers, then we all signed. There was a storm coming in over the cliff. Remember the lightening hitting the bluffs?"

Deke leaned back in the chair and took a swill of beer, his eyes distant. "Yeah. I also remember being jacked up on mescaline so bad that I thought my skin had turned blue."

Joe laughed, remembering Deke's insistence that he had transformed into 'Drummer Smurf'. Then his smile dropped, his gaunt face becoming somber. "The shadow moved past the tomb we were sitting on. We all saw it. Vincent dropped the contract when he ran off with you, the both of you screaming like women and giggling. I picked it up and stuffed it in my coat before the rain started. I've had it ever since."

Deke shook his head, then shrugged, handing the paper back to Joe. "Good times. We're lucky we didn't burn our brains to a crisp with all those drugs we did." He frowned at Joe. "What about you? How are you doing?"

Joe glanced at the paper in his hands, then lifted his eyes. "Not so good, Deke. Not so good. That's what I came to talk to you about."

Deke looked uneasy. "Well, if it's money you need, I can't really help you. I've got two kids and a mortgage. I'd love to, buddy, but I'm strapped. Go see Vincent. He's loaded now, did you hear?"

"I don't want money. It's about the contract here. Do you remember what it says?" Joe tried handing the paper back to Deke, who didn't take it.

"I thought I was turning into a Smurf that night. I was drinking Jack Daniels on top of a mescaline buzz. My Blood Blister years are a blur of nightclubs, titties and acid."

"But you remember what we wrote here."

"No, I don't," he said, turning away and swatting at a bee.

"Read it," Joe said, shoving the paper at him.

Deke's face darkened. "I don't want to read it. I don't care what it says. That was almost twenty years ago. Now it's been great seeing you, but frankly you're starting to freak me out."

"Vincent turned forty last month," Joe said.

Deke finished his beer and let out a sigh as he crushed the can. "Woopty-freekin-do."

"You turned forty last week."

"Yeah, so I did. My wife threw me a surprise party. What's your point?"

"We made a promise to each other that night. A stupid promise. We said we'd never change. We said we'd always play music, we'd never be...well, like this," he said, gesturing to Deke in the lawn chair.

Deke chortled. "So does every nineteen-year old punk. Life is sweet before reality sets in."

"We swore that if by this age, we'd become everything we despised, we'd do something about it."

Deke eyed him warily. "Yeah, we said we'd throw ourselves off the Anchorage Cliff on your birthday. It was juvenile, drug-trip punk talk. So what?"

Joe folded the contract, placed it back in the envelope and stuffed it in his trousers. He stood, looking down at Deke. "Something heard us that night."

Deke laughed, making a face. "What?"

"We raised a demon, Deke."

Deke stood, tipping his chair over. He pointed at Joe. "You're off your tree!"

"I turn forty in five weeks, and if we don't jump off that cliff, it's going to come for us."

Deke raised his eyebrows in mock concern. "I see. A demon is coming for us, is it?"

Joe nodded. "That's right. It's a Time Demon. It lives in my calendar at the moment."

"Get some help, Joe. Get some serious fucking help."

Joe clenched his teeth. "You'd better listen to me! You're in this as much as I am!"

"Get off my property, Joe."

"You signed in blood! This is your fault too! Fat arrogant bastard! I'm warning you, you'd better honor this contract!"

"Lacey!" he called out. The dark-haired woman came to the deck door. "Call the police."

"You were supposed to stay out of trouble, Joe. That was the deal we made. I can't keep bailing you out like this. You're going to end up back in rehab. Or worse."

"The deal we made was that I don't do drugs and exhibit disorderly conduct. I didn't do drugs, and I didn't hit anybody. He hit me," Joe said, patting his swelling eye with an ice pack.

Eunice had been Joe's social worker for months, an unwanted addition to his life. He'd acquired her as part of a bargain made in court after he popped too many mushrooms one afternoon and attacked a clerk in a local music shop. The mangy little weasel had asked for it, calling Joe a has-been and laughing at him.

"I'm concerned, Joe. Your behavior is self-destructive. I fear that you want to harm yourself, and this is why you provoke others."

"I don't want to harm myself! Can I go now?"

"How's your job going?" she asked, insisting on prolonging his agony. As if it wasn't bad enough that he detested his life, he had to sit and dissect it with this woman every other week, have it shoved in his face like a wicked mirror that showed all of his flaws, inside and out.

"My job sucks. But I go there and eat shit every day, just like I said I would. Can I go now?"

"I must advise you against paying a visit to Vincent Rizzo. That would be a very bad idea."

Joe sneered. "Who?"

Eunice pursed her painted lips. "Vincent Rizzo. Your former bass player. After what happened today with Mr. Martin, I fear you might attempt to contact Vincent as well."

"You fear a lot, Eunice. You ought to see someone about that."

Her eyes narrowed as she struggled to maintain her docile, social worker face. He smiled at her. "May I go now, Eunice?"

Finally she stood and walked him to the door. "I'll see you in two weeks. And I pray that fate does not bring us together before then."

"That makes two of us."

The afternoon sun assaulted his fair skin as Joe strode down the city sidewalk toward the towing garage where they were keeping Road Bastard. The demon was everywhere, taunting him. It was in the shop window signs that read 'FORTY percent off sale!' Then it was in an old woman chatting with a friend at the bus stop. "You'll have to come over FOR TEA soon!" A street vagrant ranted about God and floods and rain for FORTY days and FORTY nights.

Joe was sweating when he handed the garage worker his cash, and received four dollars and forty cents back in change. He climbed onto Road Bastard and headed out of the neighborhood, toward Westford, the posh section of town where Vincent Rizzo lived.

Joe stood blinking before the enormous fountain in the center of the elegantly landscaped lawn. His head swiveled toward the house, which was more like a mansion, then he looked back at the fountain. Sculptures and lush shrubberies dotted the edge of the lawn where a stone wall made a boundary. He couldn't seem to move his feet. He checked the address on the scribbled post-it again, then looked back up at the house.

"This can't be the place," he muttered, then made his way toward the porch.

The front door opened as he climbed the steps, and a tanned, handsome man appeared on the stoop. His black hair was tied back into a ponytail that ended at his mid-back. He wore faded blue jeans, cowboy boots, with a peach silk button-down shirt that accentuated his healthy olive skin and blue eyes, a thick gold chain visible at the open collar. He was older, and the bones in his face were thicker, but it was Vincent.

Joe and Vincent faced each other for a long moment, saying nothing, each taking in the other's appearance. Finally, Joe broke the silence. "Well. At least you're not fat."

Vincent grinned, a line of perfect white teeth. "Joe. Why don't you come inside?"

Joe cocked an eyebrow. "You been expecting me?"

Vincent sighed, then tightened his lips. He nodded. "Deke called."

Joe looked down. "Right. Of course he did." He looked at Vincent. "And you're still inviting me in, then?"

Vincent smiled. "Yeah, Joe. I'm still inviting you in. Come on."

Even after seeing the impressive exterior, Joe was flabbergasted as he followed Vincent through the rooms of his palatial home, tastefully decorated, with high ceilings, gleaming wood floors and thick oriental rugs. The furniture was modern, earth tones, the walls stark white with abstract paintings the size of small cars. Joe was pleased to see a string of polished bass guitars lined up in the vast study Vincent led him into, though they looked to be more decorative than functional, not a fingerprint or a spec of dust on any.

Joe attempted a cocky sneer when Vincent gestured him toward a soft, leather chair by the fireplace, but he was having trouble disguising his awe.

"What are you drinking these days?" Vincent asked, moving to a liquor hutch in the corner and grabbing two glasses from the display.

"These days I'm not drinking," Joe said. "But I'll have tequila if you've got it."

Vincent poured Joe a short glass of tequila along with one for himself, then crossed the room and handed Joe the drink, seating himself in an adjoining chair. "To Blood Blister," he said, raising his glass.

Joe raised his glass uneasily. "Right," he said, then took a long swallow of the burning liquid.

"So," Vincent said after a sip of his drink. "Tell me about this demon in your calendar."

Joe scowled. "You think I'm a bloody lunatic."

Vincent raised his hand as if to ward off Joe's toxic sneer. "Now hang on, Joe. I'm not your enemy."

Joe shrugged and took another swig of tequila, draining the glass. Vincent sighed, resting his elbows on his knees. "What's going on with you? Talk to me. Deke said some strange shit on the phone today. He said you were on about suicide and deals with the devil."

Joe's eyes drifted around the fancy room. "If anyone here made a deal with the devil, it's you. How did you get all of this, Vin?"

"Well," Vincent said, grabbing Joe's glass and moving to the hutch to refill it, "I was one of the lucky ones. Software stock, back at the start of the technology boom. I got in tight with a financial guru called Stan Badley." He returned with Joe's drink and sat back down. "Old Stan Badley ended up being Stan Goodly, for me. He pointed me in the right direction. Took what little money I'd saved from Blood Blister's sales, and made me rich."

"Imagine that. Never would have seen that coming with you. Money used to slip through your fingers like water."

Vincent laughed. "No kidding. That's why I put it in someone else's hands. What about you? What are you doing with your life?"

Joe looked at the floor, swirling his drink. "Well I'm not living in a mansion, I can tell you that. I've had some bad luck, Vin. Life's been a pile of shit, if you want the truth."

Vincent stared at him hard, his expression pained. "I love you, Joe. You know that, right? Time hasn't changed that."

Joe smiled. "But?"

He sighed, leaning back in his chair. "I'm not jumping off a cliff with you, Joe. I haven't got enough anarchy left in me to run a stop sign."

Joe eyed him, his face tightening. "Then I guess I'll be dying alone."

"Oh come on!" Vincent said, standing. He circled the room, running a hand across his forehead. "What the hell are you doing?"

"There's a Time Demon, and it wants payment from us. The contract we made—"

"Oh shut up, Joe!" he said, stopping before the chair and looking down at him. "I don't want to hear about your God damned demon. Your life! What are you doing with your life? Do you think I haven't kept tabs on you? You think I forgot all about you and never checked around to see how you were doing?"

"Well I know you never threw any cash my way," Joe said, trying to lighten things up. Vincent stood over him, angry and emotional. He abruptly turned away and began pacing the floor again.

"Do you see those bass guitars over there? I never touch them. At least not often. I like having them. I like looking at them. But I never play anymore."

"So you've got enough cash to buy worthless toys. What's your point?"

"My point is that I can live without music. There was a time when we were young that I never thought I'd say those words, but it's happened. I don't care anymore."

"You were, good, Vincent. You were really good."

"But you were great. This is what I'm trying to tell you. I can live without creating, Joe. But you can't."

"Huh," Joe said, crossing his arms. "That's funny. I seem to have been doing just that for nearly twenty years."

"Oh really? You call what you're doing living? I know you work at that butcher shop. I know where you live. I know you've been in and out of rehab, in trouble with the law. And I don't know for sure, but I suspect you haven't picked up a fucking guitar, or written a single note or lyric since you can't remember!"

Joe bounded out of his chair. "You're one to talk! Look at you! With your fountains and your gold chain and your...whatever that thing is over there," Joe said, pointing to an odd ceramic statue of two horned women making love. "You've got five top-of-the-line basses sitting against a wall, not gathering dust because your fucking maid dusts them ten times a day!"

Vincent leaned into him. "I don't need it, Joe. I loved composing with you, I loved playing, but it's not who I am. It's not part of my make-up. You? You're a genius. Every cell of your body screams for it. I remember how you were, I watched you for years. None of us were worth a shit without you." He turned away, retrieving his drink from the end table. "It's in your fucking DNA."

Joe turned away, running his fingers through his red spiked hair. "Maybe you're right," he muttered. "Maybe you're right." He turned about. "And then I'm dead already."

Vincent spread his arms. "Why? You can still create. You're still young. You're only forty, for Christ sakes. Some guys out there are–"

"Thirty-nine!" Joe said, pointing. "I'm thirty-nine, Vincent."

Vincent scowled. "Okay, thirty-nine. Whatever. You're miserable. So miserable that you're inventing demons, making yourself insane so you've got a reason to quit life. And all because you're denying who you are."

Joe put his hands on his hips and swaggered toward Vincent. "The demon is real. And I know who I am. I'm Joe Blood. I'm a punk. I'm not denying that. But guess what? Punk is dead. And any form of music that was a close facsimile of punk is dead. You tell me to make music? For who? For what?"

Joe's voice elevated, echoing off the cathedral ceiling. "I hate today's music. Electronic beat samples, twiddly-diddly guitar solos, whining, crying, marble-mouthed vocals? You tell me, Vincent. Where does Joe Blood fit into that?"

Vincent frowned, opened his mouth, then closed it again. He sighed and turned away. Joe nodded. "Uh-huh. I see. You got nothing to say. Because you know I'm right."

"You're a genius, Joe," Vincent said, turning to face him. "You created something unique once. You can do it again."

Joe checked the clock on the wall, then met Vincent's eyes. "Dead men don't play guitars. It's been nice seeing you, but I've got to go to work."

Joe left the room and Vincent followed him out, calling after. "Okay, stay in denial. Go cut meat. Talk to demons."

Joe turned back once as he pulled open the door. "The demon is real, Vincent."

Vincent flinched as the door slammed. He turned away, rubbing the bridge of his nose. "Shit," he said. He looked up the sound of the refrigerator door opening, and saw his son digging for food. At eighteen, Max was the image of his father at that age, despite the brown eyes he'd inherited from his mother. Maxine had died ten years before, and Vincent had been struggling to raise the boy in a fashion he thought would have pleased her. Though he doubted she'd be pleased with the outcome. Despite his attempts to guide Max toward college, his son had chosen the one road his mother would have disapproved of. Max wanted to make music. As much as Vincent tried to show his support, he saw the inevitable unfolding. His spoiled, lazy Max did not have what it took, beyond taking great care in adjusting his appearance to look the part.

"Getting any work done down there?" Vincent asked, moving into the kitchen. Max looked up at his father as he closed the fridge, an armful of sandwich supplies in his grasp. He swung his long dark hair behind his shoulders with a careful jerk of his head, a practiced habit.

"Some. I gotta get back down. The guys are hungry."

Max made out of the room with Vincent following. He glanced back over his shoulder. "You want something, Dad?"

"Well that's an interesting question, Max," Vincent said, trailing his son down the stairs that led to the in-house studio. "There are a lot of things I want. I want world peace. I want the Red Sox to win the World Series. And after a year of watching you screw off with your half-baked buddies in the rehearsal studio I so graciously funded for you, I want to see some results. So if you'd be so obliged, I'd like to accompany you to your lair, and check on your progress."

Max stopped before the studio door and sneered over his shoulder at Vincent. "You want to come inside?"

Vincent feigned a cordial bow. "If that's okay with you of course, Your Highness."

A quick look of alarm passed over Max's face, then the jaded scoff returned. "Whatever."

Vincent stepped into the studio behind Max, where a cloud of marijuana smoke hung like ghostly snakes in the air. His boot crunched something, and he looked down to see a trail of potato chips scattered across the floor. He lifted his eyes and looked to the left, where empty beer bottles lined the top of the high-priced mixing board. Max's bass player Peter, or 'Pez' as he'd chosen as his music persona, lay on the floor in front of the drum-kit, gnawing on a Snickers bar, his feet up on a speaker amp. His long orange hair spread out on the floor like ginger fire.

Shane the drummer, a quiet little waif with chin-length dark blond wisps and wide gray eyes that always looked spooked, stepped out from behind a curtain with a joint in his hand, which he dropped when he saw Vincent. Max threw the sandwiches on the floor in front of Pez, then went and picked up his guitar, as if Vincent would believe at this point that they'd been actually practicing.

"Good afternoon, boys," Vincent announced. Pez sat up in a flash, choking on the glob of Snickers in his mouth, his fire-red hair a disheveled curtain in front of his eyes.

"I see you've been quite productive today. Perhaps I could hear a sample of one of your songs."

Shane stomped out the joint, then looked to Max. Pez swiped the hair off his freckled face and jumped to his feet. "Mr. Rizzo. How's it going? Good of you to come down here. We can always use your advice."

Vincent stepped further into the room, chips crunching under his feet. "I've had my ass kissed enough for one lifetime, thank you anyway, Pez." He turned to his son, who pretended to be deeply enthralled in the tuning of his guitar. "Just tell me this, Max. Have you got anything? One song? A part of a song?"

Max looked at him and shrugged. "We've got some stuff in the works. Relax, Dad."

"I'd like to hear it."

Max looked to Shane, who appeared about to wet his pants. Shane pointed to Pez. "Pez has some lyrics written. Don't you, Pez?"

Pez swung his orange hair over his shoulders and assumed a cocky pose. "Yeah, I've got lots of lyrics."

"No you don't," Max said.

"I do!" he said. "You've seen them, Max!"

"It's crap poetry, Pez, the kind of stuff I wrote in grade school. We're not using it."

Vincent made a steeple of his fingers and rested his chin on it, circling the room. "Let's just cut the bullshit, boys, and get this over with. You've got nothing. You've been down here for a year, and you've got nothing. Just say it. Look at me," he said, stopping to peer down at the timid Shane, "and tell me you've got nothing."

Shane's lip quivered as he looked up. "We've got...almost nothing," he said. "But we do jam, and that could lead to something."

Vincent stared the boy down for a moment, then turned to his son. "I'm pulling the plug, Max. Go to college, get a job, do whatever you'd like. But I'm not funding this free-for-all anymore."

Finally showing emotion, Max slung his guitar off and stormed at his father. "That's not fair! These things take time!"

"You've had plenty of time!"

"I've been practicing my riffs! I'll get around to writing music when I feel confident in my sound!"

"Mr. Rizzo," Pez piped up, still gnawing his snickers bar. "Max is an awesome guitarist. No shit."

"It takes more than talent to make music!" Vincent said. "It takes drive, and discipline and desire! You've got to want it! You've got to dig your teeth in, and–"

"Oh, here we go," Max said, rolling his eyes.

Vincent moved toward him, backing him into the wall. "Here we go? Do I bore you, Max?"

"Not everyone can do what Blood Blister did!" Max yelled. "For some people it takes time! You expect me to bang out ten songs overnight, and I just don't work that way!"

Vincent turned to leave the studio, then paused in the doorway. He remained there for a moment as the thought puzzled its way into his brain. Slowly, he turned and stepped back into the room. "Maybe you need help," he said.

Pez shook his head. "Nah, we auditioned three singers. They were stupider than us. I mean..."

"Come upstairs, all of you."

They eyed him curiously, but didn't move. Vincent raised his eyebrows. "Do you want a second chance?"

Shane and Pez nodded. Max shrugged.

"Then come," Vincent said.

Vincent finished talking, and the three eighteen-year olds stared up at him from the leather couch, matching expressions of unease pinching their faces.

"Joe Blood?" Max said. "Your old band-mate? The one that works down at the butcher shop in a fucking cow suit?"

"He's got exactly what you need," Vincent said. "Drive."

Max laughed. "Well dad, I'm sure he *used* to have drive in the Blood Blister days. But have you seen him lately?"

"I heard he's a mental patient or something," Shane said.

Vincent scowled at him. "He's not a mental patient." He paused. "Not yet, anyway."

"I heard he once ate a baby onstage," Pez said.

Vincent grimaced. "Oh for the love of God, Pez."

Max shook his head. "Dad, come on. The guy's a crackpot. What does he know about our music?"

"Your music? Last I checked, you didn't have any music. Do you know anything about Joe Blood?"

"Just that he ate a baby," Pez said.

"He did not eat a baby!" Vincent yelled. He caught himself, took a deep breath, and raised his hands. "Look. I'll admit to you, Joe is a bit off center. Manic, to say the least. But whatever backwards, chaotic mix he's got flowing through his brain fluid, when it comes to music, it's the right mix. Put him out in society, and he's a lost soldier on an enemy battlefield. Put him in a studio? He's a general. A drill sergeant. A master composer. The things he can accomplish...the things he drove us to accomplish! It's almost superhuman. You want to kiss that last breath of life into your dying dream, boys? I tell you with all honesty, Joe Blood is your best chance. And it's my only offer. Take it or leave it."

"Will he do it?" Shane asked. "I mean, will he agree to help us?"

Vincent shrugged. "I don't know." He turned to his son. "But it's worth asking. So what do you say, Max?"

Max was staring at the floor, silent. Finally he looked up. "Dad. The guy wears a cow suit to work."

Vincent frowned. "I know, son."

"Good afternoon. Cow can I help you?"

Joe stood behind the counter in his white and brown spotted bovine uniform, hooded ears and stubby horns shrouding his red spikes. The front door made its deep mooing sound every time a customer entered, and it was busy this evening, so the single cow mewl was escalated to a herd, one moo after the other. The crowded store made it even harder to deal with Irving, the new trainee that had made Joe's life even more of a hell than usual since his boss, David, had assigned Joe to mentor him.

Irving's uniform was a lamb. With his short, pudgy frame and captain-of-the-math-team glasses, Irving looked like an overgrown special needs child that had been given a part in a grade school play for sympathy reasons. But Irving was not shy, much to Joe's agony. Twenty years old, Irving sought a career in the butcher business, and took on his new job of scooping salmon loaf and weighing turkey slices with an unparalleled enthusiasm. His fuzzy, lamb form inadvertently bumped into Joe as he carried a perfectly wrapped package of roast beef to the cash register.

"Oh, sorry there, Joe! Guess I should have asked you to moooove over, huh? Get it? Moooove over!"

Joe curled his lip at Irving, then turned to the woman approaching the counter. "Good afternoon. Cow can I help you?"

"Um, is the Captain's cut Cod fresh today?" she asked, wrinkling her nose at the display of white fish.

"No, ma'am," Joe said. "I believe it's three weeks old and rotting with maggots."

She gasped, eyeing him with shock. "What did you say?"

"I said of course it's fresh, ma'am. Our fish comes in fresh every day. Just like the sign says. There are more fish choices in the next room."

She stared at the fish display, her brow furrowing. "Oh. I think I'll have the smoked ham."

The evening rush finally cleared out and Joe was content with slicing logs of meat and avoiding Irving, who was like a drug-trip nightmare in his fleecy woolen costume, like some perverse erotic fantasy for hardcore computer geeks that lived in their parent's basement and had three cats named Kirk, Spock and Bones. As Joe mindlessly carved the meat, Irving approached, compelled to make irrelevant banter for the simple reason that he could not shut his peach-fuzzed, adolescent-looking mouth for more than five minutes or his sheepy form would explode; sis, boom, baaa.

"Hey, Joe! Good thing that crowd cleared out huh? I mean, that was chaos!"

Joe ignored him, robotically slicing the turkey loaf.

"I have to say, I love it when it gets like that. I mean, it's such a rush, you know? People shouting orders at you. Tickets flying. You're trying to remember everyone's order and you're moving, moving, moving, you know? It's like...wow!"

Irving replenished the displays. Joe sliced.

"This place is great, I have to say. I worked at Pig Bellies, and between you and me, Joe? This place blows it away. I mean, I've made tuna salad before, but," he shook his head. "Never anything like this."

Joe sliced.

"Hey, Joe. I'm sure you heard that assistant manager's job is opening up, right?"

Joe sliced the turkey loaf, bowing his cow head as Irving tried to meet his eyes.

"I just thought I'd tell you, I plan on applying for it. I mean, I can tell you that, with us being buddies and all. I want to be straight on. Honest. I just want to make sure I'm not stepping on your toes here. Or your hooves, as the case may be!" He let out a high-pitched giggle, slapping his fleecy thigh. Joe sliced.

"I wanted to tell you I was going for it, you know. In case you wanted it instead. Because if you're going to apply, I'll withdraw my application. I mean, you deserve it. You've been here longer than I have. Besides, you must be thinking of advancing your career. What are you, like forty?"

Joe stopped slicing. His eyes widened, and he turned his bovine head. Irving's fuzzy lips puckered as Joe grabbed his fleece and slammed him up onto the wall.

"I'm THIRTY-NINE!" He slammed him again. "Do you hear me, you fucking meat puppet? THIRTY..." *slam* "FUCKING..." *slam* "NINE!"

The door went moo. Joe let go of Irving and he dropped to the floor.

"Cow can I help you?" Joe said, turning toward the customers.

"Joe?"

Vincent stood at the counter with a teenaged boy. The boy had long dark hair and wore jeans and a concert tee shirt. Joe's jaw fell as he gazed at the boy, who looked nearly identical to Vincent when Joe had first met him. Finally tearing his eyes from the teen, he looked at Vincent. "Vin. What are you doing here?"

The teen sneered at Joe, then shook his head. "I'll wait in the car, Dad." The door mooed as he left the store.

Joe looked at Vincent. "Dad?"

"My son," he said. "Are you about done here? I want to talk about something."

Irving climbed up off the floor, gave Joe a fearful look, then ran into the back room. Joe glanced at the clock. "I've got to clean up and lock down."

"I'll wait for you outside," Vincent said. He turned to leave, then paused and looked back. "Nice outfit."

Joe gave him a snarl, its impact falling short in the cow uniform. "I'll be out in fifteen."

David, the shop owner stepped into the back room as Joe was pulling the horned hood off of his head, running his fingers through his blood-red hair. "Can I have a word, Joe?"

"You're the boss," he said, unzipping the front of the costume. He struggled with it, tugging the furry shoulders down.

"Joe, I've had a few complaints. It's not just Irving, though he's reasonably upset by your treatment of him. Some of the customers have expressed a lack of respect exhibited by you. You've got to temper your attitude, Joe."

"Respect?" Joe said, peeling the costume down his hips and stepping out. "You make us dress like this, and you talk to me about respect?" In his underpants, Joe pulled his pink and black leopard spandex out of his locker and stepped into them, pulling them up. "How can I have respect for the customers when I can't even respect myself?"

"Well..." David said, eyeing Joe's trousers.

"I have pride in my appearance, David," he said, pulling his tee shirt over his head, then covering it with the green neon vinyl jacket. "I care about the presentation I give to the world. You can't have me dress like a freak and expect me to be treated like a professional." He pulled on his fluorescent orange boots, then twisted his hair, refining the tall spikes. "You've got to get respect to give respect. And if you walk around dressed like a clown, nobody's going to take you seriously."

"I see," his boss said, raising his eyebrows at Joe's boots.

Joe completed his outfit by attaching a black, spiked dog collar around his neck. "I've got to run, I've got an appointment. But remember." Joe reached his hand inside his spandex trousers and adjusted his privates. Satisfied, he tucked in his tee shirt, wiped his nose with his wrist, and then patted his boss on the shoulder. "It's about dignity, David. Dignity. G'nite then."

Joe left the back room, leaving his boss to stare after him, brushing his shoulder with a handkerchief.

Joe approached Vincent, who leaned against a shiny silver sports car. He could see the teen sitting in the passenger seat inside. "So," he said. "That Maxine's kid?"

Vincent nodded. "We got married right after he was born. You know about..."

"I heard, yeah. I'm sorry, Vin."

"It's been ten years. I'm okay. But thanks, Joe. Go for a walk?"

They wandered across the shopping plaza lot and sat down on a sidewalk thirty feet from Vincent's car. Joe listened, expressionless, staring at the pavement as Vincent pitched his idea. When he'd finished, Joe remained placid.

"Joe? Say something."

Joe looked at him. "No."

"Just like that? Hear me out."

"I heard you out, and the answer is no. You're asking me to baby-sit your kid, Vin. I ain't no baby-sitter."

"I'm asking you to do what you do best. Take a group of raggedy, downtrodden musicians with moderate talent and mold them into something. It's what you love! Come on, Joe. This could be good for you."

Joe stood. "Good for me, huh? I haven't seen you in almost twenty God-damned years, and you're gonna tell me what's good for me?"

"Okay, then, do it as a favor. Do it as charity, I don't care! I've got money. You'll have the best instruments and equipment at your fingertips, and I've already told the boys that you have full reign. You'll be in charge."

Joe walked away from Vincent, heading back to the butcher shop where his scooter sat. Vincent followed him. "Christ, you're stubborn! Come on. Give me a break. Would it be so bad to create something again? Do it as a favor to me!"

Joe stopped and turned back. "Jump of Anchorage Cliff with me on my birthday."

Vincent stopped. "I have a kid, Joe."

Joe turned and kept walking, reaching his scooter and swiping the kickstand with his boot. "I gave you my answer, Vincent. I don't make music anymore. Now go on. Get in your fancy sports car and go back to your mansion. You've got basses to polish."

Max sat with arms crossed in the passenger seat, looking sullen and apathetic when Vincent got in and shut the door. "No go," he said.

Max turned to him, his face forgetting to sneer in his genuine surprise. He looked childlike in the shadowy lighting. "He said no?"

Vincent turned the keys in the ignition. "He said no."

"But why?" Max asked. "I mean, did he give you a reason?"

Vincent looked at his son. "I told you, Joe's unpredictable. He's got issues. You sound disappointed. I thought you didn't want him."

Max crossed his arms again and shrugged. "Well I don't, but...I mean...what the hell is his problem? It's not like he's got anything else going for him."

"Why don't you ask him?" Vincent said.

Max looked at him. "What? Me? Ask him?"

"He's getting on his scooter. You'd better hurry up."

Max looked out the window at Joe, swinging a leg over the seat of a shoddy-looking moped.

"Go on. See if you can catch him."

Max looked back and forth between his father and the window, his mouth agape. His brown eyes had the look of a cornered animal.

Vincent raised his eyebrows. "Your call, Max."

Max looked back at his father, his lips tightened. Then he grabbed the door handle and stepped out, slamming it behind him. Vincent watched him put on his cocky swagger as he made his way toward Joe. He chuckled. "Oh, this ought to be good."

Joe did a double take when he saw the kid walking toward him. He was about to start up Road Bastard, but he paused, scowling at the approaching teen, who looked eerily like an eighteen-year old Vincent in the dimly-lit night.

"Hey," the kid said, swinging his hair behind his shoulders. "You Joe Blood?"

Joe made a face at him. "Who wants to know?"

The kid froze, looking unsure of himself. Then he stepped forward, offering Joe his hand. "I'm Max Rizzo. Vincent's son."

Joe shook his hand, eyeing him suspiciously. "Good to meet ya. Now what ya want?"

"Why won't you play with us? Your ego too big?"

Joe was first stunned by the kid's brazen attitude. He took in the shifty swagger, the half-sneer, the arrogant tilt of the head, and he grinned. "Well. Ain't you a saucy little bugger? What sort of music you play?"

Max shrugged. "Alternative, mostly. Some death metal. Some cross-over stuff."

"Crap," Joe said under his breath as he adjusted the side mirror.

Max took a step toward him. "What did you say?"

Joe looked up and stuck his chin out. "I said, CRAP. That's what you play. C-R-A-P. And if you can't learn to write crap on your own, you got no business looking for help writing real music. Give it up, kid."

The kid's face scrunched in rage. Joe smiled sweetly at him. He was about to kick up Road Bastard again, when Max said, "Well you should know from crap. I've heard the Blood Blister albums."

Joe froze, his eyes lifting. "What did you say?"

Max stood defiantly, but said nothing. Joe dropped the kickstand, climbed off the scooter and walked toward him, his lanky arms curved at his sides, his sunken chest puffed out.

Max stood firm, puffing out his own chest. "I said I've heard your music. It was nothing but fucking noise!"

"Which album?" Joe asked.

"Gluttonous Starvation."

"Really," Joe said. "I'll have you know, that fucking noise took three months of day in, day out studio rehearsals to get so bad. We tried every possible combination of atonal, vile chord combinations in our repertoire. Would you disagree that the first song, *Arses*, was the ultimate puke to the ears? Nothing short of noise pollution perfection?"

Max shrugged. "Okay. So?"

"We wanted a sound that invoked disgust, and we achieved it. Bad is not to be confused with amateur."

"What's the difference? Sounds like you just threw it together regardless."

Joe moved closer, his face inches away from Max's. "Do you realize, YOUNG MAN, that there were twenty fucking million bands out there, trying to create an innovative sound? And do you further realize that there are eight notes in an octave, twelve with the sharps and flats, so the chances of writing an original riff and STILL maintaining the simplicity and aggression we so desired was virtually nil, and decreasing by the day?"

"But you did it," Max said.

"You're fucking-A right we did!" Joe said, throwing his head back in pride.

"But you can't do it again," Max said. "You're all tapped out. Finished. You're telling me that if you had the resources, you couldn't spin out another song list with another unique combination of notes and chords and lyrics. That you had a limited amount of music in you, and now your well's run dry."

Joe laughed. "Couldn't? Listen, moppet, I could compose music from now until the end of time and never run out of combinations. I can do it with my fucking eyes closed and one hand tied behind my back. I can do it in my fucking *sleep*."

Max stuffed his hands in his pockets. "I've got a studio, and every piece of top-of-the-line equipment you could ever dream of. I want to make a deal."

Joe stepped back and crossed his arms. "I don't gamble."

"My equipment, my band, with your music. You call the shots, final say on every song. I play lead, and I have a bassist and drummer. You can do whatever you want."

Joe scratched his chin, then took a slow step forward. He leaned over and whispered in Max's ear. "I'm...not...interested! I don't do music anymore."

Max stepped back, looking angry. "Fine. Then I guess that makes two of us." Max kicked the ground.

Joe studied him. "You gonna quit then?"

"Yes," Max said. "I have no choice. Dad holds the purse strings, and he's cutting them. Unless I get you to help."

Joe looked over at the silver sport's car. He grinned, then looked at Max, who stood with shoulders slumped, looking defeated. "Well you spoiled little shit."

Max's eyes widened. "What?"

"Have you never done anything on your own, lad? Daddy pulls his money, so you can't play anymore? Do you know what your dad and I went through to get equipment? To get rehearsal time? Do you have any idea some of the crap we had to eat because we never had any extra cash? Do you—"

"Oh great!" Max said. "You're just like my dad. I should have known. Never mind then. You're too OLD anyway."

Joe frowned at the boy, then looked over at Vincent's shiny sports car. He glanced over his shoulder at the butcher shop, at Road Bastard, then back at Max. "I am not like your father. I am *nothing* like your father."

Max let his eyes drift over Joe's outfit. "No. I guess you're not."

Joe turned around and strode back, climbing onto Road Bastard. He started it up and revved the engine.

Max walked over. "My dad says you're a master composer. Is that true?"

Joe revved the engine.

"My dad says you're like a general. A drill sergeant. We could use your help. I've got two of the laziest band-mates in the history of the world."

Joe glanced at him. "So get rid of them."

Max laughed. "And end up with someone even lazier?"

"Nobody's lazier than your dad and Deke were before I got my hands on them. I assure you."

"So that's your final answer, then?" Max yelled over the motor. "Are you in, or are you out?"

Joe gave Road Bastard more gas, then punched up the stereo, blasting a Ramones song. He glanced at Max, as if just remembering that he was still there. "Okay, Death Metal Boy. See you on Tuesday," he said, and sped off.

The calendar was smoking a cigar when Joe walked into the apartment. Ignoring it, he went directly to the kitchen and threw his keys down along with the bag containing his purchases. He grabbed a beer from the fridge and popped the cap on the counter, taking a long swallow.

YOU'RE NOT SUPPOSED TO BE DRINKING, the calendar beast called out from the study.

"What the fuck difference does it make? I'll be dead in a month!" he yelled back. Joe's face broke to a frown, then he crumpled over the counter, resting his head on his arm. He fought tears.

IF EUNICE FINDS OUT, YOU'LL BE BACK IN REHAB. THAT COULD HINDER OUR AGREEMENT. YOU CANNOT BE UNDER LOCK AND KEY ON YOUR BIRTHDAY.

Joe moved into the study and went directly to the television remote, flicking it on and raising the volume to drown out the voice of the beast. A cereal commercial came on, boasting about being FORTI-fied with vitamins and iron. Joe flicked the channel. An infomercial showed a woman slathering a mask of cream on her face. "*When I turned forty, I started to see fine lines.*" Joe clicked the television off and tossed the remote. The calendar laughed.

Joe approached the beast. "I told you not to smoke in here," he said. The beast blew tufts of smoke into his face. Joe grabbed the red marker as he waved cigar trails away.

WHAT ARE YOU DOING? TOMORROW HAS NOT YET COME. The days of the week chomped the cigar.

Joe dug the pen into tomorrow's date, and made a heavy red slash. "I won't be coming out of my room tomorrow. I've got work to do."

REALLY, JOE. WRITING MUSIC? DON'T BE A FOOL. DO YOU REALLY WANT TO SPEND YOUR FINAL DAYS WITH THOSE TEENAGERS? THEY'LL SEE THROUGH YOU. YOU CAN'T HIDE YOUR NOTHINGNESS.

Joe glared at the beast, his breathing becoming erratic. He wound up and punched the calendar hard in the week of the sixteenth. Pain shot through his fingers. "Ah!" he yelled, shaking his hand out. He looked up. The days of the week had smoothed out. The beast was gone. For now.

Someone knocked hard. Rubbing his wounded hand, Joe moved to the door, pulling it open. Donna from down the hall stood before him, her face pinched. "Are you smoking cigars in here? Because it stinks! I can smell it all the way down the hall, inside my apartment."

"I'm not smoking cigars!" Joe snarled, but as he brought his sore hand to his chest, there was a lit cigar between his fingers. He stared at it, then looked up at Donna. She crossed her arms and smirked.

"Nice try. Put it out or I'm gonna call the landlord. Have a little respect, Joe. Jesus."

Joe slammed the door, bounded into the kitchen and ran water over the cigar, then tossed it into the trash. He grabbed his bag of newly purchased notebooks and made off to his bedroom. As he closed the door, he could hear the beast laughing jubilantly down the hall.

Max, Pez and Shane polished their Harley Davidson motorcycles near the garage at the top of the driveway. Pez straightened up, looking toward the street. The others followed his gaze as a strange sound cut into the silence, like a chainsaw backed by drumbeats.

Joe Blood turned in at the bottom of the long driveway, the scooter bucking and whining, thrashy guitar sounds bellowing from his speakers. The wind had not altered his red spiked hair, points standing erect like bloody volcanoes. He seemed to be having some trouble with his engine. The scooter lurched and bucked, edging closer to them in a jerky crawl.

He wore red, iridescent trousers that matched his hair, with heavy, black, spiked boots. A sleeveless denim jacket covered his white tee shirt. The multitude of rusty safety pins glittered strangely in the morning sun, creating a mirage of speckled lights shooting out of Joe's lanky body.

"Holy fucking Christ," Pez said. "Is that him?"

Max rounded his motorcycle and watched Joe's approach. "Yeah. That's him. The legend. Aren't you impressed?" he asked with sarcasm.

"Legend?" Shane said. "More like a relic. What the hell is he riding? A lawnmower?"

Joe made it within ten feet of them, then his motor backfired with a puff of smoke, and died. The sound was so like a gunshot that the three instinctively dropped, ducking behind their Harley's. Joe hopped off his scooter and looked over at the bikes, hands on his hips, frowning. Slowly, the three rose to their feet.

"Hi," Shane said.

Joe stared at them for a moment, his brow knit in confusion. He rounded the back of his scooter, ducked down, then slowly raised himself up. "Hi," he said.

Vincent came out the front door looking cheery and casual in a pair of jeans and a black tee shirt. "Joe! You made it." He trotted down the walk and wrapped an arm around Joe's shoulders, walking him toward the boys.

"Max you've already met. And this is Pez and Shane. Boys, this is Joe

Blood."

Pez stepped up, his ginger mane tied back under a bandana, his freckled face grinning. "Hey, man." He offered Joe a hard slap on the arm. Joe nodded, rubbing where he'd been slapped.

"Hi, I'm Shane," the gaunt, skinny kid said. He seemed frightened to move from behind his bike, and studied Joe with spooked gray eyes.

"What say we show you the studio?" Vincent asked. "I think you'll be impressed."

Joe followed Vincent through the house and down the stairs to the rehearsal studio, with the three boys trailing behind. They stepped into a spacious, high ceiling room, filled with equipment. Joe's eyes widened. "Fahkin hell, Vin. You've got this in your own house, and you don't even use it?"

"Not bad, huh? My son here has no concept of what it's like to scrap around on the street, begging for rehearsal time in a dirty mill studio."

"Jesus, Dad," Max said. "Do you ever stop? I know. It was hell when you were my age. Dirty rehearsal studios. Walking to school barefoot in the snow, uphill both ways."

"I cleaned the place up for you, but I'm sure these three will have it trashed again in no time if they can. I'm gonna leave you to it then." Vincent patted Joe on the shoulder. "Thanks for doing this, Joe."

"I didn't say I was doing nothing," Joe snarled. "I just came to check it out."

Vincent smiled. "Okay, Joe. Just take your time."

Vincent left, and Max, Pez and Shane stood awkwardly by, watching as Joe circled the room, examining each piece of equipment diligently.

He looked up at Max. "A harmonizer?"

Max nodded. "You can make it sound like three guitars when you only have one."

Joe raised his eyebrows, then moved on, touching things, kneeling down, looking behind the equipment. He stood, brushed himself off, and looked at Max again. "Is that a dual rectifier?"

"Triple," Max said.

"Uh-huh," Joe said, frowning. He stepped over a snake of cables, and kneeled down, running a finger down the side of the instrument. He looked up at Pez. "Are you aware that your bass has five strings?"

Pez made a face. "That would be on account of it being a five-stringed bass."

Joe pursed his lips, nodding. "I see. You play slap-bass?"

Pez swaggered over and picked up his bass, switching on the amp. He tossed his red hair back and hit the string with his thumb. The amp farted. He looked at Joe, frowning, then hit it again, twice. The sound was the same. "I think there's something wrong with the amp. I mean, I've slapped it before, and that's never happened."

"There's nothing wrong with your amp," Joe said, and moved on to Max's guitar. Pez stared after him, looking wounded.

"Nice guitar," he said to Max. "Let's see what you've got, then."

Max made a face. "I feel like I'm auditioning for my own band."

Joe raised his eyebrows. "Aw, you shy? How you ever going to play in front of a crowd, if you can't even show my narrow white ass what you've got?"

Looking both intimidated and spiteful, Max stormed over and picked up his guitar. He spent several minutes on tuning, then threw his head back and began to play. His fingers flew up and down the neck at an uncanny speed, wild sounds spilling out. The sound was good, accurate, and in tune. Intensifying his solo, Max slung his hips forward, arching his back until his long dark hair brushed the floor. He ended with a whining high note, pushing the guitar outward from his hips, then he cut it.

Pez clapped. "All right, Max! That was awesome."

Max looked at Joe, a cocky smirk tilting his lips. "So. Whatcha think of that?"

"You've got talent," Joe said.

Max nodded, grinning. Pez gave him a high five.

"But," Joe said.

Max turned to him. "But what?"

Joe pulled the guitar out from where it hung at Max's mid thigh, then let it drop. He stepped back and examined him. "Do you know what I've always hated? Stupid twats that hang their guitars round their knees to look cool, but can barely reach the strings to play. I tried it once, just to see if it was possible, and I ended up giving myself carpel tunnel. Also, twiddly-diddly guitar solos are a poser, cop-out substitute for good writing. And finally, if I EVER see you do that David Lee Roth backbend again, I will personally disembowel you. Is that clear?"

Max scowled at him, and Shane giggled in the corner.

Joe spun about and pointed at Shane. "You!"

Shane's face dropped. "Me?"

"Yes, you, little drummer boy. How do you count out the start of a song?"

"I hit the sticks four times," he said.

"Well don't!" Joe shouted, and Shane jumped. "Use your fucking hi-hat. Now, I've come up with eight songs for you little abortions to learn. I've decided I'm going to help you wankers make something of this mess, but only under the following conditions. What I say goes. When I say it's time to practice, it's time to practice. I don't care what your weekend plans are, or whose panties you're trying to pull off. If I say a song's not good enough yet, it's not good enough yet. If I say we need to do it again, and again, and again, and again, then I expect you to do it. Again, and again, and again, and again. If these conditions pose a problem for any of you princesses, please speak now. If you're not serious about this, then don't waste my fucking time."

Max scratched his head. Pez looked at Shane, who nodded. He turned to Max. "Max?"

Max looked up. "Yeah, yeah we have a deal. You're the boss, Joe. But," he shook his head, "where did you get eight songs for us to do?"

"I wrote them," he said.

"When?"

"Yesterday."

Shane stepped up, tilting his head. "You wrote eight songs in one day?"

"That's right. Just music at this point. You can add lyrics later. I'll be back in two days, then it's go time."

Pez bounded off and retrieved a notebook from the floor, then stomped over to Joe, his eyes wild. "Hey, Joe. I write lyrics."

Joe raised his eyebrows. "You do?" His eyes shifted to Shane, who stood behind Pez, mouthing the word 'no' to Joe, shaking his head.

"Yeah, man. I write lots of lyrics. I'm a natural born poet, and I can't *wait* to get my words out through our songs."

"Pez," Max started.

Pez held a hand up, signaling for silence. "It makes me cry, Joe. It makes me cry, I want it so much."

Joe took a step back, frowning as the boy's freckled face took on a maniacal gleam.

"Here, take a look." He handed Joe the notebook.

Joe held it up, reading the words with a frown. "My mother can kiss my ass. She thinks she's the boss. And my father is a dork. I hate them both..."

"Yeah man, these lyrics saved me from suicide when my eight brothers and sisters died in that awful train wreck. I don't mean to boast, but I KNOW they're brilliant. I believe I was visited by God when I wrote them. I felt divine, man!"

Joe read aloud. "When I was small, the bastards wouldn't let me have a puppy. But my sister had a pony. This was before the train crash."

Pez moved in closer to Joe, his hands gesturing wildly. "You know, between you and me, Joe, I'm not all that stable. I sometimes slip into the black void." He twisted his face up. "It's the depression that puts my hand in the drawer and guides the revolver to the roof of my mouth. The MONSTER RAGE that pushes my trigger finger to fractions of a millimeter from blowing my genius brains all over my ungrateful parents. It would only take another disappointment, like having my band-mates REJECT my beautiful lyrics, to make the rage prevail and the dark side send demons into my bedroom SCREAMING my name! Dig?"

There was a long pause. Joe frowned down at the page. Finally, he looked up at Pez. "Um, can I hang on to these for a day or two?"

"Sure man. Just don't lose them." Pez snarled and snapped his teeth before turning away.

Joe looked over at Max. "Well. This has been...fun. I'll see you all in two..." Joe paused, staring at Max. "What is that thing under your lip?"

Max touched the gold stud just above his chin. "It's a piercing. I got it done last night. Pretty cool, huh?"

Joe walked over and examined Max's lip. He pulled it open and studied the underside, while Max stood wincing. "Well, isn't that tidy. You do it yourself?"

Max jerked his head back from Joe's grasp. "No, man. I got it done at the piercing studio. It's totally safe. Brand new needles, all sterile jewelry. I just have to clean it a lot right now so it doesn't get infected. It's a little sore, but in a few weeks I'll be able to pull on it and not even feel it."

"Lovely," Joe said, and turned to leave.

"Are you so old you've never seen a body piercing?" Pez called out.

He froze in the doorway. Slowly, he turned around. The freckled-faced teen grinned at him. Joe walked back into the room, and stopped in front of Pez, his face inches away. Pez's smile dropped.

With eyes locked on the bassist, Joe unclipped a safety pin from his jacket, and held it before his eyes. Max and Shane moved behind Pez to watch.

Joe held it there for a moment, then pulled the side of his mouth open, and jammed it through his cheek, in one, swift movement.

"Aww MAN!" Shane said, turning away.

Max laughed. "Holy shit!"

Pez's eyes widened as Joe dug the pin over until the point met the inside of his lip, then he clasped it.

Pez sighed. "Jesus!"

Joe grinned, the pin grotesquely gracing the edge of his mouth. "Hey Pez?"

"Yeah?"

"We're not using your shitty lyrics. Okay?"

Pez nodded. "Yeah. Okay."

"Good then. I'll see you all Thursday."

The cliff was beauty, rage and death, swirling in a cacophonous shifting of imagery and emotion. Joe stood at the edge, watching the waves slam the sharp black rocks below, tips of his boots teetering on oblivion. Quite a drop. No chance of surviving a fall from this height.

He spread his arms out wide, closed his eyes and felt the ocean breeze tugging at him, pulling him this way and that, making him sway. Perhaps he should leave it up to the breeze. If it pulled him forward, he would jump. If it pushed him back, he would retreat.

RETREAT TO WHAT? YOU HAVE NO LIFE.

The beast was there with him. He'd sensed it just after he arrived, a black stain, stretching out from behind a tree, stealthily moving from branches to rock shadows, gliding across the grass behind him, watching.

IT IS NOT YET YOUR BIRTHDAY. WHY ARE YOU HERE?

Joe ignored the beast. Eventually it gave up its taunting and retreated to the shadows of the wooded cemetery. Eyes closed, he circled his arms, relishing the sea air, softly singing an old Blood Blister song.

"How long can I be
King of this
Destiny
If I jump
I will not fly
But to stand still
While life goes by,
I'd rather die..."

The beast shadowed by, curious, but silent. "*I'd rather die...*" Joe sang, twirling his arms, swaying in the breeze, dangerously close to the edge of the cliff.

An out of place sound prompted Joe's eyes to open. Drum beats. Close. Ten feet to his left, a sudden, rhythmic thumping. Arms pin wheeling, Joe stumbled back when he saw the source. A man stood near the edge of the cliff, his back to the water. For several moments Joe simply blinked, the wrongness of the man's sudden appearance rudely disturbing his suicidal serenity zone.

And it wasn't simply the suddenness. It was the wrongness of the man's appearance in general.

He wasn't exactly naked. Some sort of feathered loincloth covered his privates, a breastplate of bones and teeth covering his otherwise bare chest. Colored paint slashed in stripes across the reddish-brown skin of his face, arms and ribs. The black hair was tied into a braid on either side. But the savage costumed appearance wasn't what chilled Joe's blood. He circled around so that he could see the stranger's face, full on. The black eyes stared ahead at nothing. At least they seemed to. But Joe wouldn't have known if the savage was looking at him, for there was only black in the eye. No iris, no pupil, no white. Those ebony eyes, those *wrong* eyes seemed to focus ahead as he repeated a solemn drumbeat, banging bound sticks on the single bongo that hung from his neck.

Bdrump...bump...bump. Bdrump...bump...bump. Joe moved cautiously toward the drummer, who kept his rhythm with mechanical precision. He did not stop drumming when Joe spoke. "Okay, mate. What the hell are you doing here?"

Bdrump...bump...bump. Bdrump...bump...bump. "Playing a death march for you."

Joe flinched. He hadn't really expected to get an answer, as he suspected this bloke an illusion, perhaps concocted by the beast. The inky black eyes stayed focused, staring, either with purpose or involuntarily, there was no way to tell.

"A death march, eh? And why would I want that?" Joe asked, struggling to sound un-rattled.

"How should I know?" the stranger said, a matter of fact tone. *Bdrump...bump..bump.* "It's YOUR subconscious."

Joe took another step, putting him alongside the stranger. "My subconscious. That where you're from, then?"

"Yes."

Joe stared at the man's bare feet, then his eyes traveled up to his black eyes. "Am I going crazy?"

"No."

Joe let out a breath. "Could have fooled me. So what's this then? With the drum, and the war paint and the...fancy underpants."

Bdrump...bump...bump. "I'm a member of the long dead Rjiashowa Tribe. We practiced ritual suicides to appease the Gods of the sea, to make fishing plentiful and storms scarce. On the day of the sacrifice, the tribal member closest to the chosen would play this death march in honor as the sacrifice jumped from the cliff and into the sea."

Joe wagged his finger. "Ah ha! All that stuff you just said? I don't know a thing about it. Never heard of the...whatever tribe before. Therefore, you CAN'T be from my subconscious."

The stranger stared. "When you were a small boy in school, they showed you a film strip about the Rjiashowa Tribe. I was the chief. It's stored in your subconscious with all the other crap you can't remember."

Joe tentatively reached out to touch the chief's shoulder. His fingers breezed through the flesh. The stranger was a phantom, not solid. Joe pulled his hand back and flexed it into a fist, wincing. "What about the demon?" Joe whispered.

"What about it?" *Bdrump...bump...bump.*

"Is it from my subconscious too, or is it real?"

The chief stared. "The demon is from your subconscious. But the demon also real."

"I don't understand."

"The demon has been let out to manifest. It has become a reality."

"How? Why?" Joe demanded.

The chief drummed. "Because you're no longer in control."

"In control of what?"

"Of your mind," he said.

Joe scratched his head and walked a small circle across the grass. He turned about and pointed at the chief. "You're contradicting yourself! You said I wasn't going crazy! Now you tell me I'm not in control of my mind."

Bdrump...bump...bump. "That is correct. You're not *going* crazy. You've been crazy for some time now."

Joe looked down for only an instant. When his eyes lifted, the chief was gone. And the drumming had stopped. The cliff was silent save for the wind and the waves.

"I'm pleased you came to see me, Joe. But I must say, I'm confused. You've never asked for a meeting before. In fact, I believe coming to see me is dead last on your list of favorite things. So tell me. What's wrong?"

Eunice chewed the stem of her eyeglasses, her brows lowered. Joe stared at her curly black hair, trying to avoid her eyes, lest she see the truth in his. That he was completely off his tree. He'd lost the plot. Loony, batty, not right, nuts, bonkers, and a thousand other adjectives that meant he was crazy.

"Eunice, you're not a real doctor, right? I mean, you're not a shrink."

She shrugged. "Okay. I suppose that's true. I'm a social worker. But I'm studying to become a *real* doctor. Why does this concern you?"

"So you can't...have me committed. I mean even if you wanted to."

Eunice crossed her legs, adjusting her position in the chair. Joe guessed she was buying time while she considered her answer. "I suppose I can't, but Joe, you're not making any sense. Why would I want to have you committed?"

Joe leaned forward, wringing his hands. "Eunice, you study this stuff. Tell me something. If a bloke were to start...seeing things. Like...hallucinations. Would that automatically make him a nutter? Or could it be something else? I mean, is there a pill for that sort of thing?"

"Are you afraid you're having hallucinations?" she asked.

"Honestly? I'm more afraid that I'm not."

"I can recommend a specialist."

"No," he said. "No doctors. Just your opinion. Tell me straight. From what you know of me. Do I seem crazy to you, Eunice?"

Eunice studied him carefully, looking conflicted. Finally she sighed and put her glasses down. She met his eyes. "Okay," she said. "Off the record, you want my opinion?"

Joe nodded. "Please."

"I think your problem is drug-related."

"I don't do drugs anymore."

"Nevertheless, you once listed for me all of the recreational drugs you used in your past, and with what frequency."

Joe frowned. "So what you saying?"

"I'm saying that if I had to guess, I'd say you're experiencing what is known in layman's terms as acid flashbacks."

Joe eyed her, warily. "These acid flashbacks. Do they tend to be...detailed?"

"Not usually, no. Are your hallucinations detailed?"

Joe let out a humorless laugh. "They smoke cigars and play bongos. So, yes. I'd say they're rather detailed."

Eunice looked disturbed by the comment, but struggled to remain stoic. "Tell me something, Joe. Are you happy?"

"Happy with what?"

"With Joe Blood. With yourself."

Joe stared at the floor for several moments. Finally he lifted his eyes to Eunice. "You want the truth?"

"That would be nice for a change."

Joe let out a long sigh. He looked at the floor. "I don't like who I am. I only like who I was."

Eunice nodded. "But what if who you were, and who you *are*, are the same person?"

Joe considered the question for only a moment, before he was distracted by something on the wall behind Eunice's desk. Her serene, seascape-themed wall calendar was smoking a cigar. It grinned at him when it saw him noticing it. The beast.

"I've got to go to work," he said, and bolted out of Eunice's office before she could protest.

"Good evening. Cow can I help you?"

The butcher shop was filling up, a line of rush hour dinner planners forming before Joe. He felt worlds better without the hideous cow costume. He'd reached an agreement with David, that he'd be more respectful to the customers if he could wear his own clothes. David had agreed, despite his futile protests about Joe's current outfit; black leather pants, black and red *Exploited* tee shirt, complete with dog collar and sleeveless denim vest. Joe didn't understand what all the fuss was about. He'd toned himself down considerably from his off-duty style.

Sam Barnsley stormed into the room from the adjoining fish department, as well as a man could storm while wearing a giant crab costume. "This isn't fair! Why does Joe get to wear his own clothes! I've been asking for out of this stupid crab costume for months! David never let *me* wear my own clothes!"

He waved his pincers furiously at Irving, who had forgone his lamb uniform for a pig this evening, curly pink tail bouncing as he shuffled about, jubilantly scooping ham salad as though it wasn't indicative of what he, in his current pig persona, would look like after being forced through a meat shredder.

"Joe made a deal with David," Irving said to Sam. "Besides, don't be so glum, chum! David's ordered you a sardine uniform, so you can switch off, like me! It should be in any day now."

"A sardine? I don't want to be a f..." Sam glanced at the growing line of customers, and seemed to think better of using whatever colorful adjective he had in mind. He turned his girth and waddled his crustacean form back into the adjoining fish department. Ironically, the uniform was too wide to fit through the doorways, forcing him to sideways shuffle most of the time.

Joe made chicken salad at the side counter, allowing Irving to man the front alone, which brought no complaints from the career-minded little porker. Still, Joe felt eyes on him. He glanced over at the line of customers, and saw two young men staring at him. They looked in their late twenties. One was a chubby, long-haired, beer-drinking type in a 'Ski Naked' sweatshirt. The other had a shaved head and wore yellow sunglasses, leaving them on inside the shop, either unknowingly or as a fashion statement.

Joe gave them a toxic sneer, which to his dismay, only intensified their stares. One whispered to the other, then they both turned back to Joe. He went back to his chicken salad, ignoring them.

As the line moved up, Joe tuned into the conversation between the two young men, who if he had to guess, were stoned on Cannabis. Not only did they have the vague, skunky odor, but their eyes were bloodshot, and Joe had heard enough weed-induced conversations in his life to recognize one taking place three feet from him.

"I swear to God, man. I know that guy from somewhere! He's somebody famous," Ski Naked said.

"I think it's Adam Ant," the bald friend said.

Joe gave them a seething look, then turned back to his celery chopping.

"Idiot! It's not Adam Ant!" the other said. "It's someone, though. Damn, why can't I place it?"

"Bowie. Looks like David Bowie."

This time Joe gave them a worse look, let it linger, then went back to his celery chopping.

"Bowie? Are you nuts? David Bowie is like a thousand years old."

"I know, I mean when he was Ziggy Stardust. Kind of looks like that guy."

"You're not listening to me, dumb-ass. I'm not saying that guy just *looks* like someone famous. I'm saying he actually *is* someone famous. I'd bet my life on it."

"Well if he's so famous then why is he working here?"

Joe scooped the contents of the cutting board into a tray and set it in the bin behind the glass counter. The twenty-somethings had moved to the front of the line, and were giving their order to Irving. The second of the two leaned over and narrowed his eyes at Joe. "Hey, excuse me?" he said. Joe ignored him. "Hey, you with the spiky hair, can I ask you something?"

Joe turned away.

"Joe? I believe this gentleman is speaking to you," Irving called over his shoulder.

He turned around slowly, and Irving appeared about to wet his pig suit for the glare Joe gave him. But the damage was already done.

"JOE BLOOD! That's it!" Ski Naked called out. "I knew it was someone in music, man!"

Irving looked at Joe, a puzzled frown beneath his pig snout. Joe realized then for the first time, not that he'd thought about it much, that Irving had never known who the hell he was. Of course Irving wasn't exactly punk rock material.

Joe looked up at the two men and shook his head. "You're mistaken. I'm nobody. Trust me."

"Ha!" Yellow glasses said. "You're British. He's right, you ARE Joe Blood! Holy shit!"

"No, I'm not," he said.

Irving's pink-eared head swiveled between Joe and the stoners. "Joe? Why are you denying who you are? These gentlemen obviously know you from somewhere."

"From *somewhere?*" Ski Naked said, staring at Irving incredulously. "Don't you know who this guy is? Man, I had every Blood Blister album, listened to them all through college! Remember, Jay?"

"Hell yeah!" Yellow Glasses said, then to Joe's horror, broke into song. Badly. "*You're a useless pile of cells! I don't give a crap if you burn in hell!*"

The friend chimed in, the two of them air-guitaring, thrashing their heads. "*You're useless! Useless! Arses!*"

"Please stop that," Joe said.

"*Arses!*" The stoners chimed.

"Seriously," Joe said. "Stop."

"*Arses!*"

"Not kidding, now."

"*Arses!*"

"I'm warning you."

"*Arses!*"

Joe was almost unaware of his hand grabbing the butcher's knife from the cutting board. It was an automatic motion, synchronized by the bopping heads of the stoners as they performed their abominable imitation of his song. It felt...right. He lifted the cleaver over his shoulder and tilted his arm back, considering which bobbing head he wanted to remove first; imagining it flying from the neck and landing in a bin of potato salad.

Then a foot-long red claw snapped shut on Joe's wrist, and the cleaver slipped from his fingers and clattered on the floor.

The twenty-somethings ceased their singing, awed anew by the sight of a giant crab dragging Joe Blood away by his spindly arm. "If you'll excuse us a moment," Sam Barnsley said to the customers, as he pulled Joe, stumbling into the back storeroom.

"Let go of me, Barnsley!" Joe yelled at the crab.

"Come on!" Sam shouted, and tugged Joe into the storeroom, tossing him inside. He slammed the door closed behind him, and blocked the exit with his costumed bulk.

"What the hell do you think you're doing, Sam?" Joe shouted, recovering his footing.

"What am I doing? You need to get a grip, Joe!"

"Get out of my way."

"Not until you calm down!" He said, pointing a claw. "First you attack Irving the other night, now you're pulling knives on customers! May I remind you that you're on probation? That you need this job?"

"That's none of your business, Barnsley. Now move your crab ass out of my way!"

Sam raised his pincers, spreading himself in front of the door. "Make me."

Joe clenched his jaw in rage and charged at Sam Barnsley. Sam shoved his body to meet the blow, and Joe bounced off his Styrofoam crab belly and landed on his ass. He climbed to his feet and went at him again, but this time Sam cracked him across the face with his long red claw. "I said calm down, Joe!"

Joe rubbed his face, then put up his fists. Sam put up his pincers. They boxed awkwardly, but even ducking and weaving, Joe couldn't get past the giant claws that swiped at him. He took two more in the jaw, then fell back, dropping to his knees, exhausted. He touched his lip, where a small trickle of blood had erupted. He examined the red wetness on his hand, and looked up. "Well. Never got my ass kicked by an entrée before."

Sam lowered his claws and sighed, sliding his bulk down the door and sitting against it. He was panting from the altercation and the hindrance of the costume. Joe eased himself back and sat against the opposite wall. He dropped his head in his hands, breathing heavily. After a moment, he looked up at Sam. "I wasn't really gonna throw the cleaver," he said.

Sam looked sympathetic. "What's wrong with you? You've always been uptight, but lately? I don't know, man. You looking to get yourself thrown in jail? Or worse? One of these days you're going to cross the wrong person with these antics. Someone's gonna kill you. Or is that what you want?"

Joe sneered at him. "What do you care?"

"I'd be left alone with Irving! That's what I care. You're a nut, Joe, but if I have to work alone with piglet out there every day, I'll hang myself."

Joe laughed, the last of his rage leaking out of him. He looked at Sam, his face growing serious. "Let me ask you something, Barnsley. If you only had a month to live, what would you do? With the rest of your time, I mean."

Sam shrugged. He lifted a pincer, then let it drop. "I don't know, man. I guess I'd figure out what I love to do more than anything in the world. Then I'd do that, every day until the end."

Joe stared at the floor thoughtfully, then looked back at Sam. "What if..." He paused. "What if you knew what you loved to do, more than anything, but that thing caused you pain. Unbearable pain. Because it reminded you of what you used to be."

Sam scratched his cheek with a pincer. "I think I understand. But consider this. If you do that thing, that thing that reminds you of what you used to be, then wouldn't you be that person again? I mean, what if what you used to be, and what you choose to become, are the same thing? Then you don't have to miss it, because you'll be it."

Joe stared at him. "Interesting. Someone else said that same thing to me, just today."

"Hey, I don't know. I'm trying to reason with a punk who just tried to hatchet a customer."

"Right," Joe said, climbing to his feet. "And I'm taking philosophy lessons from a crab."

Sam tried to work himself to a stand, but his awkward shell held him down. Joe grabbed a claw and helped him to his feet. "Thanks," Sam said. "Now if I let you out, do you promise not to kill anyone?"

Joe patted Sam's Styrofoam shoulder. "Not to worry, Sam. You have my word, if I feel compelled to murder, I'll take it out on the turkey loaf."

Sam opened the door, and gestured with his claw. "After you."

When Joe pulled Road Bastard into his driveway later on, the three neighborhood pre-teens were on his porch, digging through his mailbox. They scattered as he hopped off the scooter. "Hey!" Joe yelled out. "God-damned gypsies!"

"Fuck off, loser!" one of the kids called out, tearing off down the sidewalk, one of Joe's music magazines tucked under his arm.

"You little abortions!" Joe yelled after him. "I knew you'd been stealing my magazines! I catch you and I'm gonna..." It was useless. The little bastards were gone, ducked off into the maze of urban alleyways. He shook his head. "Gypsies!" he spat, and climbed the stairs to his building.

A man stood in the hallway before Joe's apartment door, holding a birthday cake. Joe froze when he saw him. He was spindly, balding, wearing a cheap pinstriped suit. The man's eyes widened when he saw Joe, and he did a quick scan of his appearance, looking alarmed. Joe approached him, an eyebrow cocked. He looked at the birthday cake he held, then at the man's face. "Who are you?" Joe demanded. Then in a whisper, "Are you from my subconscious?"

The man's lip quivered. "No. I'm from New Jersey. Verne!"

Verne stepped through the door at the other entrance at the end of the hall, pushing his Clark Kent glasses up on his nose as he approached. "Joe. I see you've met my brother. You want to come down for cake? It's my birthday."

"Your brother?" Joe asked, relieved.

"Yeah," Verne said, stepping up next to the cake guy. "Paul, this is Joe Blood. Joe, my brother Paul."

"Pleased to meet you," Paul said, though he didn't sound pleased at all. Joe frowned at the two of them, then stepped into his apartment and closed the door.

He took a glance at the wall calendar, pleased to see nothing animated happening there. The Beast was incognito. He moved into the kitchen and picked up the phone, dialing Vincent's number. Vin picked up on the third ring, and Joe explained his wishes to have all the boys spend the night there, with Max. Vincent agreed without question. He was familiar with Joe's tactics.

"So you're going to do it then," Vincent said. "You think my spoiled son and his half-baked band have something to work with?"

"We're gonna find out, Vin. We're gonna find out," he said, and hung up. He dialed the second number on his list and spoke to the booking agent he'd contacted earlier.

"Yeah, hey Joe. You're all set. But I had to pull some strings for this, so it better be good."

"Don't worry, Hal. I'll see to it."

"All right then, Joe. See you in June."

Joe went straight to bed after that, setting his alarm for 5:00 A.M.

Something pulled Max out of a dream. He'd been far under in a deep slumber, then suddenly...something. His eyes peeled open and scanned the room. Still dark, but a crest of blue light cut a dull beam through the blinds. Dawn. Couldn't be more than 5:30 in the morning. He heard a snore and looked to his left, rubbing his eyes. He'd forgotten Shane and Pez had stayed the night. Pez was on the pull-out couch on the other side of the room, and Shane was in the spare bed next to him. The soft sounds of foreign sleepers must have been what startled him awake at such an hour, his subconscious alerting him that something was amiss.

With a sigh of satisfaction, he eased himself back down on the pillow, and pulled the blanket up around his bare shoulders. Shane snored.

Someone ripped the blankets off Max. He bolted up in bed, watching the sheets tumble to the floor. He blinked to adjust his eyes, and saw Shane tumble out of bed, onto the floor as the mattress flipped.

"What the fuck!" Shane yelled as he rolled.

Max watched Joe Blood cross the room to Pez, pull the pillow out from under his head and beat him with it three times. Pez cried out

"Jesus Christ, Joe!" Max said, digging around for his sweatpants to cover his underwear-clad form. "What time is it?"

Pez sat in the pull-out bed, rubbing his temple and grimacing at Joe, who walked to the wall and switched on the light. The room brightened and Shane groaned, covering his eyes.

"What time is it? It's time to get up!" Joe yelled.

After pulling on his sweats, Max stood blinking at the vision of Joe, dressed in camouflage pants, combat boots, and a black sleeveless tee. A red bandana was tied around his head, Rambo style, and his gaunt face was striped with black and green paint. He slapped a rolled up magazine on his palm.

"It's the crack of dawn!" Max yelled. "Why are you here so early, you psycho?"

"Gather round boys," Joe said, and took up position in front of Max and Shane, who stood scratching his ass, his chin-length hair a pile of sleep knots. Pez stayed where he was. Joe glanced his way, and screamed, "I said GATHER ROUND!"

"Okay, okay!" Pez said, climbing out of bed and crossing the room in his boxer shorts, his long ginger hair a curtain over his face. "You're a fucking lunatic, Joe! What's the big rush?"

Joe waited until all three of them were together, and urged them to sit on Max's bed. Then he opened the magazine and held it out before them. "Do you know this band?"

The three simultaneously leaned forward to view the open pages. "Naphula," Pez said. "Of course we know them, they fucking rock!"

Joe panned the open magazine in front of Shane, then Max. "And you two?" he said. "You share this opinion?"

"Yeah," Shane said.

"Naphula is our favorite band," Max said. "Is there a point to this? Because I've got to take a leak."

Joe slapped the magazine shut. "On June eighteenth of this year of our Lord, the band known as Naphula will be playing a sold out show at the King's

Ring Concert Club in downtown Boston. We will all be there."

Pez jumped off the bed, smiling. "No shit? Joe, you got us tickets? I am SO sorry I called you a lunatic, man! You're my hero!"

"We do not have tickets."

Pez's smile dropped. Max leaned forward. "Then why will we be there?"

Joe looked each of them in the eye. "Because we're opening for them."

"Naphula?" Pez gasped.

"That's not funny," Max said. "You're kidding, right?"

"No joke, young man. We are now on the bill as 'to be announced', seeing that we do not yet have a name."

"Not have a name?" Shane cried. "We don't even have a band! We don't have a single song, and that's..." He counted on his fingers. "Just over four weeks away!"

"Well then," Joe said. "We have work to do, don't we?"

Pez sat back down on the bed. "I'm gonna throw up."

"Cut the shit, Joe. This is *impossible* and you know it," Max said. "We can't be ready to open for a band like Naphula in that short a time."

"We can, and we will," Joe said. "It's already booked."

"I'm gonna throw up," Pez said again.

Joe circled the room, slapping the magazine on his palm, head held high. "Forget everything you think you know about yourselves. Forget everything anyone else thinks they know about you. It's all bullshit. The human mind is built to achieve great things when focused and *especially* when under great pressure. "

"Rome wasn't built in a day!" Shane said.

Joe turned to him. "We are not Romans. We are musicians. Or at least I am. That remains to be seen for the rest of you."

"Exactly!" Pez said, then frowned. "I mean we are musicians! But we're not magicians! And I cave under pressure!"

Joe made a mock whimper. "Oh boo hoo! Mommy I can't go to school today, I have a fever! Bunch of poofs. You've got a chance here to do something you'd never be able to do without me to pull the strings for you. There is no trying. There is no crying. There is only doing, or not doing. It's that simple."

Max laughed and shook his head. "Look, Joe, this is a great chance, I'll give you that. But not everyone can do the things you did with Blood Blister. I mean not everyone can create something from scratch overnight."

"You're right. Not everyone can. And if you think I have the slightest desire or intent to rebuild Blood Blister with you manicured mop of masturbators, then your egos are grossly inflated, chums. There will NEVER be another Blood Blister. Nor do I want there to be. Our job is to create our own sound."

"I'm gonna throw up," Pez said again.

"What if..." Shane quivered. "What if we get to June eighteenth and we still suck?"

"Sucking is not an option."

Shane shook his head. "Well we can try, but..."

"No!" Joe pointed at him. "You don't try. You either DO IT or you DON'T! So make a decision, and make it fast. Vincent has coffee ready in the kitchen. I'll be down in the studio. If you are not there in fifteen minutes, I'll assume that you have embraced musical failure, and I will walk out of here and never set eyes on you princesses again. If you walk through that door before then, however..." Joe put his hands on his hips. "Then be ready to hand over your souls at the door." He slapped the magazine on his palm once, then left the room.

Shane looked to Max. "He's nuts!"

Max stood and pulled on a tee shirt. "Yeah. He's nuts alright."

"So what are we gonna do?" Shane asked.

Max pulled his hair back into a ponytail and turned to Shane. "We're going to open for Naphula on June eighteenth. That's what we're gonna do."

Pez threw up.

By noon, Joe had nearly made Shane cry twice, and was well on his way to a third. Working the song like puzzle pieces, he opted to focus on one instrument at a time, and to Shane's misery had started with drums. Max and Pez watched, wincing. It was like standing by silent while a friend was beaten and tortured, and not lifting a hand to help.

"One, two, three, four, again!" Joe stood beside Shane, coaching, sometimes waving his hands like a classical composer, sometimes air drumming the beats along with him, often ripping Shane's sticks from his hands and breaking them over his knee in frustration. Trying to feel useful, Pez retrieved a new set after each incident, and obediently handed them over to Shane.

"There, that was better. Now if we could only HEAR you, we'd be all set! Don't fairy-tap those drums, boy, HIT them! Four-four snare beats sound poppy and programmed. If it's not a blast beat, make it original or hit yourself in the head as a suitable alternative to the snare."

"I have to go to the bathroom," Shane said pleadingly.

An hour later, Shane had finally adjusted the rhythm to meet Joe's expectations, and looked so relieved when Joe said so that both Pez and Max sighed along with him. Then Joe said, "Okay, now do it in double time."

After a late lunch, it was Pez's turn. It seemed at first that the bassist's sentence would be lighter, as Joe expressed his pleasant surprise that Pez had basic talent and could follow instructions with quick accuracy. Joe stood by, arms crossed, nodding as Pez hatched out the full sequence for the first time with no interruptions from Joe. When he'd finished, he looked up expectantly.

"That was perfect," Joe said, and Pez sighed. "You've learned your part. Okay. Now let me hear you actually play it."

Pez frowned. "What do you mean?"

"I mean play it. Play it like you would if this was a real gig."

"But I just did. Play it."

"You tickled it, lad. I want you to slap it. Slap, don't tickle."

Pez nodded, though his brow furrowed in confusion. "Slap, don't tickle," he said.

"That's right," Joe said patiently, nodding. "Now go on. Let's hear it."

Pez took a deep breath and began playing the sequence again. Joe stopped his hand. "Pez? That wasn't slapping."

"What do you want from me?" Pez asked, frustrated. "This line is too soft. It's like a coffee house number or something. What is this anyway?"

"When you hear it together with the rest of the song, you will understand. It only sounds slow now. The bass guitar is an instrument in itself, and by its nature will add weight to the rhythm section, so bass lines need to deviate radically from the guitars. And slap-bass can be heard clearer than plucked bass amid other instruments. So get funky! Let's go!"

Shane and Max shifted on their feet nervously as Joe's patience with Pez showed its first sign of wavering. Pez took a deep breath and swallowed, then began the sequence again. Max winced. It was musically perfect, but Pez played it as delicately as he had before, and Joe's face was turning colors. He stopped Pez's hands again. Pez lifted his eyes to Joe, his face stiff.

Joe leaned in and placed a hand on the bassist's shoulder. "Pez, how much did that bass cost you?"

Pez snickered. "You don't want to know," he said.

"It was quite a lot of money, wasn't it?"

"You got that right!" he said. "This is top-of-the-line, man."

"I see," Joe said, moving away, fingering his chin. "And is this why you're so afraid of it?"

"Excuse me?"

Joe looked at him. "I said is this why you're so afraid of it? Do you think you're going to break it?"

Pez shrugged, making a face. "I'm not afraid of my bass."

"But you are conscious of its value, am I right? You take great care in keeping it shined and polished? Tune it up and gently tuck it into bed every night with a kiss?"

"Well, it is a nice bass," Pez said, defensive now.

Joe smiled. "Yes," he said. "It is. May I have a look?" He reached out. Pez hesitated. Joe stood in the same position, reaching. Finally Pez un-strapped the instrument and handed it to Joe.

Joe let out a long whistle. "You're right. This is a nice one. A real beauty."

Pez grinned. "Fuckin A right," he said.

"Uh-huh." Joe lifted the bass and slammed it into his own head three times, making a hideous gong.

Pez stepped forward. "Hey!"

Max moved over to Pez and held him back gently.

"It's a nice bass," Joe said. "It's also SOLID FUCKING MAPLE!" he said, and whacked it against the wall.

"You mother fu-"

Joe wound up and whacked the bass again. "SOLID...(whack)...FUCKING...(whack)...MAPLE!"

Pez shrieked in rage, struggling to get at Joe while Max held him. "Joe!" Max said. "Cut the shit, man!"

"Why?" Joe asked innocently. He held the bass up, examining it, then turned it to show the others. It gleamed in the light, unscathed. "It's perfectly fine. Here you go, Pez."

Max reluctantly let go of Pez, who immediately snatched his instrument back from Joe. He looked it over, turning it this way and that, stroking it like a baby. Finally he looked up at Joe. "You're lucky," he said, pointing. "If this had broken–"

"I'll break it over your fucking head if you don't stop TICKLING the damn thing and SLAP it already! Now do it again!"

When all had calmed, Pez played the sequence three more times, his freckled face still flushed with a simmering rage. The anger seemed to flow through him, and into his fingers. The sound was clear. The sound was loud. The sound was slap-bass. When he finished the third run, Joe Blood clapped.

"Bravo!" he said.

Pez allowed a smile to curl the edges of his lips. "That was good?"

"Good?" Joe said. "That was fucking fabulous, my boy."

Pez let out a long sigh, and fell back into a chair. He wiped his brow. "Son of a bitch," he said softly.

"All right," Joe said. "Now do it in triple time."

It took both Max and Shane to keep Pez from strangling Joe with a cable wire.

At the dinner table, they sat with Vincent, the haggard looking boys stuffing ravioli into their mouths. They were silent as the grave, while Joe was alert and chipper, joking and chatting with Vincent. When they'd finished eating, Joe clapped his hands. "Okay boys, let's get back down there."
"Don't you have to go to work or something?" Max asked hopefully.
"Not tonight. Don't worry, Max old boy. I wouldn't dream of leaving without teaching you your part."
"Lucky me," Max said. He slumped off out of the kitchen, with Pez and Shane following, grumbling softly to each other.
Joe smiled at Vincent. "I'd say it's going rather well."
Vincent nodded. "They look positively miserable. I'd say it must be going better than rather well."

Max deviated only once in the sequence Joe had given him. It was more a force of habit than a voluntary misstep. He'd been playing around, jamming haphazardly on the guitar for so many years, his fingers now naturally succumbed to his own style, holding a note here, adding a little twiddle there. But as soon as his fingers strayed on their own accord, his shoulders tightened, and he looked up at Joe.
"What the fuck are you doing to my riff?" Joe shouted.
"I'm sorry," Max said. "I didn't change anything. I was just adding a few frills."
"You want frills? Go buy a dress. Now remember, you do this riff eight times, then you'll be following the drums in the time change. Now do it again! And do it right this time."
Max shook his head. "Yes sir," he snapped, and started again.

It was midnight when Joe Blood blessedly announced that they were done 'for the day', and hopped on his scooter and left. Pez and Shane left as well, stumbling out of the house without bothering to tune or polish their instruments.
Vincent was on the couch reading when Max stumbled into the study and flopped down on the couch beside him, sliding into a horizontal position. "Dad?" he said.
"Yeah, Max."
"I hate Joe Blood."
Vincent patted his thigh. "I know, son. I know."

A beam of sunshine cut through the window like a spotlight, framing the wall calendar. Joe held the marking pen, frozen. His lips trembled as he gazed upon the beast. It breathed, loud and raspy, the days of the month swelling and retreating. It was the last day of May. Joe was anguished about flipping the page over to reveal June, the month of his death, yet this was not what caused him pause.

The lines that separated the days of the month had a mossy growth protruding from them, black and rotted looking, like dead vegetation was pushing its way through the calendar from the back. The calendar breathed. Despite his wariness to welcome June, Joe was anxious to turn the hideous page. Mustering his courage, he made the slash across the last day. The pen came back with some of the black gunk on it, and Joe examined it, his face scrunching in disgust.

I DON'T LIKE IT! The beast shouted, and Joe jumped, taking a step back.

I DON'T LIKE IT ONE BIT.

Joe looked at the gunk on the pen, unsure if this was what the beast was referring to. "You don't like what?"

YOU! It hissed. *COMPOSING MUSIC. USELESS ENDEAVOR.*

Joe took a step toward the beast, cocking his head. "What do you care? And what's wrong with your...um...face?"

THE TIME IS NEAR. I AM BEGINNING THE TRANSITION.

Joe glanced at the pen again, then wiped the gunk off on his trousers. "What transition?" he asked, grimacing up at the beast.

THE TRANSITION INTO YOUR WORLD. It took a deep, labored breath, then the pregnant swell retreated and flattened out. A few flecks of the black weeds fell like ashes to the floor. *I HOPE YOU'RE NOT HAVING SECOND THOUGHTS, JOE BLOOD.* The weeks munched together. *I WILL HAVE MY PAYMENT. FROM ALL OF YOU.*

Joe's body trembled. "But Deke...Deke and Vincent. I asked them. They don't want to jump. They'll not do it."

THEY WILL.

Joe's breathing quickened, fear lilting his stance. In a quick motion he reached in and flipped May up, securing it to the wall, then he stepped back. He breathed a hesitant sigh. June was clear, flat and white. His eyes fell to the nineteenth. *Joe's Birthday. Joe dies.* Shaking off the trembles, he sagged his shoulder, and replaced the pen.

SHAAAAAAAAAAAAAAAA!

Joe tumbled backwards, screaming as the blackened face erupted on the month of June. He whimpered as he looked up from where he'd fallen. The beast grinned. The calendar days were only visible along the edges of the month now. In the center, it had become a face. Not like the vague, toothy-month impression of a face it'd been before, but an actual face, with large yellowing teeth and white eyes buried in contrast with the flaky, weed-covered blackness.

JUNE NINETEENTH. COME FOR ME. OR I'LL BE COMING FOR YOU. JOE BLOOD!

The beast laughed, a phlegm-filled hissing that crawled over Joe's skin, yellowed teeth dripping black gore onto his carpet. Joe scrambled backwards and climbed to his feet. He snatched his keys and ran from the apartment, the giggles of the beast still clinging to his skin like fungus.

The crawling skin feeling did not subside until he was blocks away, pushing Road Bastard's motor to its weak maximum, then he pulled over to catch his breath. Pedestrians glanced at him as he hopped off the scooter and squatted down beside it, holding his face in his hands.

"Fuck!" he whispered. "Oh, fuck, fuck, fuck."

David gave Joe a curious shrug, then a nod when he told him he'd like to begin wearing his cow uniform again. Since he'd stopped, four more people had recognized him as he worked behind the deli counter. One expressed sympathy for his plight, while another claimed to admire his music. A third had thought he was dead. The last broke into song, as the two stoners had days before.

On his off time he worked with the boys. Production had ceased briefly when the blisters on Pez's fingers had begun to bleed, and needed tending. By the third rehearsal, all three had learned their separate parts to precision on the first song. But then Joe was faced with another obstacle. Their hopelessness.

"We've been talking, Joe. We can't do it. I mean, do the math. How are we going to learn enough of these songs to be ready for the Naphula show? It's not going to happen."

Joe refrained from tossing Max across the room, as he desired. Instead he took a deep breath and forced himself to calm. They simply hadn't felt it yet. The connection. The buzz. The magic of bringing the puzzle together and viewing the picture whole, in all its glorious shape and color. It was time to show them.

"You're ready to do the song now. Let's play it."

"You're not listening," Shane said. "We know what we're capable of, and we can't—"

"You don't know SHIT," Joe said. "Until you've merged your parts. You haven't even heard the full bloody song yet. Now pick up your sticks." He took a breath, wondering if he should gamble on his next statement. He examined the three. Negativity radiated off of them. They were musicians, all of them. They had natural talent. He only hoped this would be enough to awaken the feeling inside of them, and turn the negativity to excitement. As glum as they looked, it was most likely his only hope at any rate, so he decided to chance it.

"If after playing the song together, you still feel the way you do, then I'll cancel the gig. And I'm out of your lives."

The boys looked at each other. Max hung his head.

"You're feeling weathered and worn," Joe said. "It's understandable. You're pushing yourselves further than you ever have in a matter of days. But your bodies will adjust. Shane, your sore arms will become strong within a week. Pez's calluses will harden and his fingers will adjust to playing faster. Max? Your brain will learn to stop sending your hands off to Disney Land whenever you play a riff. That's why they call it practice."

Max looked at him. "This may be all we've got, Joe. We're beyond the edge of our abilities here."

"Then step off the edge! See what's out there in the abyss. Let's do the song, lads. What do you say?"

There were several moments of stillness, then Shane picked up his drumsticks and seated himself behind his kit. Pez stared at Shane for a moment, then went to his bass. Max picked up his guitar, still radiating negativity, shaking his head.

When they were all in position, Joe strapped on the guitar Vin had given him to play rhythm. He looked over at the drummer. "The time change comes when Pez hits a slap-bass chord once, then you roll down your toms and bring us into the heavy part with the blast-beat. Let's go."

Shane hit his hi-hat four times then started a funk-rock beat, followed by Pez's rhythmic pounding on the low E. After twelve bars of drum and bass, Max came in with an odd, distorted bluegrass rhythm over the top.

They were slightly out of time, but could hear what was supposed to be happening, and their faces showed this. They glanced at each other, and the music started to tighten up as they worked together. The music merged.

Eight bars further, Joe and Max looked at Pez and Shane, waiting for the chord and the drum fill. Pez played the chord in a moment of perfectly timed silence, then Shane rolled down the toms and they all moved into a thrashy, blast-beat unison. In contrast to the bluegrass funk, it sounded heavy as donkey balls.

When the time change happened, Pez looked up, wide-eyed, and Max smiled. Shane hammered the drums with vigor, and Joe joined in on rhythm.

That was the last of the eye contact. After that they simply played the song, heads down, lost. Max closed his eyes. A while into the thrash rhythm, the tempo doubled and Pez's head started to bob up and down. Max looked in a state of ecstasy. They all turned to Shane, waiting for the snare roll, and then everything stopped except for Shane tapping his hi-hat in a 1940's style jazz rhythm while Joe twanged out a high-pitched funk rhythm again.

Pez ran up and down the fret board playing a solo while Joe and Shane kept the rhythm in a cool, unobtrusive undertone. It sounded amazing.

The music shifted and turned, slowed down then burst forward, separated then came together again. When it was done, the silence hummed in the studio, carrying a weight of its own with the absence of sound.

A throat cleared, and they turned to see Vincent standing in the doorway. He stared at them, at the instruments, then at Joe. He raised his eyebrows, and Joe raised his in return.

"Did you want something, Dad?" Max asked.

Vincent pursed his lips, and shook his head. "No, not really. I just...heard the music."

Max looked at his father. "Well, can you shut the door? We've got more songs to learn."

Joe bit his lip to stifle a smile. Vincent nodded respectfully. He offered Joe a glance, then left the room, shutting the door behind him.

Each day, Joe vacuumed the black shreds of crud that flaked off of the month of June. The beast was there all the time now, never retreating, growing more hideous as the days passed. It would retract only momentarily, giving Joe the chance to make his mark on the day's block, then the black, fern-encrusted face would return, its white eyes, its yellow teeth.

And it rarely remained silent anymore, laughing hideously, constantly reminding Joe of how many days he had left, calling him a loser, and repeatedly stating its objections to his latest music endeavor. It threatened the lives of Vincent and Deke, and assured Joe that one way or another, they would all be true to the pact they'd made that night in the graveyard so many years before. Joe spent as little time at home as possible now, stopping in only to sleep and vacuum up the mess left by the ever-changing beast in his wall calendar.

He went to see Eunice on his scheduled day, and told her the lies the beast had ordered him to. That he wasn't seeing things, that he felt fine, and that the hallucinations had gone.

When he wasn't at the butcher shop, he was at Vincent's. Rehearsals with the boys were going well, and day by day they grew closer to composing a full song list. He was in a battle with the boys over the lyric scenario now. Joe insisted that they do all of the writing, as this was a group endeavor, and to be a true band they must have some of their own influence on the songs they played. This caused a lot of whining, tantrums, arguing amongst themselves. Though their optimism and confidence had increased considerably with their excitement over the songs they'd learned, they shut down stubbornly each time the subject of lyrics was brought up.

Vincent gave Joe an office room near the studio to spend time in when he wasn't working with the boys. He'd told Vincent his apartment complex was too noisy for him to contemplate the music, but the truth was he'd do anything to avoid going home to the beast. It was here in this office that Joe, kicked back with his feet up on a desk, began to hold an odd sort of court. Despite his sneers and insistence that he wanted to be alone on breaks, one of the boys was always popping in, taking the seat across from him and sharing their thoughts, angst and eighteen-year old wisdoms with him.

Pez came in with the revelation that he wanted to write a song about tits. Joe reminded him that every wanker in the music business wrote about sex, and that he was a stupid unoriginal sod that should sooner hang himself with a bass string than consider writing another line of verse in his life.

Max popped in and talked about the woes of having long hair, and whether or not he should switch to a more expensive conditioner to remedy his split ends.

As the days wore on, his break time sessions with the boys became less surface, and they began to share more of themselves with him. This was when Joe began to jot down pieces of their conversations on his doodle pad as they spoke.

"I wouldn't mind knowing when I was going to die," Max told him one day while he worked his long brown hair into a braid. "I mean, then you can plan things, you know? If the end is near, then the road becomes clear, right?"

Joe wrote 'if the end is near, the road becomes clear' on the note pad.

"You wouldn't spend so much time fucking about which road to take. Just plow on through with your head on straight and your heart on a plate, dig?"

Joe wrote 'heart on a plate'.

"It's my parent's fault, no matter what I choose to do," Pez ranted in a later sitting. "The fuckers *made* me, man. They created me, and even if I destroy myself, they're to blame. I blame them for my destruction. Even if I'm ninety when it happens. They're not just responsible for my life, man. They're responsible for my death! By the act of giving me life, they have also condemned me to die!"

Joe wrote 'blame for my destruction' on the note pad. If these pampered little fuckers wouldn't give him lyrics voluntarily, he'd take the lyrics right out of their mouths.

Shane slinked in one afternoon after a hearty song session and slid into the chair across the desk. Joe tried to ignore him, but after the third heavy sigh, he finally looked up. "What?" he yelled. "Somebody steal your purse? Stop that sighing for fuck sakes!"

Shane lifted his sad gray eyes. "Joe, you're older. Tell me something. There's this woman, see."

"Women?" Joe said, straightening up. "You're asking me about women? Shane, look at me."

Shane frowned. "So?"

"I couldn't lure a cow to bed with a bell and a bag of feed. Do you know why that is? Because I'm a sad lonely sod. And do you know why that is? Because of women."

"But–"

"Listen to me very carefully, Shane. It is better to have never loved at all, than to have loved and lost."

Shane shook his head. "I think that saying goes the other way around. That it's better to have loved and lost, than to never have loved at all."

"WRONG!" Joe said, standing and circling the desk to kneel in front of Shane. "Do you see this here?" he asked, curling his fingers to a half fist. "This is a butter knife. Do you know what a butter knife is?"

"Of course."

"It's dull right? It ain't sharp?"

"Right."

"So this is loneliness. Your dull, blunt ache, like a butter knife." He thumped Shane's shoulder with the fist. "It ain't too pleasant to be poked with it all day, but it ain't gonna kill ya either, right?"

Shane rubbed his shoulder. "So loneliness is a butter knife."

"Right. But this..." He made a spade of his hand. "This is the dagger! This is heartache, my boy. Sharp, penetrable, searing pain. And it comes at you like this!"

Joe stabbed at Shane's abdomen with his spaded hand. "Ah ah ah! Can you feel that? Ah ah ah!"

"Ouch!" Shane said, grabbing his gut. "Okay, I get it. You can stop now!"

Joe stood, looking down. "So you tell me, lad, which one of these hurts you want. This?"

He held his left hand up in a half fist. "The dull, throbbing numbness of a lonely man? Or this."

He held up the other, making it a spade. "The knife that rips open your gut, and scoops your intestines out, leaving a hollow, bleeding, wounded, half-dead shell of the man you once were. Choice is yours."

"Are we still talking about women?" Shane asked warily.

"Yes we're still talking about women! They will cut you open so they can taste your insides, lad!"

"But," Shane said, rubbing his ribs. "Why do they want to taste my insides?"

"Because that's what women do. Now get back in there. We have work to do. I'll be right there."

Shane stood and walked to the door. He stopped and gave Joe an odd look. "Thanks," he said, and left, shaking his head.

Joe went back round the desk and wrote 'Why do you want to taste my insides' on the notebook. He slapped it into a top drawer and went to join the boys in the studio.

"Come on, Joe. Forty's not so bad," Vincent said as he poured them both a drink. Joe was slumped in a leather chair, solemn. He wanted to be happy. He'd achieved a miracle. In just over a month, the boys had learned all of the songs, and were tickled pink when Joe presented them with the lyrics he'd concocted unknowingly from their rants. They'd gone through the entire set list earlier, with Joe singing. It was perfect. He dared even say they were ready. He should be happy.

But he had less than a week to live. Vincent handed him his drink and took the chair next to him. "Forty is just a number. I've been forty for a month, and I don't feel any different than I did last year. I mean, hell. When you're sixty, you'll be wishing you were forty."

"Will you PLEASE stop saying the F-word?" Joe shouted.

Vincent took a swallow of his drink, his eyes on Joe. "Is the demon still around?" he asked, keeping his voice light. Joe turned his eyes to him.

"Yes, Vincent. The bloody demon is still around. You want to talk about it?"

"If you do. Will that make you feel better?"

"Oh fahk off, Vin! I've already got a therapist."

"I'm sorry. I didn't mean to be condescending. It's just...disconcerting to hear you talk about it."

Joe laughed. "Oh, Vin. You have no idea how disconcerted you'd be if you knew what it's been saying lately."

"Tell me."

Joe eyed him. "You don't want to know."

"Yes I do. Tell me. I want to hear about it."

Joe laughed, and tossed his drink back. He walked to the bar to refill it. "Okay, Vin. I know you think you're humoring me, but since you asked, I'll tell you." He turned to face him. "The demon, as it were, is beginning to manifest in the flesh, and I use the term flesh lightly. The closer we get to my birthday, the more real, and the more monstrous it becomes. And now, not only has it vowed to come after me if I don't fulfill my promise and sacrifice myself to it by jumping off the Anchorage Cliff, it also wants you and Deke. So there you go. Feel better now?" Joe lifted his glass, and took a long swallow.

Vincent looked at the floor, rubbing his chin. "So Deke and I are part of this."

"Well, hello! I've been trying to tell you. You signed in blood, Vin. The demon remembers. You think I enjoy this little fantasy? You think I like going home every night and cleaning shreds of demon shit off my carpet?"

Vincent frowned. "It shits?"

Joe shook his head, waving his arm. "No. No, it doesn't shit. At least not that I know of. Look, this is irrelevant. You don't believe me, and that's fine. I'm not going to ask you to jump with me anymore. I don't particularly want to jump myself, though no one will believe that. But I've got to face this thing. And I'm doing it alone. So whatever you do, stay clear of the cliff. I'd say that goes for Deke too, but the fat bastard probably never gets out of his lawn chair, so we need not worry about that."

"Joe, promise me you won't do anything stupid. You can't lay this on me and expect me to forget about it. You're talking suicide."

Joe shrugged and drained his glass. "We all talked suicide once, Vin."

"That was a long time ago."

Joe snatched his vinyl jacket off the chair. "I've got to go. I'm gonna pick up some cheap beer and then head down to Shane's garage. The boys are thinking up a name for the band tonight, and as much as I'd rather get a root canal than be a part of it, I need to be there. I dread to think what they'll come up with on their own."

"Why the beer? You never have more than a couple drinks anymore, and we just downed two."

"Why? Because I just turned a sloppy trio of rejects into a decent band, I work in a butcher shop wearing a cow suit, and I've got a fuckin demon living in my calendar. I think I've earned the right to get rip-roaring drunk later on if I so desire."

"Yes," Vincent said. "I suppose you do."

"Besides," Joe said, throwing his jacket on. "Pez gives me a headache. Fahkin kid never stops talking."

"Hold on a second," Vincent said. He went to his liquor cabinet and pulled out a bottle, then walked over and handed it to Joe. "I got this in Mexico. Best damn tequila I've ever had, and it cost a small fortune. Forget the cheap beer. Tie one on in style, tonight."

Joe took the bottle and smiled. "Thanks, Vin! That's mighty kind of you."

"And do me a favor, will you? Try to enjoy yourself tonight. You've got a good life, Joe."

Joe patted his shoulder. "Right. A good life. See you later, Vin."

Joe tucked the bottle in his saddlebag and made off on Road Bastard, enjoying the night smells and the warm wind on his face. He wanted nothing less than to stop at his apartment. But his clothes were sweaty from rehearsal, and he had to take a leak before riding the ten miles to Shane's house. He mentally prepared himself as well as he could for another taunting from the beast as he pulled into his driveway and killed the engine.

He opened the apartment door only two inches and reached in to flick on the light. It was bad enough in there without walking into the beast's lair in the dark. Letting the door swing open, he gasped, and lilted in the doorway.

The black head of the beast protruded two feet out of the wall on what appeared to be a long, trunk of neck. The strange ink-colored ferns seemed to shift and move over its surface, giving the impression of thousands of bugs crawling over each other in a frenzied dance. Like an ancient, rotted figurehead on a sailing ship, it jutted out from the wall. Joe swallowed hard and stepped into the apartment, closing the door.

He knew he had to walk past the thing to get to the bathroom. He struggled to convince his mind it was a mere statue, made of iron or black stone, but the shifting of the ferns contradicted the image. "Screw it," he whispered. "I'll deal with the stinky clothes, and I'll fucking piss outside."

With a terrible, snapping creak, the head turned on the neck, and white eyes seemed to focus on Joe. He slammed his back into the door. "Bloody hell!" he yelled.

The thing grinned, bearing its yellow teeth. *BLOODY HELL*, it said. *THAT'S WHERE YOU'RE GOING IN FOUR DAYS.*

Joe fumbled with the doorknob. Finally able to open the door, he tore out of the apartment and down the hallway. His heart thudded, and his bladder throbbed. Once outside on the front porch, he looked around. The sidewalk looked empty, so he ducked behind a shrub and relieved himself. As he was zipping up, he heard a child's giggle over in the driveway, then footsteps, running. He finished buttoning his fly, then stepped out from behind the shrub, rounding the porch toward the driveway. Gazing ahead down the street, he saw the shadowed figures of three boys, growing smaller.

He turned to his left and saw Road Bastard, still there, and he sighed. Then his eyes focused on the saddlebag. Open. He ran to it and dug inside. The bottle Vincent had given him was gone. He felt his fear from the beast transform into rage, and he shook his head. "Oh no. Not tonight, you little bastards!"

Joe sprinted down the sidewalk as fast as his skinny legs could take him. Under a street lamp thirty yards up, he spotted the pre-teen thieves turning a corner. He ran across the street, making chase. Sweat streamed down his face and under his arms, degrading his already ripe condition. He turned the corner where the boys had gone, and was met with an empty street. He ran down it anyway.

"Where are you?" he yelled. "Little fuckers!" A giggle came in the distance somewhere, but he couldn't determine its origin. He sprinted further down, passing houses and mailboxes and alleyways. His heart pounded against his chest, his lungs threatening to explode. "Christ!" he puffed, his pace slowing, first to a jog, then finally to a walk. Bending over with his hands on his knees, he caught his breath.

Straightening up, he examined the darkened street. The kids were gone by now, he was sure, slippery little bastards. He clenched his teeth.

"Damn you!" he screamed, his voice echoing against the buildings. Taking vengeance on a nearby trashcan, he kicked and kicked until his foot exploded in pain as his big toe jammed.

"Fuck!" he yelled, hopping on one foot now. His rage un-subsided, he began to punch the metal can. Still hopping on one foot, he jabbed repeatedly at it, making sharp dents in the aluminum. When his knuckles came back bloodied, he stopped, and lowered himself to sit on the sidewalk, panting. "Gypsies," he whispered, wiping the sweat from his brow. "Lousy, stinking gypsies."

Shane stood before a large, schoolhouse blackboard, holding a stick of chalk. Max and Pez had pulled mop buckets from the corners of the garage and made seats in front of the blackboard like a pair of bedraggled students. A list of names graced the board in yellow chalk, one beneath the other. 'Monolith, Junk Puppies, Lick Me, Scamsters, Piss Ant, Mass Destruction, Tomb Fetus.'

"Well if you don't like any of these, then think up some more! We've got a gig in three days, we need a name!" Shane said.

Max leaned over on his bucket, rubbing his temples. "My brain hurts."

"How bout 'The Ball Sacks?'" Pez said

Shane grimaced. "Cut the shit, Pez."

Pez shrugged. "Okay. I like Ball Sacks, but if you want a band called 'Cut the Shit', that's fine by me."

The garage door lifted with a loud scrape, and they all turned. Joe Blood stood in the rectangular entrance. His red spikes were askew on his head, two of them matted down in the front with sweat, giving him a double Eddie Munster point on his forehead. His clothes were dirt-stained, the shirt under his armpits darkened with sweat. His hand was bleeding. He remained there, breathing heavily.

Max said, "Joe?"

"GYPSIES STOLE MY TEQUILA!" he screamed.

They stared at Joe for a moment, then Max turned to Pez. Pez shrugged, then nodded. They looked up at Shane.

Shane raised his eyebrows. "Huh," he said, then turned to the blackboard. With his sleeve he wiped the other names off the board. Then in large, yellow letters, wrote 'Gypsies Stole My Tequila'. He turned back to the others, grinning.

"I like it," Max said. "I like it a lot."

Joe took an extra long shower, though he had showered the night before when he got home. His body was sore from chasing the gypsies and his street fight with the trashcan. After dressing in torn jeans, bright red leather boots and a white tee shirt covered in safety pins, he spiked his hair, fastened his dog collar and made into the study. Stopping short, he examined the calendar. He blinked. The beast was not there.

He walked over to it, and tapped on the month of June. The paper fluttered, then fell back into place. He leaned in close and examined the page.

The paper was clean and white, the days of the month unsoiled. He frowned.

THREE DAYS, a voice called from behind him.

Joe wheeled around. In the corner of the room was the beast, a black, spinning cyclone that stretched from ceiling to floor. The bulbous head remained on top, eyes white, yellow teeth visible, slithering ferns for hair and beard. From there down it was an inky black funnel, spinning clockwise. Joe held his breath. He couldn't move.

The beast funneled over in front of the window, blotting the beam of sunlight. The white eyes stayed on him.

BE AT THE CLIFF ON THE NINETEENTH, it said, horrible mouth shifting in the blackness.

AND JOE? IF I DON'T GET A CHANCE TO TELL YOU...HAPPY BIRTHDAY! The beast roared with laughter, then retreated backwards, sucking through the glass window. It hovered outside for a moment, grinning at him, then shot upwards.

Joe ran to the window and looked up. He slid it open and stuck his head out. The day was bright and sunny, the sky clear. Birds flew by. There was no sign of the beast.

He worked the early shift at the butcher shop so he could pep-talk the boys later that night after stopping by the King's Ring Concert Club to check on final preparations. Everything was in order. The sign outside read 'TOMMOROW NIGHT: NAPHULA', and in small letters beneath, 'With Gypsies Stole My Tequila'. He stood before the sign, hands on his hips, shaking his head.

"Bloody stupid name if ya ask me," he said, then hopped on Road Bastard and headed to Vincent's.

Max, Pez and Shane sat on the floor in the studio, waiting nervously for Joe to arrive. "What if he kills us?" Shane asked.

"He's not going to kill us," Max said, though he didn't look so sure. "Just let me handle this."

"What if he kills us THEN eats us?" Pez said. "He ate a baby onstage once, you know."

"He didn't eat a baby. My dad said that's bullshit," Max said. "Just don't worry about it. It's no big deal. I'm sure he'll understand."

"Yeah right!" Shane said. "Because Joe's such a warm fuzzy kind of guy."

"Look," Max said. "Joe got us to this point, and we're forever indebted to him for that. But now that we're here, do you really want to blow it for ourselves? We have to reason with him. He said himself he doesn't want to be another Blood Blister. He'll understand this!"

"I hope he eats you and Shane first," Pez said. "Maybe he'll be too full to eat me."

Joe came through the door looking as fresh and chipper as any thirty-nine year old punk could look. He stopped short when he saw the boys sitting in a circle on the floor.

"We praying, then? Because I should let you know, I'm an atheist."

Max jumped to his feet, forcing a smile. "Joe! Hey, man. I've got something to show you."

Joe looked suspicious. "Yeah? What's at then?"

Max dragged over the box and pulled out a white, ruffled shirt, black trousers and bright red and white headscarf. "We thought we'd all wear these for the gig. It would look cool, don't you think? Like gypsies. Get it?"

Joe snatched the shirt and held it up, sneering at it. He looked at Max. "Oh, no no no. We're not going to play dress-up. If there's one thing I can't stand, it's bands that dress up like Vikings or gothic warlords or vampires or...fucking gypsies for Christ's sake."

"We like them," Pez said, trying to sound cheery. "Right, Shane?"

"Yeah, why not?" Shane said. "It will be like our theme. I think people will dig it."

"I think people will laugh and throw things," Joe said. "No flogging way. I wear a cow suit to work, chums. When I get up on that stage, I'm gonna be dressed as nothing but me. Joe Blood."

Max looked to the others. Pez widened his eyes, urging him on. Joe noticed. "You got something you want to say to me, Max?"

Max shifted on his feet. "The thing is, Joe, you're pretty well known. So we were thinking that in order to introduce ourselves as a fresh new band...um..."

"Oh," Joe said, his face darkening. "I see what's going on here. You want me to disguise myself. You don't want any of your little death metal wanker friends to know you've got Joe Blood, the old punk sod as your front man. Is that it?"

Max held his hands up. "Look, Joe. It's not that we're not happy to be playing with you. But...you have a reputation. And not all of it is good. I mean, this isn't so bad!" he said, taking the ruffled shirt from Joe and holding it up to him. "And look!" he said, laying the bandanna over Joe's head. "This will hide your hair, so nobody will see that you're...um..."

"So that nobody will see it's me," Joe said.

"Come on, Joe," Pez said. "It's not like you wanted any of this for yourself, anyway. We were your guinea pigs."

"You were frogs," Joe said. "And I turned you into princes. I gave you all of my time. Worked day and night, wrote all of your music, made all of your dreams come true with this gig tomorrow. And now?"

He took the shirt and bandanna and tossed them to the floor. "You want me to dress up like Lord of the fucking Dance because you're ashamed to be on the same stage as me. I ask you, boys. In what universe is that supposed to make sense to me?"

Max looked to Pez and Shane, then back at Joe. "It's what we want, Joe. Please."

Joe turned away, giving them his back. He scratched his head. This went on for several minutes. Pez looked up at Max and shrugged. Max shook his head. Finally Joe turned around. He smiled at them.

"All right then," he said. "If that's what you want, then that's what you want."

"And...you're okay with it?" Max asked.

"Fine!" Joe said, grinning. "I'm fine with it. May I have my costume please? I'd like to try it on tonight. Make sure it fits. After all, we want everything to be perfect tomorrow night, don't we?"

The boys stared at him, frowning. Joe kept the sugary smile. "Um, okay," Max said, and handed Joe the clothes. "Are you sure you're fine with this?"

"Fine!" Joe said again, then took the costume and left.

When he'd gone, Max looked to the others. "I don't have a good feeling about this," he said.

Shane shook his head. "Me either."

Joe stopped home and found Verne, who agreed to let him borrow his car. When he got to the butcher shop he pulled it round to the rear shipping door and backed it in. Leaving the trunk open, he used his key to get in and went to the refrigeration closet. The gizzards were in white plastic buckets marked 'Excess'.

As he loaded the buckets into his trunk, he grumbled to himself. "Mop of masturbators...no good little...I'll show them who...rotten wankers...gonna see how it feels..."

"Joe?"

Joe turned. Sam Barnsley stood in the doorway, dressed in a silver sardine costume. His head peeked through the open fish mouth. "Oh, hey Sam. Like the wardrobe change. Canned fish suits you."

"Oh, thanks," he said, smoothing his gills. "What are you doing with all the gizzards and crap?"

Joe loaded the last bucket into the trunk and slammed it shut. He turned to Sam. "Um...I got a puppy."

"A puppy? Joe, you've got like twenty buckets of intestines there. It's cow guts, man."

Joe wiped his hands on his jeans. "I got a puppy," he said, and turned away, hopping in the driver's side and slamming the door.

Sam watched him drive off. He shook his head. "Thank God that guy never reproduced," he said, and went back inside.

The stage was set at the King's Ring, and people were starting to filter in. Max walked into the long darkened club from backstage and approached Shane, who was speaking with the sound technician. "Everything all set?" he asked.

The muscular black man fiddled with his dials. "Yes. For the sixteenth time, everything is all set. You've been here since noon. And I do this for a living. I think I've got it covered."

Shane gave the tech a foul look, and Max grabbed him by the elbow and led him away. "Come on. Joe says we have to start getting ready."

"That sound tech's a prick. He thinks we're amateurs."

"We are amateurs, Shane. Now come on. It's almost show time, and I need you to help me calm down Pez. He threw up on the stage manager."

In a room backstage, Joe Blood adjusted his red and white bandana in a full-length mirror. The white ruffled blouse puffed around his bony chest, making him look like a marionette. He smoothed his black trousers and spun around, clicking the heels of his boots. He seemed in high spirits. "What ya think?" he asked Pez. "Lord of the Dance got nuthin' on me, eh?"

Pez sat on a nearby couch in his own costume. It was identical to Joe's aside from a royal blue bandana. His ginger hair spilled out down his shoulders. His freckled face was sheet-white. "You look great, Joe. I just wish I felt great."

Joe patted his shoulder. "Buck up, chum. You'll be fine. This is the good part."

Max and Shane stepped into the room. "You okay, Pez?" Shane said.

"I'm feeling better, thanks. But I owe the stage manager a new shirt."

"Get dressed!" Joe shouted to them. "It's almost show time!"

Shane and Max went in the back, and returned in full gypsy regalia, Max with an emerald green bandana, Shane with a black and white. A young man stepped into the room, his dyed, platinum-blond hair just brushing his shoulders. He wore dark blue jeans and a sleeveless white tee shirt. Tattoos covered both arms like a black and blue rash. His eyes drifted over the four of them and he grinned.

"Well. Don't you all look pretty? You're NOT going out on stage like that."

Pez jumped to his feet, the color returning to his face. "Simon Maul! Shit man, you rock. Your bass playing is what made me pick it up in the first place, four years ago."

The platinum-haired bassist eyed Pez from head to toe, sneering. "You look like one of the Village People," he said. "Are you going start with YMCA, or Macho Man?"

Pez turned to Joe. "Joe, this is Simon Maul, from Naphula!"

"Charmed, I'm sure," Joe said, turning to the mirror and adjusting his bandana.

Simon glanced over at Joe and cocked his head. "Who's the Brit?" No one answered. He moved over and stood beside Joe, studying him openly.

Joe turned to him. "Have you fallen in love with me?"

The bassist laughed. "Christ, man. You're old enough to know better. These outfits your idea, Bones?"

"Yes, I agree," Joe said. "These outfits ARE ridiculous." Max turned and walked out of the room.

The bassist laughed again. "You got that right!" he said. "But I'd go with nightmarish."

"I know," Joe said, turning back to the mirror and fluffing his shirt. "How humiliating this must be for you."

Simon made a face. "For ME? I'm not the one wearing that. Why would I be humiliated?"

Joe turned to him. "Because tomorrow morning, you'll be forced to read the entertainment section of the newspapers. About how Naphula was upstaged by their opening band. A bunch of poofy twats in gypsy costumes."

The smirk left the bassist's face, replaced by a cold stare. "Do your worst, Tinkerbelle," he said, and turned to leave.

"Have a good show, Britney!" Joe called over his shoulder.

Simon muttered a curse then disappeared out the door.

Pez gaped at Joe. "Jesus Christ, Joe! Do you know who that was?"

Joe stormed at Pez, gripping him by his ruffled collar. He pulled his face in, their foreheads touching. "Do you know who I am, PEZ?" Pez looked shaken. Joe shoved him. "It's show time. They're playing our song."

Joe stormed out of the room. Max came back in, his eyes wide. "Our opening music! It's on. Come on, we have to go!"

Shane stepped out of the toilet, and paused when he heard the music, a festival carnival polka they'd chosen. "Oh shit. Is it time?"

To the backdrop of carnival music, Gypsies Stole My Tequila walked onto the stage. The crowd was there for Naphula, and it looked like only half of them had arrived, but there were still a good lot of people milling about, hanging at the side bars, some congregating in front of the stage. They were a scramble of styles and ages, some death metal types in dark clothing, some tattooed, some college, a few older yuppies. No punks that Joe could see as he adjusted his microphone and picked up his guitar.

Shane climbed behind his drum-kit. Max and Pez picked up their guitars, flicking the amps from standby and testing the volume. More people drifted toward the stage, curious. Especially when the caught sight of the costumes, illuminated under the red and blue stage lights.

Joe turned around and checked on the boys, waiting until he got a nod from each one of them. Then he gave the signal to Shane. Shane gave them four on the hi-hat and they blasted into their first song, *The End is Near*.

Joe wailed out the vocals, remaining stationary before the microphone while he played rhythm. One ear was tuned to himself, the other listening to every note coming from Max, Shane and Pez. He felt a welling pride as he heard them pounding forth, their timing perfect, their sound flawless. Then he remembered that he hated them.

As they moved into the middle of the second song, the concert club began to fill up, and the crowd before the stage thickened. Someone hooted encouragement to Pez as he banged out his solo part, and he visibly brightened and began bobbing his head, his ginger hair wild where it leaked out of the bandana.

As Joe shouted out the chorus, he began to feel at home. Being on stage, screaming his lungs out, the guitar in his grip, stimulated memories from his past, and he began to move about, bouncing, bending whichever way the music moved him. It felt natural, a long lost friend possessing his body, and he allowed it to take hold.

They moved through each song on the set list as if they'd been playing together for years. One flowed into the next, and it was relaxed and full of vigor as if they were at home in Vin's studio, practicing.

Time seemed to speed up, and before Joe knew it, they had blasted through six songs and were nearly done with the set. Joe had a decision to make.

Max, Shane and Joe fell silent at the close of the second to last song, and as rehearsed, Pez kept up the bass line while they gathered themselves to move into the final number, the number Joe had been waiting for; *Taste my Insides*. He looked back at Shane, who was sweating profusely, but offered him a solid nod. He looked over at Max, who smiled.

Then he glanced over at the stagehand, who stood ready with the pull-chord. Joe had a moment of hesitation. Could he do this to them? He forced himself to recall the conversation with the boys the night before. They had shamed him. They had hurt him. They had infuriated him. But most of all, they had reinforced every festering fear and misery that plagued his heart and mind. Nobody wanted Joe Blood anymore. Joe Blood was dead.

With Pez's bass line deviating and melding into the beginning of *Taste my Insides*, Joe puffed his bony chest out and gave Shane the nod. Screw it. He was going through with it. He was Joe Blood. He was not a nice guy. He was a punk. And he was going out with a bang. Or a splat, more like it. Stephen King's *Carrie* would look like a prom night picnic compared to this.

Shane rolled in right on time, and the thick, heavy rhythm of the song began. By now the floor before the stage was packed tight, and there was no question that they were enjoying the music. Heads bounced, arms thrashed, feet stomped and bodies danced. Joe belted out the song like it was his last breath of life, which in a way, it was.

"Why do you want to
Taste my insides
Why do you want to
Cut me open
Why do you want to
Taste my insides,"

Shane's drums slammed the beat, as Max and Pez followed Joe with their back vocals, their voices harmonizing a gravelly snarl. They played it with all the vigor of a final song after an ass-kicking set. After the third and final stanza, Joe sang the chorus once more, and Max and Pez went into their final bout of back-up vocals, which led to the final jam that ended the song. "*Taste my insides! Taste my insides! Taste my insides! Taste my insides! Taste my insides! Taste my insiiiiides!*"

The moment had come. Joe gave the stagehand the nod.

"TASTE THIS!" Joe screamed into the mike, a second and a half before it began raining intestines all over the stage. Joe made sure he turned his head to the right as it happened. More than anything, he wanted to watch Max's reaction as the guts showered onto his perfectly conditioned head. And it was glorious. A wash of pink and red chunks completely blotted out Max's face momentarily before the innards slid down his body onto the floor.

Joe glanced behind him, as the buckets dumped from above, creating a mess of bouncing guts all over the stage floor. Along with Max's position, the most concentrated streams were over Shane and Pez, and Joe watched as the same phenomenon happened, their faces disappearing in a flood of gore for a moment as the crap slid down their bodies. Then, he tilted his own head back and let a stream of guts hit him in the face. He shook it off, but could feel the bloody wetness, clinging to his skin, painting it red.

He glanced at Max, who shook his head like a dog. When he finished, his eyes glared at Joe, the whites standing out against his newly-painted red skin. And it was pure, feral rage. Joe smiled.

"How do you like the taste of THAT?" Joe yelled into the microphone, his eyes on the seething Max. The crowd assumed his question was for them, and responded in hoots, cheers, and jubilant screams. Surprised, Joe turned to face them. He hadn't even thought about the crowd. Hadn't thought beyond dumping twenty buckets of cow intestines on Max, Pez and Shane. But now the crowd jumped and cheered, which was probably the only thing that prompted the boys to actually finish the song with the unexpected smears of gizzards dripping down their arms.

Joe glanced over his shoulder at the band, secretly impressed that they'd kept playing, amused as Shane watched a gizzard pop up into the air off his drum as he hit it.

He looked at Pez, who mouthed, "Fuck you" at him, and by the look on his face, it wasn't a good-natured ribbing. The crowd screamed and Joe remembered that he was onstage, at a show, and he owed him his attention.

"Can you taste my insides NOW?" he yelled to them, then held the mike out for them to scream into. They did not disappoint, yelling their enthusiasm. He scanned their faces, wrought with glee, laughing, shrieking, wincing in delight as cow guts slipped off the stage. Then he looked to his band-mates, on the final notes of the song. Each met him with a cold stare. He raised his middle finger to each them, which brought another cheer from the crowd, who hadn't the slightest idea the gesture was sincere, and not good-natured.

He ripped off his bandana, his red spiked hair plunging up under the yellow lights, matching his blood-painted face. Then he tore off the white ruffled gypsy top, leaving him naked from the waist up. He glanced at Max, held the shirt up, then dropped it onto a pile of cow slop on the stage beside him, grinding it in with his boot heel. With a slap of the bass and a blast of the drums, the song came to an end. The crowd cheered wildly. Joe pulled the mike to his mouth.

"We'd like to thank you all for coming out tonight. Max Rizzo on guitar, Pez Langley on bass, Shane Brewer on drums. My name is Joe Blood!"

The crowd cheered and threw intestines at him. Joe pogo-jumped, deflecting the gizzards with his chest. He walked down the front of the stage, slapping the hands that reached up for him. When he turned back around, the boys had already left the stage. The show was over, but now was the time to face the music. Giving a final wave to the crowd, he stepped over piles of innards and made his way back stage.

It was difficult to discern who was yelling loudest. Although Joe was pretty sure it was the singer for the band Naphula, Max was a close second, followed by Pez. Joe was in the center of a screaming crowd of ten people. The voices swam over each other in a sea of fury.

"-all over my equipment, before our show even starts!"

"-asshole, Joe! Have you seen my guitar? It's ruined now!"

"Fucking guts! All over my amps! Fucking guts!"

"You had to do it, didn't you?" Pez. "Had to let them all know it was you."

"-any idea how much this guitar cost?" Max again.

"-have any idea how much those people paid to see Naphula? Now we have to delay the show to clean up—"

"Fucking guts!"

"My guitar!" Max shoved the instrument in Joe's face. It was slick with gizzard juice.

The wolves began to scrap among themselves then as Naphula's drummer grabbed Max by the shirt. "Shut up about your fucking guitar, punk! I've got amps and an entire drum-kit on that stage! You little fuckers better—"

"Get the fuck off him!" Pez grabbed Naphula's drummer, and Naphula's guitarist grabbed Pez. Shane grabbed Naphula's guitarist, and was then grabbed by Monty, the stage manager. Naphula's drummer released Max, who then grabbed Joe by the shoulder.

"You son of a bitch!" he yelled, his face folded in rage. "Look at my guitar, Joe! Just look at it! Look at it!"

Having had enough, Joe snatched Max's guitar from him. He shoved his way out of the middle of the crowd, and with four solid, over the shoulder wind-ups, whacked and smashed Max's guitar to oblivion all over the floor of the back stage room. Wood splinters shot out, strings popped, and the sound was so loud that the entire crowd fell simultaneously still, leaving silence.

When it was done, Joe looked up at the huddle of faces that stared at him. He took a deep breath, smoothed his spiked hair, and handed Max the broken neck of what had once been his guitar. Max took it, and dangled it before his eyes, wincing.

"You're a rich kid," Joe said. "Buy yourself another fucking guitar." With this said, Joe Blood left, disappearing from the room, from the club, and from their lives.

"I thought it looked cool as hell," Vincent said as he sipped his coffee. Shane and Max both lay on their backs in front of the fireplace, moping. Shane had shown up early, unable to sleep late despite having to spend the wee hours of the morning cleaning gore from his drum-kit. Max hadn't had that problem. His guitar was in pieces, thanks to Joe.

"Dad, you're just saying that because Joe's your friend. He totally screwed us."

"Nevertheless," Vincent said, looking up over his sports page. "I was in the audience, and I saw it from that perspective. There wasn't a single person in that crowd that knew the intestine-dropping wasn't planned. And the sight of you guys up there, your eyes white, your faces painted with blood, singing 'Taste my Insides', was one of the coolest things I've ever seen. So sue me."

"Naphula might sue *us*," Shane said.

"Fuck Naphula," Vincent mumbled.

"Now you sound like Joe, Dad. Fuck Naphula, fuck us, fuck the world, fuck it all to hell."

The doorbell rang and Pez called in from the foyer. "Anybody home?"

"We're in here, Pez," Max yelled.

Moments later, Pez came bopping into the room, a wide smile on his freckled face. "Morning girls. I hold in my hands the entertainment pages from *The Phoenix*, *The Globe*, and *The Sound*. Read 'em and weep," he said, tossing three newspaper sections onto the coffee table.

Still lying on the floor, Max and Shane simultaneously lifted their heads only. "What is it?" Shane said.

"Reviews of the show," Pez said.

Max and Shane jumped up, scrambling across the floor, fighting to get to the papers. Vincent reached down to grab the third, and the three of them frantically flipped through the pages, while Pez grabbed a muffin from a paper bag and stuffed it into his mouth. He grinned at them as he watched them read.

"'Gypsies Stole My Show, says Naphula?'" Max cried. "Oh man. Naphula's telling everyone we fucked up their set!"

"Read the article," Pez said. "It ain't about us fucking up their set. It's about us mopping up the floor. With them."

Max frowned at Pez. "What do you mean?"

"Holy shit! Listen to this," Shane said. "Gypsies Stole My Tequila played their literal and figurative guts out at the King's Ring last night. A unique blend of sounds combined a heart-pumping thrash beat with a stylish, jazz undertone, bringing the crowd to their feet, and making the headlining Naphula show feel anti-climactic!"

"It's good," Max said, unbelieving. "We got good reviews."

"Listen to this one," Vincent said, leaning forward, paper in hand. "'Guitarist Max Rizzo, rumored to be the eighteen-year old son of former Blood Blister bassist Vincent Rizzo, sounded like he was born with a guitar in his hands. And considering his musical lineage, this may just be the case.'"

Max made a face. "You just read that because it mentioned you," he said.

Vincent smirked at him. "Well I was there when you were born, hotshot, and the only thing in your hands was your little pecker."

"How 'bout this here," Shane said, reading. "'On rhythm and lead vocals was none other than Joe Blood of the late punk trio 'Blood Blister'. Seeming to have fallen off the planet over the past fifteen years, Blood was in top form, and proves himself to be in outstanding condition despite reports of bouts with drugs and alcohol. If Blood were not in control of his life, then he'd no doubt have spilled the secret of this unique musical project, which had to have taken months, if not years of preparation. But Joe Blood took everyone by surprise, including his band, who rumors claim were unaware of a stunt which rained actual animal intestines onto the stage during the final number.'"

"Where the hell is Joe?" Vincent asked suddenly.

Pez shrugged, finishing his muffin. "Don't know. I went by his place after I picked up the reviews. I was gonna show him. But he wasn't there. He wasn't at the butcher shop either."

Vincent jumped to his feet. "Oh shit! What's the date?"

"June nineteenth," Max said. "Why?"

Vincent slapped his hands to his forehead. "The nineteenth! Holy Christ! It's Joe's birthday!" He leapt over the coffee table and dove for his keys.

"Dad? Where are you going?"

"Joe's birthday!" he yelled as he headed toward the door, realizing suddenly that he had no shoes on, and running back to retrieve them. "I'm so stupid! I can't believe I forgot!"

Max frowned at his father. Pez and Shane stared as he dropped to the floor, rolled back and pulled on his shoes. "Dear God," he said as he fumbled with the laces. "Dear God, don't let me be too late."

"Dad?" Max said. "What's wrong?"

Vincent jumped to his feet, snatched his fallen keys, then stopped. "Deke. I've gotta go get Deke. Yeah, Deke's a part of it. I'll need him. For psychological reasons. Shit. I hope I've got time. What time is it?"

Shane gave him an odd look. "It's nine thirty. Mr. Rizzo, are you okay?"

"Nine-thirty. Good. I'll get Deke, then I'll find Joe. Christ, don't let it be too late," he said, then ran out of the house, leaving the door wide open.

Max went to the front window and watched as his father ran down the walk, hopped in his silver sports car and squealed tires as he backed out of the driveway and sped off down the street. When the car was out of sight, he turned to his friends and scratched his head.

"Huh," Pez said. "I guess he forgot to buy him a card."

"No way. No how. Not in this life, or any other, Vin. He's a lunatic, and I don't care if he jumps of the cliff. Now get the hell out of here. You're blocking the TV."

Vincent stood before Deke, who lay on his living room couch in a gray sweat suit, eating a plate of pancakes. "You're not listening to me, Deke. I think he's really going do it."

"And again. How does this concern me? Oh yeah. It doesn't."

"It does in Joe's mind, and that's why I need you there with me! If we show up, and it's the three of us there, like when we made the pact, I think it will trigger something in him. Together we can talk him out of this! Now come on!"

Deke sat up and placed his empty plate on the floor. His wife Lacey came into the room and picked it up, then left again. "Vincent, I am not going to Anchorage Cliff. I don't care if I ever see Joe Blood again. And I sure as hell never want to see that fucking cliff again. Or that graveyard." He shuddered.

Vincent's lips tightened, then he pointed. "I don't believe it! You're scared."

Deke made a face. "Fuck off!"

"You are!" Vincent said, his eyes widening. "You're scared to go to the cliff! To the graveyard!"

Deke tried to look past Vincent at the television. Vincent stepped to the left, blocking his view. "Oh my God, Deke," he said. "You *are* scared!" He checked to make sure Lacey was out of hearing range, then lowered his voice to a whisper. "You think the demon is real!"

"Oh kiss my fat white ass! Is that supposed to appeal to my macho side? Because I haven't got one. Now take a hike."

"Deke..."

Deke stood. "Read my lips, Vin. I am not going to that cliff. And that's the end of it."

"I'll give you five thousand dollars."

Deke gave him a scowl. "Fifteen."

"Ten."

"Fourteen."

"Twelve. Final offer."

Deke studied his feet for a moment, then looked up. "Okay. I'll get my coat. It's getting windy out there."

Joe's black leather boots teetered on the edge of the cliff. Waves crashed against the rocks below. He looked up at the sky. Black clouds moved in over the ocean, shifting, the wind pushing them toward land. In the distance, thunder rumbled. He held his arms out straight at his sides, and closed his eyes, letting the wind tug him this way and that, beating against his face, fluttering his tee shirt.

A tribal drumbeat cut into the wind, and Joe opened his eyes and looked to his left. "About time you showed up," he said.

The chief with the black eyes stood solemn, beating out the death march. *Bdrump...bump...bump.* "I wouldn't miss it for the world."

"What's with this weather?" Deke asked, peering through the windshield as leaves flurried like snow across the path of the speeding sport's car. "I didn't hear anything about a storm."

Vincent maneuvered the car along the secluded winding road that led up to Anchorage Point. "No," he said. "Neither did I."

A purple spider web of lightening brightened the sky ahead. Vincent pressed down on the gas pedal, the motor humming up an octave as the road climbed. The first droplets of rain spattered on the windshield.

"Oh fucking great!" Deke said. "It's raining."

"You're not going to melt," Vincent said as he took the turn onto the narrow dirt road that would take them to the cliff. The rain came down harder, pelting against the metal. Vincent winced at the sound, switching his wipers to high. Wind rocked the tiny vehicle, and he gripped the wheel tighter. Thunder clapped overhead.

"Jesus, look out!" Deke cried.

Vincent slammed on the breaks as a small tree swooped down in front of them, blocking their path. "Holy shit," he gasped, catching his breath, adrenaline speeding his pulse. He put the car in park and shut the engine off, turning to Deke. "We'll have to walk the rest of the way."

"Walk? Fuck that!"

"It's only a half-mile up to the cliff. Now come on, Deke! We have to get to Joe before he..." Vincent paused. "If he hasn't already."

A pinging sound started, and they both turned to see hail stones popping off the windshield. "Hail? What the hell is this?" Deke said. "Screw it, Vin. Keep your twelve grand. I'm not walking up that hill through a hail storm."

Vincent took a deep breath. "I'll give you twenty thousand."

Deke turned. "Thirty."

Vincent sighed and rolled his eyes. "Twenty-five."

"Twenty-eight."

"Twenty-seven. Final offer."

Deke looked out the window, up at the black clouds. Hail pelted on the windshield. He turned back to Vincent. "You'd better pay up."

"You have my word. Now let's go."

They climbed over the fallen tree and made their way up the narrow dirt road, arms in front of their faces to ward off the hail. The wind rocked them, and they had to push against it to keep moving. Leaves and twigs swirled through the air.

When they finally got to the clearing beside the graveyard, they were soaked through their clothes. Deke stepped under a tree and used his wet jacket arm to wipe the rain from his eyes. He looked up. "Holy Mother of God," he said.

Vincent followed his gaze. The lithe, rain-soaked form of Joe Blood stood on the edge of the cliff, looking down.

Joe saw the beast coming across the water. At first it appeared as just a small black funnel cloud, bending and twisting, making a figure-eight pattern as it moved ever so slowly toward the cliff. Then he saw the white eyes, the yellow teeth. The face of the beast hovered just over the top of the miniature tornado. It looked menacing. It was angry, and Joe knew why. He hadn't jumped yet, so it was coming to help him along, bringing the wind and the hail with it to encourage his resolve, to threaten him. The tribal chief remained, drumming, but the beat was lost in the sound of the storm. Joe looked down at the rocks, then back up at the beast. He took a deep breath.

"Joe!"

His name echoed through the wind, and at first he thought it was the beast, calling to him. Then it came again, from behind him. "Joe!"

He whirled around and saw Vincent and Deke walking toward him. Vin's long black hair was drenched, hanging around his shoulders. Deke looked like a fat rat in a gray sweat suit with a brown leather jacket thrown over. "No," Joe whispered. "No, go back."

They ran to him, closing the gap, and Joe held his hands up. "Stop right there!" he shouted. "Vin, I told you not to come here!"

They approached him cautiously, faces pinched as the elements pelted them. "Step back from the cliff, Joe," Vincent yelled. "Come on, now."

"You have to get out of here!" Joe yelled. "It's coming! The beast is coming!"

Vincent and Deke's eyes lifted, looking beyond Joe, out at the sea. "Tornado!" Deke screamed.

Vincent's eyes widened in terror. He took a step closer. "It's a tornado, Joe! Now come on, we have to get out of here!"

"It's the beast!" he yelled back, wiping his matted red hair out of his eyes. "I have to face it. Now get out of here, you two! Get out of here now!"

"It's not the beast, you stupid son of a bitch! It's a fucking twister, Joe! A fucking twister! Now give me your God-damned hand!"

Joe turned toward the sea. The beast spun a hideous dance across the water's surface, closing the distance. It grinned, white eyes glinting as a bolt of lightening whipped the sky above. "Come and get me, you fucker," he said softly. "You're gonna have to come and get me."

Someone grabbed his arm and jerked him about. He looked up, saw that Deke had hold of him, and then his boots slipped. His knees cracked the edge of the cliff as his body went over.

Deke was pulled down onto his stomach with a painful slap against the earth as Joe's legs slipped over the edge of the cliff. Deke gripped his right arm with both hands, screaming. Vincent dove down and got hold of his other arm. Joe was slippery as an eel, his pale skin slick with rain. He began to glide through their hands.

"Hang on to him!" Vincent screamed as Joe's shoulder slid through his fingers, down to his elbow. Joe looked up at them, his blood-red hair saturated flat across his forehead. His eyes rolled back, showing white as he lost consciousness. His weight seemed to double, and Vincent screamed in panic as his arm slipped further. He clung to the bony wrist as Joe's thin body dangled off the cliff, twisting in the wind.

Then the weight lightened suddenly, and Joe's form began to move toward them, upward. Vincent squinted through the rain and saw Deke's fingers gripping the dog collar around Joe's neck, pulling. It gave Vincent enough give to get an arm under Joe's shoulder, and with another heave, they dragged him back up onto the grass.

Joe's pale, drenched form looked broken, sprawled out on the wet grass. Hail and rain pelted them all. They took only a moment to catch their breath, then Deke yelled, "Graveyard!"

Vincent nodded, peering toward the neighboring cemetery. He eyed one of several stone-roofed tombs. "Let's go!"

Deke lifted Joe and worked his body up until he was able to sling him over his shoulder, then he began to move in a strained, half-jog toward the graveyard.

Vincent offered a final glance out at the sea, where the miniature tornado twisted toward the edge of the cliff. "You can't have him," he whispered. "He's staying here." Then he hurried off after Deke.

Deke carried Joe down a set of cement steps that led to a large tomb. The entrance door was locked, but the stone awning overhead covered them and kept the elements out. They huddled close to the door on the bottom step.

Leaves and twigs hurled by the opening on a furious current of wind and rain. They huddled around Joe, the three bodies becoming a single lump of flesh, and they waited out the storm. Thunder clapped, shaking the ground.

After twenty minutes, the wind began to slow, and the rain became a steady, non-threatening trickle on the earth outside. Joe groaned, and they pulled back, releasing him. Vincent gripped his jaw and lifted his face, wiping the hair back off his forehead. His eyelids fluttered open.

"You okay?" Vincent asked.

Becoming aware of himself, Joe's body stiffened, struggling to sit. Vincent let him go, and he scrambled back, looking at the two of them. He looked toward the opening of the tomb, at the subsiding storm, then back at Deke and Vincent.

"Where are we?" he asked.

"In a fucking tomb," Deke offered.

Joe looked up at the stone awning over their heads and rubbed his arms. He lowered his eyes to them. "Are we dead, then?"

Vincent laughed. Deke grinned and buried his head in his hands. "No, Joe," Vincent said. "We're not dead. We're very much alive."

"Ah," Joe said. He pulled his knees to his chest, shivering. Looking at Vincent, he said, "Odd that. Don't you think?"

"What's that?"

Joe shook his head, water flying from his matted hair. "Life and death. We're alive but we're sitting in a tomb."

"Brilliant observation," Deke said, his voice muffled in his arm.

"Supposed to be opposites," Joe said. "Life and death. Supposed to be opposites. Why do they always walk side by side?"

Vincent shook his head and shrugged. Joe wiped his face with his hands, then rested his chin on his knees, hugging himself. They sat like that for several minutes, silent.

"I'm forty years old," Joe said. "Forty fucking years old."

Deke lifted his head. "Yeah," he said. "So are well all."

Joe looked off into the distance. He shook his head. "Jesus," he said. "How'd that happen?"

They left the question hanging there, unanswered. Vincent looked out at the day, relieved to see a gradual brightening of the sky. "Rain's stopping," he said.

Deke looked outside, then back and forth between Joe and Vincent. "Hey," he said. "I've got a nail clipper in my pocket. Anybody wanna make a blood pact?"

Vincent dropped his head and laughed. Joe stared at the ground for a moment, then he too began to snicker. The giggles escalated, their frayed nerves helpless against it, until they were three, hysterical voices, echoing peals of laughter out of the yawning mouth of a graveyard tomb.

"Not enough drugs in the world for that," Joe said. "Not enough drugs in the world."

Two Years Later...

"Turn it up, I can't hear it," Pez said, shoving Max with his elbow as he wiggled into a spot on the couch.

"Shane, you're closest. Turn it up," Deke said from the recliner chair.

Shane crawled forward from his spot on the floor and grabbed the remote, raising the volume of Vincent's big screen television. Joe Blood's red spiked head looked huge on the giant screen. He sat in a circular chair, smoking a cigarette, the dog collar that had saved his life fastened around his scrawny neck. He wore a blood-red, vinyl top, with green and black spotted trousers, the heel of his combat boot resting on the opposite knee.

The woman sitting across from him waved a dainty hand discreetly to ward off the trail of smoke Joe expelled from his lips.

"Look at him," Pez said. "He's such a freak."

"We should have been there, man!" Shane said. "He's part of *our* band. I still think MTV should have interviewed all of us."

"Hey piss off, kid," Deke squawked from his chair. "He was our freak first. If anyone should be on the tube with him it's me and Vin."

Vincent stepped forward and grabbed the remote. "Would everyone quit arguing about whose freak Joe is, and watch the damned interview? It's half over and I've missed most of it for all your jabbering!" He thumbed the button, raising the volume further, and the voice of the female interviewer echoed into the study.

"Gypsies Stole My Tequila has had astonishing success on a first album," the woman said. Joe took a drag of the cigarette and nodded, looking bored. She continued. "And your band-mates are only twenty years old, am I right?"

"Yeah, that's right," Joe said.

"And you are how old?" she asked.

"I'm forty-two," Joe said, wiping his nose with his wrist.

"And how does that make you feel? Making music with a band that's half your age?"

Joe gave her a cynical smirk, and stubbed his cigarette in a nearby ashtray. "It makes me feel like I'm making music with a band that's half my age," he said.

Pez snickered. "He's such an asshole!"

"Shut up!" Max said elbowing him. "I'm trying to listen."

The interviewer leaned forward, clasping her hands. "You've had quite a life," she said to Joe.

Joe raised his eyebrows. "It ain't over yet," he said.

"You were out of the music business for almost twenty years," she said. "And now this. This incredible comeback. How did you do it?"

Joe fiddled with his dog collar, and shrugged. "I almost died," he said. "Two years ago."

"Drugs?" she asked.

Joe made a sour face. "No."

"Would you like to share what happened?"

"No."

The woman crossed her legs, shifting her position, and her approach. "If you had died two years ago, what would you see having been inscribed on your tombstone?"

"Oh, Christ," Vincent said. "Joe hates the tombstone question."

"Shut up!" Max snapped.

Joe grinned at the interviewer. "Back then? My tombstone would have read 'Stupid Twat.'"

The station bleeped out the second word, but not so much that it didn't come through clearly enough. The group around the television laughed.

"What's changed?" the woman asked.

"What's changed?" Joe said. "The world. The music. Life."

"And you?"

"Me?" Joe said, and let out a puff of air. "I never change," he said, twisting a red spike on his head.

"So what about now?" she asked. "If you were to leave this world today, what would be inscribed on your tombstone?"

Joe slumped in the chair, looking down, twiddling his fingers. He lifted his eyes to the interviewer. "The more things change," he said, "the more Joe Blood stays the same."

"Interesting. And is that a true statement? That the more things change, the more Joe Blood stays the same?"

He raised his eyebrows. "*That* is a truth that used to make me nuts. Literally."

"And now?" she said. "You're okay with that?"

Joe stared at his fingers for several moments, pondering. He took a deep breath, and looked up. "Yeah," he said, and nodded. "Yeah. I'm okay with that."

The image of Joe's face darkened on the screen as the program faded to black.

Cheque, Please

So how's that grab ya? Not bad for a little mom and pop dive on the ass end of nowhere, was it? Listen, you've been a sport, and since this is your first time in, it's on the house. God knows we'll have enough time to get the rest of it out of you one of these days.

You know, kid, you remind me of someone I knew once. You ever spent any time with a dead chick before? Hey, don't get nervous, I ain't a cop. Or a shrink. I get off in about an hour, give or take. Well, actually, they don't ever let me leave. But it's pretty slow, and I could really use a bit of help reaching this case of syrup in the store room — bastard delivery guy always puts it on the back of the top shelf. And you seem pretty handy.

Hey kid, hang on, where you going?

Well, ok, I'll take a raincheck. Come back anytime.

About the Authors

J.D. Welles — J.D. Welles left the glamorous world of arts journalism to persue the work-a-day existence of a horror and fantasy writer. Her stories have appeared in the Cyberpulp anthologies, *Truth, Justice, And...*, *Dead Winter* and the upcoming, *Hell Hath No Fury*, and on several websites. Nick Brown of "The Girl in B33" is the central character of her novel-in-progress, *Coney Island Complex*, which covers events preceding "Girl."
Welles lives in Brooklyn and on the web at www.jdwelles.com. She has spent the last seven years working on Broadway in one capacity or another, in an effort to support her writing habit.

Jack Mangan — Jack Mangan is a writer, musician, Software Quality Engineer, etc., born in New Jersey, but now residing in Scottsdale, Arizona, with his wife and three children. His book review and "Mythological Idol" columns can be found at the bi-annual webzine, *Beyond Infinity* www.beyondinfinitymagazine.com. His guitar playing can be heard on the Matt Mango CD releases, "Be the Light" and "The Wishing Bridge", as well on the occasional weekend night at downtown Scottsdale cafés and art galleries.

Jetse de Vries — Jetse de Vries is a technical specialist for a propulsion company, and for this he travels around the world. In his spare time he tries to crystallise some of his warped thoughts in a somewhat understandable form such as fiction. Examples of this can be found in *In the Outposts of Beyond* and *Focus* (BSFA's writers mag); and are upcoming in *The Journal of Pulse-Pounding Narratives, vol. #2, Erotic Women, Here & Now, Peridot Books Volume 21,* and more.
Comments are welcomed at jetse@home.nl. When he really is at home, Jetse lives in the historical city that was the birth place of Hieronymus Bosch.

Adrienne Jones — Adrienne Jones is the author of many published works, in the realm of speculative fiction, nonfiction and humor. Her novel *Oral Vices*, is due out at the end of 2004. She is co-owner of Dare Cards, a comic advertising and alternative greeting card company. Adrienne lives outside Providence, Rhode Island, USA.

About the cover artist — Kris Dikeman lives and works in New York City.

About AHOP

The Amityville House of Pancakes has its humble beginnings as a web magazine, the humourous companion magazine to *the Swamp* (www.the-swamp.net). While *the Swamp* is still readily available on the Net, and has even grown into maintaining the web equivalent of a respectable circulation ("hits" in web terms), AHOP did well for a while, but finally languished from a dearth of quality humour. AHOP has always been about speculative humourous fiction, and while what it did publish in its brief two years of web life was always filled with quality, the pickings became too slim to maintain as a periodical publication.

Luckily, its name carried it onward, and it has found new life as — hopefully — an annual publication. Whether it continues, of course, depends on whether everybody else in the world agrees with the warped sense of humour maintained by this editor.

In keeping with the spirit of what AHOP stands for, there is also a team of alien hunters who have banded together under AHOP's banner to help the SETI program search for bug-eyed monsters. For more information about SETI@home, or to join the AHOP team, visit www.the-swamp.net, or http://setiathome.ssl.berkeley.edu/cgi-bin/fcgi?cmd=team_join_form&id=89265

Printed in the United States
PP668100001BC/4